Whisky Chaser

David Cantrip

To Sarah Caudwell,
who wrote elegantly, and was the only woman I ever met
who smoked a pipe.

CHAPTER 1

Poor old Manila.

Manila could have been a great place.

Style, elegance, Spanish architecture growing over three centuries of civilisation, art and culture; and modern riches on top of these. Riches not just for the fat cats in the Polo Club, the sleek, oiled limo-cruising cronies and the businessmen with sticky fingers, but an economy for all, maybe even the people who worked in it; the new miracle of the Far East, the new Taiwan, or so everybody said in the 70s. But Korea, Indonesia, practically everywhere else in the Far East leaped ahead, while the poor old Philippines stayed the same, even now in 1990; stayed stuck in the worn-out cement-grey dust of withered development, the beat-up shanty towns on the road to the airport, the smiling lazy violence, the interlocking mutual cannibalism of endemic corruption.

But still, Manila had the beauty of its girls, those pretty, oriental faces with the western eyes, the black hair, the shiny brown skin so soft to the touch. Queuing hopefully for residence permits outside the American Embassy on Roxas Boulevard, the biggest American Embassy in any country of the world; pursued by the US sailors at Subic Bay until their velvet skin crumbled and wrinkled and rotted with virus; dreaming endlessly of marriage to an American, a Briton, a Frenchman. *Any* westerner, anyone at all to be the heaven on earth they all sighed after.

Any westerner.

Even, at a pinch, Bill Seymour.

Bill Seymour. Pushing sixty. Pushing his liver into the grave, pushing what little remained of his luck until it ran out. Eyes a grubby blue in his florid face, little red veins like worms on the side of his nose, blond hair, once as rich as nicotine, now going thin and dirty grey. Thick stubby fingers; an unexpected signet ring on the little finger, gold, too large, too flash – worth a bob or two, he might confide – the index finger of his right hand pressed significantly against his nose. It was his one valuable possession, his one link with the days when he had hopes ahead of him, pretensions to parade, appearances to keep up.

Bill Seymour, now sitting in a bar on Avenue del Pilar. Well-known street to the rugger clubs, to the married men with a pink ticket, to the luckless bridegrooms dragged off to stag nights by grinning drunken friends to give of their inebriated best to those soft little mouths under the table in the time-honoured game of Manila roulette, well-known even to the pale-faced wet-behind-the-ears City types out to Hong Kong on a two-year secondment.

Bill Seymour has not been wet behind the ears for forty years. Nor does he have a salary of six figures in Hong Kong, he would cut no ice there – Manila is the place for him.

Manila, the bottom of the spiral of the Far East, the spiral round which the failed expats spin before finally dropping down the plughole.

Poor old Manila.

*

Of course, he has not always been scraping the bottom, oh no.

He has had plenty of fine chances in his life. Plenty when he was young and carefree and fit, the whole of his life ahead of him. But slowly, imperceptibly, they have become less and less with each year until now at fifty-nine he has nowhere, just one refuge after another, each one chancier than the last, decaying, squalid, no home comforts, no drink nearer than the seedy bar down the road, none of them offering anything to watch except the dying embers of a wasted life.

Until today, the first chance for eight months. The chance is sitting beside him in the bar. He is Portuguese, this chance, and earlier he and Seymour had been sitting in General Mac-Arthur's old headquarters, the Manila Hotel no less, where the Portuguese is staying. Seymour had joined him there for a drink, strolling into the vast lobby with its high timber ceiling as if he came in there every evening after work, chatting like the man of the world he had once been, watching fashionable Manila wander by, showing off his one clean barong. Never really liked barongs, Seymour would confide, even though everyone wore them, even the British ambassador. Mind you, Seymour might belch over his San Miguel, they were all right on Filipinos, but a white man looked a bit, well, *charley* in them, poncing around in a thing like a sawn-off tart's nightie, and the ambassador was living proof. But, what the hell, when in Rome… plus it was cheaper than trying to keep a blazer from being eaten by the cockroaches in downtown Pasay and it fitted in better on the Avenue del Pilar where they were now. To say nothing of impressing punters with his local knowledge. Punters like Raul, sitting beside him in his Italian pants and Gucci loafers.

Raul was a stroke of luck. A real stroke of luck, the sort that he had taken for granted thirty years ago but which now came all too rarely. An acquaintance, hell no, a friend: a friend from that best of all circles, the wine trade.

Seymour had spotted him two days ago in the lobby of the Pen, on one of his speculative walks in the hope of seeing someone who might be good for a drink. And when he looked at him, he saw more than a drink – he thought that at last, at last, he might be looking at a way out of the Far East, back to Europe, back to the stylish life he'd always craved. If only he could sell it right.

And to sell the idea that he had, what better place to take his old friend than the bar they were in now?

It was a nice bar, in its own way. At least, Seymour thought so, and he'd been through all the bars on Avenue del Pilar more times than he knew. Tasteful, he thought. Seductive. Sexy. None of the corny red wallpaper peeling in the corners, with pox-ridden tarts looking bored by the bar, standing in a cage under a spotlight grinding their pelvises in time to the music, sitting behind the one-way mirror waiting to be pulled out of the fish tank.

No. Cool decor, cream walls with dark-peach lighting, polished wood, discreet alcoves softly upholstered. Air-con wafting cool air. Hostesses softly dressed, demure in crisp white blouses and dark skirts, most of whom could keep a conversation going in English for maybe as much as two minutes at a time.

He was greeted at the door like a long-lost friend, taken by two smiling hostesses to an alcove – true Philippine hospitality.

'Scotch,' he said expansively, with the air of one who entertained every day. 'Two glasses of Scotch, Grand McCowrie, large ones.'

The senior of the two hostesses, all of twenty, walked off to see to it. Stomped off, because that was the way they walked, these pretty things, so soft and silky and elegant until they walked. Their walk gave them away, 'lack of breeding, ol' boy, still what can y'do? Not like the Chinese who waft and sway and glide with several thousand years of civilisation behind them'.

Music poured from the loudspeakers, 'I did it my way' sung off-key by a Filipino, one of the customers, his eyes shut as he gripped the karaoke microphone tight, deep in his three-minute fantasy of being Frank Sinatra.

Seymour's hostess came back after a minute with two glasses of Scotch, lots of ice, lots of whisky, water on the side. Two champagne glasses for her and her friend, charged as champagne to the customer but actually holding fizzy lemonade.

Raul was about to drink when Seymour laid a hand on his arm. 'Just a moment, old boy,' he said.

He picked up his glass and sniffed, putting on the act of an expert, his nose inhaling bulbously, rootling round in the air over the glass like a gun dog looking for a rabbit in a bush. Frowned. Took a little sip, a delicate sip, not a drinking man's slurp, a sip to impress the wine expert, wrinkling his nose, acting distaste.

He turned to his hostess. 'No,' he said, 'not this stuff. I asked for Grand McCowrie.'

Her eyes widened. 'It is Grand McCowrie, sirrr.' Delightful the way they say 'sir', the Filipinas, the soft rounding of the 'r', the loin-warming lilt in the voice.

'No, no. I can tell. Fetch me a new bottle. And a glass.'

She went off, doubtful, a little uneasy. Came back with a bottle. Seymour took it from her. Showed the bottle to Raul his friend.

'Look. New bottle, right?'

Raul looked. 'Yes, it looks okay.'

Seymour twisted the cap and poured out a slug. Handed the glass to Raul. 'Here. You try. Can you tell the difference?'

Raul took the new glass and sniffed, less show, more purpose, the practised movements of a man in the trade. Put it down and sniffed the one he had been given before.

Then a sip from each in turn. Looked uncertainly at Seymour. Tasted them both again. 'No,' he said at last. 'If I must be honest, I can tell no difference.'

Seymour beamed at him. 'Exactly!'

Raul's look of puzzlement increased. 'What d'you mean?'

Seymour snorted, his fleshy nose vibrating. 'I tell you, I've been drinking this brand all my life. I know what Grand McCowrie tastes like, and it isn't like either of these.'

'So?'

'So look here,' Seymour said, picking up the bottle the girl had brought. Raul leaned forward. The girls sat still, curious about what was going on.

Seymour pointed at the neck of the bottle. 'This ring,' he said, indicating the ring broken off the bottom of the cap. 'Look at it.'

He tilted the bottle slightly. 'Now, look at the bottom of the ring.'

Raul held the bottle up so that he could do as Seymour asked. 'It's too dark, I can't see a thing.'

Seymour got a match out of the box on the table, lit it, and held it up to the bottle. 'See the little scratches, on the underside of the ring?'

Raul frowned, conscious that Seymour was attracting attention from the next alcove along, sensing the eye of another customer and taking care not to catch it. He squinted at the bottle.

'Mmm. Ye-es…'

'There you are! Explains it all.'

Seymour took the bottle from him and put it back on the table. The girls had been giggling. Now they went quiet and looked up apprehensively.

The manager stood there, impassive eyes in a smooth fleshy face. Drawn like a moth to the flame Seymour had been waving about. Customers who misbehaved were one thing, misbehaviour of a certain sort was what they came for. Customers who drew attention to misbehaviour by his barman were another.

'Excuse me sir.' His voice was quiet, but insistent, displeased.

'Ah. Just the chap.'

'Is everything in order?'

'Oh fine. Yes. Lovely girls, lovely music.' Seymour suppressed a belch. 'But not lovely Scotch, old boy. Not lovely at all.'

The music died away at the end of the song. The singer's friends clapped as he stepped down off the small stage, grinning. For a moment there was silence in the bar, silence around the table.

The manager's expression tightened.

'I am sorry sir, it is possible you may be mistaken. As you can see, it is Grand McCowrie, we have only the best here.'

'No, it isn't, old boy, as we both know very well.'

There was bravado in Seymour's voice. Thirty years ago, the bravado would have been in his heart too.

A bouncer walked slowly up behind the manager. Raul shifted uncomfortably in his seat. Shit, he thought, what is this fool trying to get us into?

'Come on,' Seymour said to the manager, 'I know this

town. I know Alonzo and his tricks, too.'

The manager hesitated. 'You know Alonzo?'

'Of course I know Alonzo. Knew him when he was behind the bar at Rosa's down the road. He showed me how he did it. Looks like he hasn't changed.'

A muscle flickered at the corner of the bouncer's eye.

'But don't worry about it,' Seymour said. 'I'm not complaining, old boy. I'm just showing my friend around.'

He waved a podgy hand at Raul, who shifted again and tried a nervous smile. The girls' eyes followed the gold of the signet ring as it circled in the dim light. The manager's tension eased a notch.

'There is no complaint, sir?'

'No, not at all. Like I said, lovely place, lovely girls.' The lovely girls smiled, nervously. 'With a real drink it'd be just perfect.'

Suddenly the manager smiled, a big smile of welcome. 'Of course, sir. It will be my pleasure, sir. On the house.'

He clicked his fingers, snapped an instruction in Tagalog. The bouncer drifted back to the door; the girls swept the offending glasses and bottle off the table, scampered to the bar and came back with two fresh glasses.

'Enjoy your stay, sir,' the manager said, and walked away.

Raul let out a breath, reached for his glass, took a swallow. 'What did you do that for? I thought…'

'You weren't worried, were you? No need, old boy, no need. They're friendly chaps, the Filipinos – always smile as they pull the trigger.' He took a drink. 'That's better.' He raised his glass to the light and made a gesture of looking through it.

'Tell the difference now?'

Raul sipped. Nodded. 'You were right.'

Those words put Seymour on a high. It was a long time since anyone had said that to him. A long time since he had seen anyone look at him with anything like respect. It was something to savour.

He held out his glass and smiled.

It looked as if this chance was going to work.

CHAPTER 2

A moorland river ran gently from one rocky pool to another, then flowed over a wide sandy stretch. Rough tussocks of grass and heather sloped gently up to one side. To the other was a manicured patch of woodland, with a large house half hidden beyond. In the far distance, a faint line of Devon hills. A watery sun shone intermittently through pale clouds. Swallows swooped overhead, chattering occasionally. Thirty yards upstream, in the pool above, a circle of small ripples appeared as a trout rose.

Hamish sighed and looked longingly towards the rising trout, sorely tempted to move upstream. Then he sighed again and turned towards the bank, where his companion sat.

'You going to try for that one?' said Nick.

'Can't,' Hamish grunted. 'It's not our beat, club waters stop at the top of this pool.'

'So? There's no one around…'

'I'm really tempted,' Hamish said. 'But I don't fancy being found poaching, thanks all the same.'

'Ha! You didn't mind a spot of poaching when we were young. Up in Scotland that time, for example…'

Hamish laughed. 'Yeah. Well. That was then. When we were young… as you say. This is now. Plus, being caught poaching wouldn't do me a lot of good.'

'Oh, now you're a respectable lawyer, you mean?' Nick said, the twitch of a smile at the corner of his mouth.

'Yep. Might get me struck off, who knows?'

'You actually think someone's watching?'

'Can't tell. Those new people at the Manor are pretty tight-arsed. That's the trouble with incomers. When my father was there, he'd have been fairly relaxed about it.'

'Hmm.' Nick went quiet for a moment. 'How is he?'

'Fine. Potters about in his cottage.' There was a note of sadness in Hamish's voice. He said nothing for a moment. Then, 'Here, you try this pool. I've got to get back to London anyway. Monday morning tomorrow, and some of us have to work for a living.'

They saluted each other, and Hamish moved off. As he turned to walk down the river he caught a glimpse of the Manor. That glimpse had the same effect as always. A remembrance of the time, six years before, when his father had moved out. It had taken him and Hamish a month to sort through all the furniture, bric-a-brac and outdated articles that had gathered in the house over the past 150 years, ever since Hamish's great-grandparents had first bought it. A mass of old furniture, respectable but not outstanding. Dulled oil paintings. Peculiar items, such as a chest of drawers no more than a foot wide and fourteen inches high, faced with elaborate inlays, the work (so Hamish had been told) of an apprentice cabinet-maker. Victorian bedpans. Accumulations of old papers. Two antique pistols, an assortment of old swords, a flintlock blunderbuss with a hinged bayonet, its trigger mechanism long rusted solid. And so on. And on... and on. Nothing that either Hamish or his father would have gone out and bought, but stuff whose familiarity, like the house itself, had given comfort. A comfort that had been ripped away after his father had been conned into an investment which had sounded so promising, but which had

proved disastrous; he had lost all his savings and been com-
pelled to sell. Six years later the thought of it still tugged at
Hamish's heart.

*

No gentle burble of the stream for Hamish on Monday
morning, but the distant buzz of London traffic. In the neo-
Georgian side streets of central London, the trout rivers of
Devon were far away. If he looked out of his window, in the
distance he could glimpse the tops of trees in Hyde Park. In
front of him were four bottles of Grand McCowrie. All of
them empty, for display only; all with slightly different labels,
as exported to the USA, Spain, Australia, Japan.

He looked up, thoughtfully, at the bookcases along his
office wall; glass-fronted, reaching up to the ceiling. Not one
of them contained a book. Only row after row of bottles. All
with a degree of similarity to Grand McCowrie, which had
been deliberately created by whoever had made them, in the
hope of getting people to mistake them for the real thing. All
of them relics of past battles in the courts of Germany, Italy,
Ecuador, South Africa, Hong Kong and a host of other
countries. Catching the people who did this was a full-time
job. Eventually they would get caught in the net of the law.
As should all fraudsters, Hamish thought. And maybe poach-
ers too, he admitted with a wry smile.

CHAPTER 3

Seymour has been on a high for three days now. Since he took his good friend Raul to the bar he has been living the life, the good life; sitting with Raul in the back of an air-conditioned limo Raul has hired from the Manila Hotel, taking Raul to the places that you go to for the weekend, if you have money. Throwing out names of the resorts down on the coast – Punta Baluarte was where Seymour suggested, and there they are now, drinking at a table with a little umbrella over it. They are in their beach clothes, Seymour's a little old and faded, though it was lucky he had them, he had almost thrown them out, thinking he would never see a beach again. Thank God he had kept them – he has no spare cash to throw away buying new ones.

'Ah, I envy you,' Raul says with a sigh, sinking back into his chair, beer sinking in his glass, sun sinking over the sea.

Seymour is startled by this. No one has envied him for some time. 'Oh? Why?'

'This place. This country. It is warm, no one works too hard, it is the easy life.'

Yes, easy the life based in the Manila Hotel, easy the life which can snap its finger for the limo to take you to Punta Baluarte. Not so easy the life in a broken-down house in Pasay with crummy furniture, the dusty vacant lot, the long, hot walk to catch the rusty bus to town, sweating after fifty yards. No one walks in this country who has money enough for anything else. That is a life not to be spoken about.

'Oh. Yes, of course. Not a bad little country really. I'll miss it in a way.'

'Miss it? Why? Do you think of leaving?'

Seymour feels a sudden tightness in his chest, wonders if he will die of cardiac arrest. He thinks of nothing else but leaving.

'Well, to do this deal of ours, of course, I would need to be in Portugal to help you set everything up.'

'Ah. But I am thinking… I think it is better, yes, if we set it up here?'

'*Here?*

'Yes, it is the perfect place. Labour is cheap. Copying is cheap. I have made some enquiries. There is no need to worry about the law, everyone tells me a few pesos in the right direction can square anything. It is near Hong Kong, Singapore, Japan, it is ideally placed for the international trade you speak of.'

Seymour shivers.

Nothing to do with the temperature, the temperature is fine, the overbearing heat of the day softening nicely into that pleasant warmth which is so ideal for dining out of doors.

It was the thought of ending his life in Pasay that makes him shiver.

'We-ell,' he says, trying to quell the alarm inside him, trying not to show his panic. 'Up to a point, I suppose.'

'How you mean, up to a point?'

'Well. On the surface, yes, what you say is true. But underneath, it's not so good. They're a lazy lot, the Filipinos. I tell you, I know them. No professionalism. No dedication to getting a thing right. If we want to get it right, absolutely right, this ain't the country to do it.'

'Hmm.' Raul puts down his glass, looks at Seymour, a quizzical look on his face. Seymour leans forward, sweat on his face.

'Europe's the place,' he urges. 'Think about it. This EEC thing, the thing you and Spain have just joined – stuff can go to France, Italy, wherever. Even send it to Scotland if we want.'

He sits back and takes a pull at his drink. 'No customs to inspect it, either,' he adds, desperate to get to Europe, anxious to stress the benefits of operating there.

'Oh?' Raul queries him. 'But why do we care about inspection? I thought you said no one will be able to spot that it is not real.'

Seymour curses himself for putting his foot in it.

'Yes. If it's done right. But that's my point,' he urges. 'You can't rely on the people here to do it right.'

Raul leans back in his chair. 'Well. Maybe. You are the local expert.' He looks at his watch. 'I'm getting hungry. Shall we eat?'

Seymour nods. Of course he will eat, he will eat any time the man suggests, this is the man who is paying the bill.

Seymour lies awake half the night, draped in the heavy blanket of the warm, humid, tropical air. *Please God, let Raul see sense.*

The next day they do little but sit in the sun, swim a little, drink a bit, and lounge.

Raul is lapping up the privilege of a weekend in the Far East at his company's expense. Seymour flops near him: a labrador drooling for a biscuit to fall from the table.

Raul does not raise the subject again until the afternoon, when they are lying on a bamboo raft in the sea.

'I am thinking. Maybe you are right. Maybe in Portugal it

will work.'

'I'm sure that's right,' Seymour says cautiously.

'Why don't you come to Portugal?' Raul says lazily. 'Then we can see.'

For three days Seymour has been waiting for this. Relief floods through him. At last, he is on his way.

CHAPTER 4

Five floors above the Calle de Alcalá, Miguel Morato settled back in the armchair behind his desk and gazed about the antique furniture beneath the high ceiling, waiting for his visitors to be shown in. Heavy curtains muffled the heat of the sun at midday. He glanced at the sideboard where the decanter of sherry rested.

Directors of Grand McCowrie had always been welcome in this room. Always in the twenty years of his time, and in his father's time before. Not that they sold as much McCowrie in his father's time as they did now. Distributing the brand in Spain had added considerably to the business of the company, had added considerably to his family's fortune. Nothing less than the best sherry from his bodega was ever served to his visitors from London.

He rose smoothly to his feet as Carmen brought the visitors in, and walked forward with arms outstretched to greet them.

'Señor Spicer. An honour to welcome you to our house.' He shook hands warmly, his eyes all smiles. 'And Señor… Freeman, is it not?' he added, turning with avuncular charm to the younger man.

His hand made a slow gesture towards the armchairs in the centre of the room while he walked to the sideboard. Reverently he poured three glasses of sherry, returning to the gentlemen with them on a small, silver tray. He had poured and carried them with his own hands, showing the dignity of one who is conferring a great honour on his guests and knows they will understand.

Adrian smiled a small smile, which he hid behind his glass, and sipped.

Morato was halfway into his chair when Simon Freeman spoke. 'Actually, I wonder if I could have a glass of Perrier.'

The words hung in midair and Morato froze in astonishment.

'If you have one, that is,' Simon added. From his tone he could have been speaking to a junior waiter in a restaurant.

Morato slowly lowered himself into his chair. He was speechless with disbelief. Never had anyone behaved in such a way in this room. Never had anyone, even a director, declined the honour of a glass before the extensive lunch that would follow. Over the years the sherry and the lunch had become a ritual. That this young puppy should say such a thing was incredible. He contained the irritation inside him, stretched out a hand for the buzzer. Carmen instantly appeared in the doorway.

'It seems,' he said as she hovered at the door, 'that señor' – he waved his hand vaguely towards Simon – 'would prefer a glass of mineral water.'

Simon looked at Carmen and switched on a smile. 'Perrier. Please.'

Carmen paused, sleek dark eyebrows raised, immobilised with surprise; then she collected herself and hurried from the room.

Morato shifted slightly in his chair, turning away from Freeman and looking directly at Spicer. 'And how is Hubert Egerton?' he asked, voice smooth once more.

'Well – I believe,' Adrian said in an offhand way.

'I am sorry not to see him here,' Morato said, raising his glass. 'Over the years he has become a close friend – a close friend.'

'Quite.' Adrian was well aware of this. It was why he had timed his visit to coincide with Egerton's trip to South America.

'He is not ill, I hope?' Morato was puzzled by his absence.

'No. There has simply been a shift in responsibilities.'

'Oh?' Morato's face showed surprise. Egerton had been the director with responsibility for Spain for fifteen years.

'Yes,' Adrian said, settling back into his seat. 'Simon, perhaps you will explain?'

Morato reluctantly shifted his gaze to the impertinent Freeman.

'Over the last few months, the board has undertaken a review of the company's distribution arrangements,' Simon recited. 'It has concluded that a leaner, more aggressive goal-oriented facility is needed for the 1990s. Minimising costs, maximising profitability and thrust.'

Morato's lip curled in disdain. One or two of his younger executives had started to use jargon like this. He thought it a sign of incompetence.

'In short,' Simon continued, 'we see the old-style distrib-utorship as a thing of the past. From now on, what we need is joint-venture arrangements with selected partners.'

'We?' Morato asked patronisingly, his glass halfway to his lips, his eyebrows raised in disbelief that Simon should iden-tify himself so closely with the board.

'Simon has been appointed Director of European Joint Ventures.' Adrian said quietly. The title of director was merely an empty commercial idiom, but Adrian omitted to say this.

Morato was just able to stop himself from snorting into his glass. *Mother of God*, he thought, as Carmen reappeared with Simon's glass of water, put it down on the table within his reach and hurriedly left the room.

'And how many European Joint Ventures are there?' Morato asked.

Simon put his finger in his glass, picked out the slice of lemon floating on top and dropped it into an antique ashtray. A drop of water fell from the lemon as it passed over the table's polished surface. Morato's glance followed it with rising annoyance.

'As you may know,' Simon said, 'our first joint ventures were established last year in Hong Kong and Singapore. We are in the middle of setting one up in Japan. We have not yet established one in Europe. However' – he stretched his legs and smiled – 'we have decided that Spain should be the first country in Europe to benefit from the new arrangements.'

'Spain? You mean *here*?'

'Exactly.'

'But… but…'

'We've worked it all out quite carefully,' Simon continued. 'We establish a joint venture to service all the marketing requirements of our brands. The share structure is split 90 -10 between us and the local interests. Profits, of course, split pro rata between the shareholders. We would like,' he said with a nasty smile, 'to invite you to subscribe to the new company.'

'Indeed. I take it that the existing distributorship agreement would then continue between my company and this new company?'

'Oh no.' Simon wriggled comfortably back into the leather armchair and put a superior smile on his already smug face. 'I don't think you've quite understood. The new company would be structured to carry out the distribution itself. Naturally,' he added with a smirk, 'we would still value your expertise, which we hope would play a significant part in the new company.'

It took Morato's brain about five seconds to absorb the truth behind the unpalatable words that were reaching his ears. It would be a substantial blow. Distributing Grand McCowrie currently provided sixty per cent of his firm's profits. As it sunk in, the sherry in his throat took on a sour taste, a stab of anxiety in his chest giving it a vinegary sharpness.

'In *place* of? You mean you wish to terminate our agreement?'

'Oh no, by no means, absolutely not. Our policy is to streamline it into a modern, structured arrangement in keeping with the company's corporate plans for the future. An arrangement in which, as I said, we would invite you to become a partner with us.'

'A partner? At *ten per cent*?' Quite apart from the financial loss, the very idea struck at the roots of his pride.

'Yes. We thought—'

'But it is an outrage! For twenty years or more we have built up the brand for you in this country. From nothing we have brought it to number two, it is poised to take over as number one – now you come and offer me ten per cent?'

'That is in line with our currently developed joint-venture policy,' Simon oozed.

'This is monstrous! It is an insult!' Morato sprang to his feet. 'I will not be dealt with in this way!' he snapped. 'I demand to see Hubert Egerton!'

'Hubert is not responsible for the company restructuring,' Adrian said quietly. 'Board- level responsibility lies with me.'

'With you! Then do you seriously expect me to listen to this, this… this nonsense?' He glared at Adrian.

Adrian stayed silent, looking up from his chair in a languid way.

'Do I take it… Miguel,' Simon enquired, 'that you decline the proposal that I've outlined?'

Morato stiffened, affronted. *To be called Miguel by such an impertinent youth!*

'Well, it's a fair question,' Adrian said. 'Do you?'

'Of course, I decline it! It is ridiculous!' Morato spat.

'Señor Morato,' Adrian said in a cheerful voice, 'I'm sorry you've decided to turn us down, believe me.' He stood up, drank the last of his sherry, cocked his head on one side and looked at the empty glass. 'Hubert's going to miss this,' he smiled, and put it lightly down beside Simon's untouched Perrier.

CHAPTER 5

Seymour yawned, stretched; he had slept well after his long flight, and now here he was in Europe once more. A dream come true. Well, perhaps not quite the dream he had imagined. He had been expecting to stay in Lisbon, but here he was in a rustic and undistinguished village. And not in its most luxurious house, either. A thin rug on pine floorboards, a mirror hanging lopsided on the wall, and the bed had sagged uncomfortably during the night. He looked out of the window, across a back yard towards the wall of a house opposite: white paint peeling from its hot, sun-baked stonework. light-blue paint flaking around its windows. From what he remembered when he had arrived, the windows of this house were pretty much the same. Not quite the opulent villa he had imagined Raul would be living in.

From the floor below he could hear the voice of Raul's wife, high-pitched and penetrating, reverberating around the house. This would not be a restful house to stay in. But it would be worth putting up with for a while, if it meant his plan would bear fruit.

*

The coffee shop that Raul drove him to was in a different league from the house. A fashionable street in central Lisbon. Shining glass window, fronting a long, dark, cool room stretching towards the back. At its right, a bar extended the whole length of the room, mirrors on the wall behind it reflecting the bar staff and clientele. Elegant lighting from overhead chandeliers; a high ceiling, divided into panels, picked out with elaborate, cream-coloured mouldings. A row of polished mahogany tables, placed at a discreet distance from each other. A delicate and seductive aroma of coffee.

Raul led him to the far end, to the furthest table, in an alcove set back from the rest of the room, where a man was already sitting; white shirt, crinkled black hair, gold chain round his neck, sunglasses. Maybe a few years older than Raul. So this was the João whom Raul had talked about.

Seymour looked down at João and smiled: the warm, calm smile of a confident man who knew what he was talking about. The smile he had been using for forty years now. He gave João's hand a firm shake and sat down opposite him. 'A perfect place,' he said, expansively, pointing around him. 'A perfect place, to design a perfect product.'

Raul smiled with him. João's face remained impassive.

Seymour got straight to it and listed all the things they needed. Bottles, the exact same shape as those used for Grand McCowrie. He took an empty bottle of Grand McCowrie out of the case he was carrying, held it upside down, pointed out the shape of the underneath of the bottle, the letters and figures embossed there. Caps – he unscrewed the cap, held it up, described it in detail: the knurling around the top edge, its exact placing and number of indentations; its slight bulge in the middle; the tamper-proof part at the bottom which had broken off when the bottle was first opened. The colour, the gold texture, the printing on the side. And then, most important of all, the two labels, front and back. He pointed out all their details of shape, colour and text. And, as always when reciting his spiel, he was subtly aware of the expression on the face he was talking to. João's gave nothing away.

'And of course,' he went on, 'there is what we put inside the bottle. First, it must be exactly the right colour. This is easy, but also, we must make the taste… acceptable. Some cheap Scotch whisky, plus some grain spirit which we get, maybe from Germany, Holland, Poland—'

'Pffft,' Raul snorted. 'We don't need to go abroad to get spirit. We have brandy, we have bagaço – why, some of our company's cheapest wine gets distilled, we can use that.'

'No, no, no,' said Seymour, keen to squash this idea at the outset. He did not want everything to come from inside Portugal; he had his own reasons for that. 'We must not use brandy. Whisky and brandy do not mix. There are people in the Philippines who try it, but you can always tell. You remember when we were in the bar in Manila?'

Raul nodded. 'When they gave us their imitation?'

'Yes,' Seymour said. 'You tasted it, you thought it was Scotch.'

Raul nodded again.

'That is because they took care to use the right spirit. Grain spirit, that's the secret. Use brandy, rum, or any of the others and the customers will know.'

Raul waved a hand dismissively. 'But by that time they've bought it, it'll be too late, why should we care?'

'Because they won't be happy. They'll complain. Then word will get out, and people will start investigating.' He turned towards João. 'I understand you…' he paused diplomatically, '… er, export, a selection of goods?'

João nodded. A slight smile, the first one Seymour had seen.

'And do you like it when people complain?'

'We do not encourage it.' Said with a stony face.

'But it's simpler if they don't?'

João gave a wry smile, a slight nod. Glanced quickly at Raul. 'He is right, Raul,' he said. 'For the plan to succeed, everything must be good. As good as we can make it.'

Raul said something in Portuguese, João spoke fast back to him. Raul nodded. Then, for the first time, João gave a proper smile. 'It is a good plan,' he said, holding out a muscular hand. 'We will make it work.' But as he gripped Seymour's hand in his, Seymour looked into his eyes; and knew this man would be a tougher customer than Raul.

CHAPTER 6

Adrian Spicer was leaning back in his chair, jacket off, blue-and-red spotted tie cascading down the front of his pure white shirt. He stared at Hamish across the wide polished surface of the mahogany table in his office. A gold pen was held against pursed lips, an expression of disdain on his smooth ex-merchant-banker face.

'That is not what I want to hear,' he was saying. 'What I want is not a lawyer who comes in and tells me I'm breaking the law. What I want is a lawyer who can provide me with advice on how I can achieve the objective that I want.'

Simon Freeman, sitting next to Spicer, nodded his head in sage youthful approval. Identical tie, identical white shirt, complete clone, Hamish thought, flicking a glance at him. *Bloody prat.*

'Look,' Hamish said, 'you've been having these cosy little chats with competitors, all aimed at carving up the market. That's illegal. That's what I've been trying to tell you for the last half-hour. I—'

'I'll thank you not to be impertinent.'

'There's no way I can tell you how to achieve an illegal objective. I'm not going to help you break the law.'

'Oh aren't you?' Spicer gave him an aggressive look. 'I thought you lawyers were there to find loopholes in the law.'

'A loophole is one thing – breaking the law's another. Have you *any idea* what the company will get fined if the

European Commission finds out what you're planning?'

'Now look here.' Spicer's tone turned smooth and patronising. 'Are you seriously trying to tell me that I can't have a discreet word with my contacts in the trade? An off-the-record conversation about matters of mutual interest? Are you really trying to say that that's breaking the law?'

'Yes. What you're trying to do amounts to a concerted practice contrary to Article 85 of the Treaty of Rome. And as for "off the record", forget it. I'll bet anything you like that one of those valued contacts of yours is going to be stupid enough to write it all down in a confidential memo. Bingo, dawn raid on them and us. In which case, don't say you didn't know, and don't say I didn't give you proper advice.'

There was silence.

He looked at Freeman, the same smooth look as his mentor on the outside, the same morals within. Now scribbling lazily on a pad.

Making up an edited version of what I said, Hamish thought. Oh well. Sort of thing you get used to after a while. Not difficult to counter, if you see it coming.

*

'Jesus,' Spicer said five minutes later, as Hamish shut the door behind him. 'Bloody lawyer!'

He strode to a cabinet across the room, a reproduction mahogany glass-fronted bookcase, bottles and glasses on the shelves where books should have been. Pulled out a bottle of Malvern water, broke the seal with a vicious twist and poured himself a large glass. He drank half in a gulp, then shook himself, a stage shiver.

'Just think what would have happened if we'd taken one of that lot to Madrid. We'd all still be there, writing memos to each other over the sherry. Trying to decide which side of the bloody glass to drink out of.'

Freeman grinned as he thought of the way he'd rejected Morato's sherry. 'All right for you to talk. You drank yours.'

'It was only one glassful,' Spicer smiled. 'When Ferguson retires you can have all the sherry you want. You'll just have to wait a couple of months.'

He put his hands on his hips and stared down at his assistant. 'And then… then we can start by sorting out young Hamish and his ilk.'

*

As Hamish returned along the corridor to his room he was collared by Alec Johnston, his boss. Dark-haired, hook-nosed and peremptory, he hustled Hamish into his room.

Papers lay all over the place: scattered on the mahogany desk, grouped in piles on the matching mahogany table in the middle of the room, stacked in boxes in the corner of the floor. Alec hustled him past a trolley which bore the remains of a sandwich lunch, grabbed a letter from the chaos on his desk and thrust it at Hamish.

Hamish was poking about on the trolley to see what was left over from Alec's lunch. He straightened up, a cluster of grapes in his hand, popped one of them in his mouth and started reading.

By the middle of the first page his jaw stopped, a half-chewed grape still in his mouth. By the bottom of the page, he was holding his breath. Halfway through page two he choked. Morato Hermanos SA was suing Grand McCowrie for unlawful termination of its distributorship agreement. What had made Hamish choke was the size of the damages claimed.

'Fifty million dollars!' he exclaimed, when he had

recovered. He was pink in the face and wide-eyed, a picture of boyish outrage.

Alec was leaning against the wall, arms crossed, looking assessingly at Hamish.

'I mean… for God's sake, that's ludicrous!' Hamish declared. 'They're trying it on, there's no way they'll get that!'

'Oh?' Alec asked in mock politeness. 'You know something about them that I don't?'

'Well, God Almighty, no court's going to award them that, they don't stand a chance.'

'Wake up. You're not in an English court now, you're in Spain. Spanish law, Spanish plaintiff, Spanish judge. We're a wicked foreign multinational, the judge'll be only too happy to shaft us.'

'Oh Christ.' Hamish closed his eyes as if in pain; then, as his brain made the connection, his gaze opened and flicked up at Alec.

'It's that oaf Spicer, isn't it? *Jesus.* God Almighty. Ever since those bloody management consultants brought him in it's been one thing after another. Why does he persist in being so *stupid?* If only people like him came and took advice first, they'd never get the company into this sort of a mess. If only people talked to their lawyers… half the cases I had at the Bar would never have arisen if my clients had the sense to take advice first.'

'Ah.' Alec smiled aloofly, twisting his lips with the superiority of his fifty years. 'You are missing the point. It is not a question of stupidity. You are simply mistaking the essential nature of the Commercial Shit.'

Hamish looked blankly at him. 'What on earth d'you mean?'

'It's what the company, plus those management

consultants who I think we can all agree to question, recruited him for in the first place. As an antidote to the complacency that has gripped this outfit, in all matters save the actual blending and selling of whisky, for the last twenty years. You wouldn't wish to see us taken over by some corporate vulture, I take it?'

Hamish shivered. He thought of his uncle, who had worked in the company for forty years. He would be turning in his grave. 'You must be joking. But what has that got to do with…'

'Think about it,' Alec said. 'I'll bet you five million pesetas to a miniature of Ecuadorean firewater that Spicer's handling of the whole situation was designed to have precisely the result that it had.'

'Oh?'

'Think, dear boy, *think*.' He spun a chair, swung his leg astride it, and folded his arms across its back. 'Spicer's job is to expand and strengthen the company. To do so by building an empire which controls distribution, makes it a stronger marketing force, and so becomes less vulnerable to a takeover. The board has decided to do all this by setting up joint ventures in key overseas markets, and Spicer is in charge of doing this.'

'Yes, yes, I know all that, I—'

'And if, conveniently, the old distributors can be got rid of in the process, Spicer can replace them with men of his own choosing. He thus removes the old loyalties and replaces them with personal influence of his own. The empire which he builds thus expands and strengthens his own position within the company. Morato is an old-style distributor whose loyalties lie with the older directors. So goodbye, Morato. A few million of the company's money is, he no doubt feels, a small price for him to pay.'

'But that's… well, damn it, it's dishonest!'

'Oh Hamish, don't be so naive,' Alec said with an exasperated frown. 'That's corporate life in the twentieth century. If you don't like it, you should have stayed in the prim cloisters of the Bar.' He gave Hamish a look of world-weary sadness. 'Besides, that's only my guess. I can't prove a word of what I've said.'

Hamish frowned. 'But if we *could* prove it…'

Alec pursed his lips and sighed. 'Your job and mine, Hamish, as lawyers to this company, is to put up a defence against Morato. Which involves proving the official version of events – that is to say Spicer's version. Start proving my unworthy suspicions and you might as well hand Morato his fifty million on a plate.'

'But—'

'Shut up and let me spell it out,' Alec said softly. 'Morato is claiming against the company. We are lawyers for the company, *therefore* it's our job to fight this claim off. So, if Spicer says that Morato is old-fashioned and out of touch, that's what we have to prove. Try to play it differently, start getting in his way, and you'll be out of a job. Got that?'

Hamish stared at him, wide-eyed.

'And remember,' Alec warned, 'friend Adrian thinks that it's worth risking a lot of cash to get what he wants. Don't get in his way.'

CHAPTER 7

'*¡Hijo de puta!* I could have killed him!'

Morato scowled through the window, squinting at the sun in his eyes.

'But you didn't,' came the reply in a light, teasing tone from the armchair behind him.

'Hah!' Morato wheeled round. 'I have seen my lawyers. They say I have a clear case. I can claim compensation of millions. Millions. Not pesetas, dollars.'

The curly-haired man in the armchair raised a lazy glass to his lips, ran a mouthful of wine slowly round his mouth and let it trickle to the back of his throat. Pushed out his legs, crossed his ankles, then raised his arms behind his neck until he felt the stretching in his vertebrae.

'Pfeugh. Lawyers, compensation – you must be getting old, Miguel.'

Morato glared at him. It was a sensitive point to a man of fifty-seven, especially when put by a man some years his junior.

'What do you mean?' he demanded.

'What I say. There was a time when you would have dealt with impudence yourself. When you would have found a more… *appropriate* way to reward an insult.'

Morato sat down and gave him a haughty glare.

'I do not need lessons from you in such matters,' he snapped. 'What do you know of the law? Fifty million dollars.

That is what I am claiming.'

'What do *I* know of the law? *You* ask *me* what I know of the law? Ha!' João's laugh rang loudly round the room. He sat up, put a hand on one thigh and leaned forward. 'You, you who have spent the last thirty years following meekly in the law's footsteps – you, an honest burgher, a… a fat merchant – you who run squealing to a lawyer, you ask *me*? I, who still dance round its lumbering footsteps in a way that you once dared, you ask me what I know of it?'

'Oh? You have done so well from this dance that you think that fifty million dollars is nothing?'

'Pffff,' João exclaimed, his hand rising from his thigh in a gesture of dismissal, 'it is as I said. You are a fat merchant, sleek in your counting-house. You think only of money. Your honour lives only in your bank account.'

Morato sprang to his feet, drawing himself up to his full height, three inches short of six foot but still the lithe figure he had had for all his adult life. 'You call me fat?' he challenged, slapping his stomach. 'You are ridiculous.'

'Not your waistline, maybe. Your mind, your spirit, your honour, it is these that are fat and sluggish.'

'This is nonsense!'

'So prove it. Leave the lawyers to their scribblings and their fawning. Let them go to court if it pleases you, if it helps to swell your bank account. All that will do to the English company will be to worry its accountants a little. It will give them no lasting hurt.'

He stretched out a hand to the bottle of white port and delicately poured more of the cold golden liquid into Morato's glass. 'If you want revenge, real revenge, that is another thing. You must hurt the company in the way that matters most to them.'

'And what do you mean by that?'

'You tell me. You know this company – you have worked with it for twenty years or more. What, above all else, is the most valuable thing to them?'

The anger left Morato's face, his frown turned to thoughtfulness.

'That is easy,' he said after a moment. 'Their brand, their markets. Without those… without those they are nothing.'

'There you are,' João said. 'Think of a way to destroy those. Do that, and I will no longer doubt your honour.' He smiled. 'I may even stop calling you a fat merchant.'

CHAPTER 8

The three men sauntered into the restaurant and paused inside the door, blinking for a moment as they stepped out of the bright glare of the day; their drive to Estoril had been hot and sweaty and they soaked in the cool atmosphere reflecting from the whitewashed walls.

The head waiter shimmered up to them, his dinner jacket a little old and battered; he greeted them unctuously and ushered them to the middle of the room. There he paused and made a slow theatrical sweep of his hand to the central table, piled high with the shellfish for which the restaurant was renowned.

'Is it fresh?' João asked, and in answer the waiter put out a hand, gripped an eyeball of the largest lobster, and squeezed. The lobster clattered and threshed about on the table in its agony. The waiter laughed, fawning. Raul winced. Miguel smiled a predatory smile.

Raul had met Miguel once before, about a year ago in João's house. He had at first thought him proud and arrogant, a man who played just a little too much the role of the patrician, who managed to project himself simultaneously as a successful businessman and as a man who was above the rest of the business world. But then Raul was always ready to detect condescension in others, he had a well-developed sensitivity to being an employee, never yet the owner of a business.

Now, however, it was different. Miguel's pride was concerned with only one thing, and that was with the slight he had suffered at the hands of the English. While it would, of course, have been improper to have come too quickly to the point of their meeting, by the time the last scraps of flesh had been picked from the claws that lay on their plates – those same lobster claws that had waved in anguish an hour or so before – Miguel's vituperation was in full flood.

A discreet silence fell as the waiters came to clear away the debris, the silence of men who do not discuss business in front of servants. As the waiters moved away, João leaned forward, approaching now the purpose of the lunch.

'I was telling Miguel,' he said, looking at Raul, 'that there are ways in which large companies are vulnerable.' He flicked his glance towards Miguel, keeping out of his expression any hint of the taunts which he had thrown at Miguel at the time. 'I thought he would be interested to hear of your friend from Manila.'

Raul looked at João, thinking of Corazon, who had made so much noise in the beach hut. He couldn't resist a smirk.

'I made one or two very charming friends in Manila,' he said. He picked up his wine glass and gave its stem a languid turn. 'Of course, I may not have told my wife about all of them.'

The three chuckled, routine manly laughter.

'The friend that João means, he does not have quite the same charm as they do. Also he is getting old and fat, and the girls complained that he does not have quite the stamina of a younger man.' Raul swaggered in his seat to show that this was not a problem where he was concerned. 'But he had an idea, an idea that I thought interesting. He seemed to know a lot about it, which is why I thought João should meet him.'

Raul told Miguel of Seymour and his plans for faking Grand McCowrie.

When Raul had finished, Morato looked at him thoughtfully for a moment. 'Of course,' he said slowly, with an authoritative wave of one neatly manicured hand. 'This sort of thing happens from time to time.'

'Yes,' João prompted. 'You sometimes read of it in the papers. Usually it is someone who sells a few dozen bottles, then somebody complains.'

'Pah,' Morato sneered. 'That is because it is done by someone who knows nothing of what he is doing. By someone who knows nothing of the whisky business.'

He stabbed his forefinger at his chest. 'All my life I have been in the business. Let me tell you how the whisky market works.'

He took a mouthful of wine, and delicately wiped his lips with his white linen napkin.

João and Raul stayed silent, waiting for him to pronounce.

'First, you must consider your customer. The whisky drinker. Few whisky drinkers are connoisseurs, not in the way that drinkers of wine are connoisseurs. Drinkers of wine drink many wines, they like to think of themselves as experts. Often they speak rubbish, they are no more expert in wine than was the lobster I have just eaten.'

He lit a cigarette and blew its smoke towards the ceiling with an expression of contempt.

'But that is because they attempt too much. They pretend to know about all wines, from Europe, America, Australia even. Drinkers of whisky are not like that. Typically, they drink only one brand. Those who do this often know instantly if they are given something else.'

'Yes,' said Raul. 'That was Señor Seymour. He was given

the wrong whisky and knew straight away.'

'And did he complain?'

'Yes. The barman looked insulted. I thought we would be thrown out. But he obviously had contacts there.'

'Well, there you are. If somebody complains, of course the whole thing falls apart.'

'Yes,' João said. 'That is what this Seymour said. It made sense.' He paused. 'In your opinion, what is the best way to make sure no one complains?'

Miguel smiled. 'Ha! First thing, don't listen to a Scotsman. They will tell you that it is impossible to reproduce the taste outside Scotland. They will speak of Highland air, of peat and heather and water from the burn.'

He laughed, a wry, nostalgic, laugh that tailed away into silence as he thought of his thirty years in the trade, of the company to which he had been loyal for so long, but had now turned against him, of how he had been parroting what the Scots always said.

'They will tell you that, but they are wrong. There is a way to fool even the expert. I will tell you how it is done.'

What Miguel told them was a revelation. He spoke of malt whisky, grain whisky, and neutral alcohol. Of congeners, of aldehydes and acids and furfural. Of alcohols, ethyl and methyl and iso-amyl and iso-butyl. Of maturation and blending, of sherry casks and tannin and caramel. He gave them a complete history of the whisky business, an outline of production methods, a summary of chemical analysis techniques.

Miguel sat back at the end of his exposition with the pleased look of someone who knows that he has placed new and valued knowledge before an attentive audience.

There had been a minute's silence while his audience digested what he had said. Sitting at the table with full stomachs, replete from the food, still savouring their wine, feeling their new knowledge cocoon them in a pleasing warmth.

It was Raul who spoke first. The satisfaction had been bubbling up inside him and could no longer be contained.

'Miguel,' he said, with a tone of bonhomie that was not natural to him but which came from a good lunch, 'this is excellent, truly excellent.'

There were smiles all round.

'But… then there is marketing. How do you distribute the product?'

There was a quizzical look on João's face. He was used to smuggling dubious merchandise. Selling it through legal channels was something he had not much bothered with.

'Oh,' said Miguel, 'that is the easy part. You simply become a parallel trader.'

He suddenly threw back his head and laughed. He laughed long and loud, while the other two looked at him, wondering what the joke was. Eventually he took a silk handkerchief from his pocket and wiped his eyes.

'For years,' he said, 'parallel traders have been the bane of my life. Buying in one country, selling in another.' He gave João an amused look. 'A bit like you, except that they pay customs duties.'

'Foolish,' João sniffed.

'No. Not so foolish. They deal in my products, they undercut my margins, they sell on the back of the advertising I have paid for. If I added up the time I have spent worrying about them, cursing them as a pestilence, thinking of how to stop them… I tell you, I have sat with Grand McCowrie for days, weeks on end, working out a strategy to eradicate this menace. Never did I think I would see the day when I would tell someone to become a parallel trader.' He looked from João to Raul and back, his handkerchief clenched in his hand, his smile becoming tighter. 'By the time we are finished,' he said, 'those fools at Grand McCowrie will come to regret what they have done.'

CHAPTER 9

Seymour has been in Portugal for a month now. It is not quite the idyll he had been hoping for. There is the language, for a start. He has always had a good ear for languages; during his time in Manila he had picked up quite a bit of Spanish, and Portuguese looks quite like Spanish when written down so he had thought he would get along. But the sound it makes when spoken, the sound is incomprehensible to him, all those different vowels and twangs. Plus of course English is not so widespread as it is in the Philippines.

He is lodging in a small flat in a village three kilometres away from Raul; Raul's wife having been quite forceful about her husband's business acquaintances cluttering up her house. He had not needed to understand the words that she spoke; he could understand the content by the shrieking tone and the unwelcoming looks. His flat looks out over the village street, which is quite noisy in the morning with scooters taking people to work, but at least it has no shrieking inside it.

He was quite busy in the first week or two, discussing all the details with Raul, boasting about his contacts in the Far East, Hong Kong, Taiwan, Singapore, suggesting people who would be likely to buy. Raul had nodded appreciatively; these were just the sort of parallel traders that Morato had spoken about. By a stroke of luck one of these, Stanley Cheng, had told Seymour he was due to drop in on Lisbon next week, and today is the day that Seymour will meet him. After that Seymour will be going to Scotland, to talk to a whisky distillery, and then there is the spirit supplier he is planning to see in Poland. But apart from that … there is nothing he can put his finger on, but he senses that Raul, and especially João, do not see him as quite so central to their plans as he would like. But then that is okay, he has a plan of his own which they know nothing about…

CHAPTER 10

Three months passed.

The tops of the trees in the distance had the full leaves of summer. Sun shone on the roof opposite Hamish's office, bringing a shimmer even to the grey slate. Hamish, his sleeves rolled up, let his concentration slide away from the dull legal matters on his desk, and looked longingly out of the window. He snapped back into focus as he heard a click from the door. In strolled a sandy-haired Scot. Iain Ferguson, sixty-four. Forty years in the whisky industry. Senior export director of Grand McCowrie, a post once held by Hamish's late uncle.

Glad of the break, Hamish put his papers down.

'Got an odd one,' Ferguson said. Hamish raised his eyebrows. 'Switchboard operator rang me. Said she had a chap on the line who wanted to speak to the chairman. He's in Scotland, as you'll know. The caller insisted on a senior director, so I took the call.

'Chap sounded a bit… breathless, I suppose, as if he'd been running. Started by asking my name, who I was, what office I held. Was I a director, and so forth? I told him; then I asked who *he* was. "Mr. Robinson," he said. Said it rather… I don't know, rather as if he was reading from a script.

'"Well, Mr. Robinson," I said, "what can I do for you?"'

He hesitated a bit, and then said he had some information of vital interest to our company. Hushed voice, bit melodramatic, sort of nonsense I can do without, quite frankly. When I asked him what it was about, he went all coy and said it was very confidential; did he have my word that it would be just between him and me? "Yes, yes," I said, and blow me, he then says he knows of a plot against our company.'

'Good Lord,' Hamish said, astonished. 'What sort of a plot?'

'He wouldn't say. Said if we wanted to know that we'd have to meet and agree terms.'

'Terms? What sort of terms?'

'Didn't say.'

'Hmm. So then what? Did you agree to meet him?'

'I did *not*,' Ferguson said emphatically. 'I've got enough to do without wasting my time on an unknown nutcase. I said I'd have to pass him over to a colleague. A *trusted* colleague,' he added. 'I told him to ring back in half an hour.' Ferguson glanced at his watch. 'Which gives you about twenty minutes to work out how to deal with him.'

'Me?' Hamish exclaimed, sitting upright in his seat. 'You want me to deal with it?'

'That's right.'

'What about that security man, that ex-policeman that Adrian Spicer insisted on recruiting? Isn't this more his sort of thing?'

'If you mean Gosling,' Ferguson sniffed, 'he's in Scotland too. Sleuthing around distilleries, sharpening the barbed wire fence or whatever he does.'

'So why me?'

'"Cos you're always dealing with shady ripoff merchants who try to poach our brand. Thought it'd be just up your street.'

*

This time, as Hamish stared out of his window, waiting for the phone to ring, he was deep in thought. No surprise that Ferguson didn't want to get involved in an offbeat mystery. Promoting and selling whisky was what work was all about. Peculiar wrinkles of life were outside his area of interest. By contrast, Hamish's streak of boyish inquisitiveness could hardly wait to hear what the man sounded like.

When the telephone rang he stared at it for a moment before stretching out his hand. The voice that announced itself as Mr. Robinson was curiously dated, with the clipped vowels of black and white films from the 1950s. Portentous phrases – *extremely sensitive, highly confidential* – rolled around like vintage claret, gently gurgling down the line, pouring unctuously into Hamish's ear.

Now he had heard the voice he was taken with curiosity to see the man behind it. He was only too ready to agree to Mr. Robinson's suggestion of a meeting. But not so ready that he turned his brain off in the meantime. There were certain precautions that it might be sensible to take first. He had been mulling these over while waiting for Mr. Robinson's call, and as soon as it ended, he picked up the phone again and dialled.

CHAPTER 11

It was a quarter to three when Robinson ambled through Berkeley Square. He looked enviously at two portly gentlemen with well-lunched paunches strolling languidly along the pavement in a cloud of claret and cognac, watched them step delicately round a motorbike courier lounging against the railings, puffing at their cigars, sniffing with disapproval. The biker, lazily feeding a sandwich into his mouth, stared back at their expensive Jermyn Street pinstripe suits with a gaze as insolent as he could manage, took a deliberately messy mouthful and blew crumbs in their wake. They pretended not to notice and strutted onwards. The biker's eyes flicked away, raking the square again from north to south, from the paths under the plane trees in the centre to the pavement round the edge.

Robinson smiled and turned out of the square, unaware of the biker's eyes returning to him as he made his way down the street.

He looked up at the buildings either side of him, as if their inscrutable facades could tell him how to steer his way through the corporate jungle that hummed unseen behind them. Halfway along the street he slowed, then stopped, drew breath; on the threshold of something he'd long dreamed of.

Oh well, he said to himself, *this is it, in you go, old boy.*

He stumped up the four stone steps into the entrance hall,

mopped his brow with a scruffy handkerchief, walked up to the receptionist. Basking in her brightly trained smile, he sat in the armchair she pointed him towards, looking around him at the Georgian architecture, the antique mirror in its gilt frame hanging on the wall opposite, the two small landscapes on either side of it, the vase of flowers on the receptionist's desk. Swallowing his tension as he waited for the croupier of fate to flick his ball into the wheel.

At exactly three o'clock an elegant girl in a blue linen dress floated into the hall, tawny-gold hair falling shinily onto freckled shoulders.

'Mr. Robinson?' she asked.

By the time he had levered himself out of his chair she was ten feet ahead, her heels clicking on the marble floor. She clipped up the cantilevered stone staircase to the first floor, swayed rhythmically along the corridor, with him puffing along yards behind her, and led him into a meeting room. He flicked his eyes about him, he always liked to get a bearing. Not quite Georgian this room, not that he was an expert on architecture, but he could tell any sort of fake by instinct.

'Mr. Robinson,' she announced, her voice cool and aloof.

He paused inside the door of the meeting room, gave another little puff and looked round with beady eyes. There was a chap already there, who strode forward with outstretched hand. Youngish chap, thirty-something. Fresh, open, honest sort of face, wavy brown hair, looked a bright sort of chap. Proper suit, he noticed. None of these mass-produced jobs. Even after twenty years knocking around abroad, he hadn't forgotten what they looked like. Just the sort of chap who'd work in a building in Mayfair. They shook hands.

'Robinson,' he said. 'Ah, Eric, ah, Robinson.'

'Hamish Mallows.' A polished voice.

Robinson took a seat and looked around him, glancing through the window. No garden, just the back of another building, plain brick, rather messy. Nothing too special compared to the front, he thought. Just goes to show, everything in life's a facade. The thought bolstered him up.

The elegant girl in blue returned with a tray holding two cups of coffee, which she placed on the table. He watched her until she left the room. Pretty girl, he thought with a sigh. As the door closed, he stretched a little, stirred his coffee, deliberately silent; always worth seeing how a chap reacts to silence.

'You said you were over here on business?' Hamish said.

'Mmmm, yes.' *Polite sort of tone. Good. Not the type to throw you out.*

'How long for?'

'Just a short while. Only till the end of this week, really.'

'Right.' Hamish squared a pad in front of him. 'Now,' he said. 'About this information of yours—'

Robinson leaned forward, paunch straining against the table, and interrupted. 'Before I start – what is it that you do in the company?'

'I'm a lawyer, actually.'

Ah. Have to watch my step.

'Oh, well, that's splendid. Know you legal chaps see all sorts of peculiar cases, used to weighing the evidence and so forth, expect you're trained to keep an open mind.'

He sat back again and sipped his coffee.

'It's like this. I'm a – I suppose you'd call me an entrepreneur, suppose I'd have to admit I'm a bit of a wheeler-dealer, really. Deal in all sorts of things, all sorts of places. Come across a variety of people in my time.'

He paused, thinking of some of them. God, what a

mixture they'd been.

'Now then,' he continued. 'A little while ago I was talking to an old friend of mine. He knows I've got contacts all over the place, he knows some of them are – how shall I put it – amenable to deals which it doesn't pay to look at too closely, if you know what I mean?'

He gave Hamish a knowing look. Hamish nodded, as if such people came into his office every day.

'He told me he was trying to sell some fake whisky. Your brand, Grand McCowrie. He wanted some help with getting rid of it. At least that's what he said to start with. I got a feeling there was a bit more to it than that. I can usually tell. Lifetime of experience, what?'

He slurped at his coffee. A little of it dribbled down his chin and he wiped it away with the back of his fleshy hand.

'Well. After chatting to him a bit, he opened up. Told me a bit more about his operation, about the other people in the plan. What it boils down to is this. They've got a factory which they've set up. It's going to pump this stuff out by the ton – five thousand cases a week.' He sat in silence. *Said enough to whet this chap's appetite. Let's see how interested he is.*

'Can you give me any evidence?' Hamish asked. 'Of where the factory is, what this chap's name is? That the fake exists?' Hamish's tone was politeness itself, no hint of anything so discourteous as disbelief.

'Ah. Evidence. Yes indeed.' Robinson fished in the inside pockets of his suit, pulled out a thin sheaf of papers and let them flop onto the shining mahogany of the table. Stubby fingers fiddled, like a man trying to roll a cigarette. He grasped a label and pushed it across to Hamish.

'There,' he said. 'Exhibit A – that's what you lawyers call it, isn't it?'

The label's green, orange and gold sparkled against the rich brown of the mahogany. Hamish picked it up, handling it delicately by the edges, gazed at it for a full minute, absorbing the quality of the printing, the clarity of the letters, the accuracy of the colour. Turned it over to see the creamy whiteness of the back, unsullied by glue, perfectly flat, unused.

'So how did you get this?' Hamish asked, eyebrows upraised.

'All in good time, all in good time,' the visitor smiled, laying his finger to his nose.

'Is this the label being used by the factory?'

Robinson nodded silently, the smile still playing round his mouth.

'Do you have a bottle?'

'Ah.' Robinson laid his finger against his nose again, a theatrical gesture which Hamish began to find a little overdone. 'It's like this, d'you see? I'm pretty well in with this group. Inside information, what? I can give you all the gen on them – you won't get it anywhere except through me.'

He paused, and leaned forward confidentially.

'But that means I've got to be careful. A bottle's a bulky thing. Can't very well stick it in my pocket, can I? Bound to be noticed.'

'I see,' Hamish said equably. 'When you say you're well in with this group, does that mean that you're buying from them? Or that you're part of them?'

Robinson avoided the question. 'Have a look at these.' He pushed the rest of the papers across the table. Hamish read them through, one after the other: telexes offering Grand McCowrie in quantities varying, from one buyer to another, of between one and five thousand cases per month.

'These don't prove anything,' Hamish said, looking at the sheaf of papers in his hand, scepticism creeping into his voice for the first time. 'Anyone can push out offers on telex. Happens on the parallel market all the time.' He flicked his eyes up to Robinson's face, then down again. 'Also, you've cut the answerback codes off. These won't take us anywhere.'

'Of course I've cut the answerback codes off,' Robinson said with a smile. He sat back into his seat, looking as if he'd made a point.

Hamish considered this for a moment, drew a blank. 'Why "of course"?' he asked.

Robinson shifted in his seat, to mark a change of gear. 'Well, there's something we ought to discuss first, isn't there?'

'How d'you mean?' Hamish's eyebrows lifted elegantly.

'How shall I put it? Add all the offers together, they add up to five thousand cases a week. Which is what they're going to push out. That could, what shall I say, provide you with quite a bit of, ah, disruption. Right?'

'Ye-es...'

'Disruption which I imagine your company would want to put a stop to, right?'

'Certainly.'

'So information – information which would let you do that – would have a pretty substantial value?' He saw the shade of a smile play about Hamish's mouth.

'In other words, you want us to pay you for this information?'

'Of course.'

In silence they gazed at each other, Hamish intrigued by this colourful eruption into his office life, this slightly shabby figure with his bizarre approach, his only-half-convincing manner. Robinson seeing an agreeable, straightforward young man with a subconsciously superior manner, of a type he would have eaten for breakfast twenty years before.

He's a lawyer, he thinks he deals in proof. He thinks that guards him against accepting anything without proof. He probably doesn't real-ise that it makes him want proof before he dismisses the story either…

'It'll save you six million quid,' he stated in a firm voice. 'A year.'

'Six million?' Hamish's voice rose in disbelief. 'How on earth d'you work that out?'

'Easy. Twenty-four quid a case, right?' He stared at Ham-ish, waiting for him to nod, drawing him into making an act of agreement. *Psychology, that's the game…* 'So, five thousand cases is one hundred and twenty thousand pounds. Five thousand a week, say fifty weeks a year – six million quid.'

'Um. If they really are producing those quantities.'

'Oh they are, dear boy, they are' - said with the plummy tones of conviction he'd been so good at in his youth.

'Hmmm. We've had nothing turn up on the market.'

But Robinson could hear a flicker of doubt creep into Hamish's voice, eating away at his scepticism…

'You wouldn't.' Almost patronising, from superior knowledge. 'As I say, it's just getting going.'

Hamish kept his face neutral before Robinson's assessing gaze.

'D'you know,' Robinson said, ruminatively, 'a few years ago I was lucky enough to find some stolen property, and I got a reward from the insurance company. Know what they gave me? Ten per cent.'

Hamish's eyebrows shot up. 'You're not suggesting we give you ten per cent of six million pounds?'

'Better than losing six million, what?' *Sit calm, chin up, old boy.*

Hamish leaned back in his chair, a look of amazement on his face.

'You come in off the street with a story like this and expect us to give you six hundred grand?'

The figure hung in the air. Robinson had been thinking about it all day; for weeks past. Dreaming of the luxuries he could indulge in, he had convinced himself of its rightness. Hearing it now, spoken for the first time by someone else, he wondered if he might have pitched it a little high. Oh well, can always come down a bit later on.

He pretended to bridle. 'What's the difference between this and an insurance company?'

Hamish gave a little laugh. 'We're not in the insurance business. Thank God. And anyway, an insurance company only pays out against property it recovers. *When* it recovers it.'

'With the information I can give you, you can take action which will shut this plant down.'

'And recover six million quid's worth of fake?'

'Depends on you. Depends on how soon you get on with it. The more you hang about the more of the stuff they'll make. Think of what you risk *not* recovering. If you want to let them flood the market, go right ahead.'

'I'm simply not authorised to make that sort of deal,' Hamish said.

So who is? Robinson thought. *Ferguson? Do I ask to speak to Ferguson? No, he's older, more experienced, a senior director, bound to be a tougher nut altogether. I'll be better off dealing with young Hamish here. Not so much guile in young Hamish.*

'Well, then,' he said, 'tell you what – you have a word with your Mr. Ferguson, soon as possible, get authorisation, then we can speak again.'

'Oka-aay.'

'And remember. I'm in a delicate situation. I need to know one way or another.'

'Mmm, yes. I do see that.'

'In fact, I'm running a hell of a risk in coming to see you at all. The people involved in this are heavy, very heavy.'

'I understand that. It doesn't alter the fact that this is a public company. I can't possibly agree without board approval.' Hamish placed both hands flat on the table, marking the end of the conversation. 'Where can I reach you?'

'I'll ring you, I'll ring you. I'll ring at midday tomorrow.'

'Very good.'

Hamish came smoothly round the table as Robinson levered himself off his chair, and ushered him to the door. He took him down the stone stairs and out onto the top of the steps. They stood in the warm sunshine, in the golden glow of Mayfair's expensive buildings; Hamish took Robinson's hand, and gave it a cordial shake. Hamish watched him potter down the steps, gave a little smile, and turned back indoors.

As Robinson reached the pavement a black taxi appeared at the far end of the street, the yellow light on its roof lit up, cruising slowly, looking for passengers.

Down in the square, a short electronic squawk came from a loudspeaker mounted on the back of the Kawasaki. The biker eased his crash helmet onto his head, swung himself onto his machine and pressed the starter.

Robinson ignored the taxi and let it pass him. His budget did not run to extravagances. He ambled down the pavement, heading towards the square.

Fifty yards behind him, on the other side of the road, a girl got out of the passenger seat of a white Ford Escort. Neat girl, mid-twenties, short brown hair, could have been a secretary or just a girl out shopping. She started walking at the same leisurely pace as Robinson, well-shaped legs swinging purposefully beneath her skirt. She saw him stop at the corner of the square and look about him as if savouring the view. By the time she had come level with him he had started moving again, crossing into the centre of the square, turning down Berkeley Street. When he came to Piccadilly he paused to look across at the Ritz, turned right and went down the steps of the subway and up the other side, emerging by the gate into Green Park. He bought a paper from the kiosk and ambled into the park, found a deckchair and sat down to enjoy the sun.

The girl bought a magazine and sat in the sun thirty yards away.

Robinson sat in the sun for the next hour. In that hour the Escort moved five times, from one yellow line to another, in a dance to stay clear of the traffic wardens that patrolled the narrow streets to the north of Green Park. The youth on the Kawasaki grinned at the Escort's exertions: avoiding wardens was easy on a motorbike.

At the end of the hour Robinson rose, stretched, ambled towards Green Park Underground. Five stops to Brixton, where he got out. Ambled five minutes to a dreary street, stopped by a grey terraced house with a B&B sign in its window, fished in his pocket for a key and let himself in.

Twenty seconds behind him the girl walked past the house and on to the next corner. Fifteen minutes later the Escort arrived. She waited for it to park and got in.

CHAPTER 12

Hamish walked purposefully up the white stone staircase which rose elegantly up across the back of the lobby, reached the first floor, turned to the left and knocked on a polished mahogany door. A grunt, muffled by the thickness of the wood, came from within.

'Your Mr. Robinson,' he said as he walked in. 'I've just seen him. He says he knows about some counterfeiting.'

Ferguson gave him a level gaze over the brim of his pipe, sat back in his chair, and puffed out a small, hazy, blue ball of smoke.

'So? That's the sort of thing you legal chaps deal with, isn't it?'

'Yes, we do. And he says he knows of a setup that's about to make five thousand cases a week.'

'Good God. Where?'

'He wouldn't say. Wouldn't say where it's being made, wouldn't say which market it's aimed at.'

'Oh? Why not?'

'He wants a reward. Wants to do a deal with us before he goes into detail.'

'What sort of a reward?'

'Well…' Hamish paused. 'He says that at five thousand cases a week, that's a quarter of a million in a year, worth about six million quid. He's looking for ten per cent.'

'Bloody hell. Does he think we're the Bank of England?'

'He says ten per cent is what an insurance company would pay.'

'Oh, for goodness' sake. We're not an insurance company. And anyway, has anyone ever made fake in those quantities before?' Ferguson asked, tamping at his pipe. 'I mean, cottage-industry stuff, a few bottles in Latin America, maybe… And he didn't give any clue about where this is supposed to be happening?'

'Nope.'

'Did he bring a bottle of the stuff?'

'He brought a label.'

Hamish fished in his pocket and dropped the label on the vast empty space of Ferguson's desk. It lay there on the gold-tooled, green leather inlay, a brazen imposter where it had no right to be. Ferguson picked it up and looked thoughtfully at it, making the small popping noises beloved of pipe-smokers.

'Anything else? Sample of what's in the bottles?'

'No.'

'Any indication who's doing it? Any hard evidence that anyone *is* doing it, come to that?'

'Not till we agree to pay him.'

'In other words, he wants half a million quid on the strength of this?' Ferguson said, holding the label in disdain between thumb and forefinger.

'Well, that's his starting point. We could probably negotiate him down.'

'Bloody easy way to earn a living, I *must* say,' Ferguson snorted. 'Nip out to the nearest printer, print someone's label, walk into their office bold as brass and demand half a million.' He tossed the label onto the desk, fiddled with a box of matches, waved a flame over the pipe and sucked vigorously, almost disappearing behind the plumes of smoke.

'What if he's just a conman?' he went on, waving a hand to clear the air.

'Maybe,' Hamish said. 'But what if he's not?'

'What d'you mean?'

'Have you thought what counterfeit could do to our market? I was talking to a chap I know in the automobile industry. Fake brake linings got onto one of their markets, word got out, their sales dropped by ninety per cent.'

'So, what are you suggesting?'

'I want your authorisation to take it further. See if we can do a deal with him.'

Ferguson sighed and examined the label again. A minute passed, his pipe puffing gently, the blue mist wreathing slowly up towards the ceiling. Finally, he pushed the label back to Hamish with a short sigh.

'And what if it turns out he *is* a conman? What then?'

'We can build safeguards into the deal, we can—'

'Earlier,' Ferguson interrupted, 'you asked why I hadn't raised it with Gosling. I told you he was in Scotland. Well, tomorrow he's back. So, we bring him in on it.'

'But that was before we knew what sort of thing we were talking about. Now we know. Brand protection, it's what our department does.'

'And dealing with crooks – that's what a policeman does. It's the sort of thing the company brought him in for. And not just *a* policeman, but a senior one. With more experience of crooks than you or I or anyone else in this building.'

'Well, maybe, but…'

'*Tomorrow*, Hamish,' Ferguson said with a thump of pipe stem on his desk. 'All right?'

'Yes,' Hamish said with resignation. 'All right.'

CHAPTER 13

Hamish passed Ferguson's secretary in the corridor at two minutes to ten. She gave a meaningful glance to the door to Ferguson's room and raised her eyeballs towards the ceiling. He smiled at her and walked in.

He saw the back of a man standing, framed by the window, looking out onto the street below. Thickset, in a dark-blue suit with overly bright pinstripes. Above the collar was a neck of suntanned, weather-beaten skin, criss-crossed with deep grooves. The man turned, revealing a round, fleshy face and slicked-back hair. His hands were deep in his pockets and there was a distrustful look in his eyes.

'Phil Gosling,' he said in a gravelly voice, his tone rising as if giving the obvious answer to a stupid question.

'I've heard your name,' Hamish said amiably.

'And I've heard yours,' Gosling said, thrusting his hands deeper into his pockets and rocking on the balls of his feet. 'Iain Ferguson tells me that – *in my absence* – you've been trying to handle some would-be informant. That right?'

Hamish looked at the man, silent for a moment while he absorbed his truculence.

'Well,' he said coolly, 'I suppose that's one way of putting it.'

'He made a demand of money, this bloke, right?'

'Yes.'

'Which you are recommending the board consider?' The

tone made it into an accusation of criminal stupidity.

Hamish flushed. 'He claims to have information about a plot to counterfeit our number-one brand. If true, that means that we—'

'Had any training dealing with informants, have you? Know the Home Office guidelines, for instance?'

'No. Of course not. I was trying—'

'Did you get him on tape?'

'No. As it happens I didn't.' The idea had not occurred to him. Gosling's manner made it irritating to have to admit it.

Gosling snorted in derision.

'Had any experience of dealing with conmen?'

'Not directly, but—'

'Ah. So, it didn't cross your mind that he might *be* a conman?'

'Of course it did!' Hamish snapped. 'It also crossed my mind that he might *not* be, that his information might be genuine, and that it might be better not to jump to conclusions.'

The door opened and Ferguson ambled in, tamping his pipe. Hamish and Gosling fell silent and half-turned towards him as he walked to his desk by the window and dropped a sheet of paper on the green leather. He called to his secretary for coffee and ushered them both round the long table at the side of his room. The three men waited silently as the secretary placed white cups in front of them, the milk jug, the sugar. As she left, Ferguson murmured a quiet thank you and started to feed lighted matches to his pipe, the moist tobacco unleashing clouds of pungent smoke.

'Now,' he said, when the fire was under control, 'perhaps we could start with Hamish updating us on Mr. Robinson.'

The diesel engine of a taxi rattled past in the street as Hamish marshalled his thoughts. He looked away from

Gosling as he recounted the meeting, trying to ignore Gosling's eyes on him, subconsciously putting Robinson's credibility in the best light to defend him against what Gosling might say.

Ferguson blew another cloud of blue smoke towards the ceiling. 'So what's your recommendation?'

'In my view,' Hamish said slowly, 'in my view, it is entirely possible that Robinson is trying to con us. It is also, I believe, equally possible that his information is genuine. Having met the man…' he paused and looked at Gosling to emphasize his advantage '… I have a feeling that the man is genuine.'

Gosling opened his mouth but was restrained by Ferguson's uplifted hand.

'And if he *is* telling the truth,' Hamish went on, 'counterfeiting on a big scale could do our company tremendous damage. So, I believe we should negotiate with him. Try to draw out as much information as we can. Aim for a deal which will satisfy him if he's genuine but which will also protect us if he isn't. I'd like your authorisation to do that.'

'Phil?'

Gosling leaned forward, a bull released from the pen.

'That's a very pretty speech but it doesn't cut a lot of ice with me. Dealing with informants is a tricky task. One of the trickiest, even for trained police officers.' He threw a look of scorn across the table, scorn at Hamish's lack of police training. 'I've dealt with a lot over my time, and let me tell you, you can never trust them. They've always got some hidden motive up their sleeve, they've always got some angle, however straightforward they seem. Sorting them out is a job for an expert.'

He flexed his bulky shoulders and settled into his stride.

'It's plain what this man's main motivation is. Money. A

pound to a penny he's a conman. I'd guess he's figured out that a company like ours is going to leap with fright at the thought of fake whisky and that we'll fall over backwards to pay him. Which we would, if Mallows here had his way.'

'I didn't say that, I made it clear what I—'

'This man's a crook. Stands to reason. If – *if* – his information's for real, he's been party to this plot. If it isn't, he's trying to defraud this company. Either way, he's party to a criminal offence, either way it's a job for the police. With my contacts in the Met, that's no problem. *No* problem.' Gosling launched into a boastful account of the senior officers he knew.

He's on an ego trip, Hamish thought in disgust. He's not interested in the best answer to the problem, he just wants to grab it for himself. He bit his lip in irritation. Until recently the company had been free of egocentric empire builders.

To his dismay, Hamish saw that Ferguson was lapping all this up. Ferguson was a whisky man of the old school, and Hamish knew he did not warm to the oily, slick-haired Gosling. But the old school meant being honest, upright, straightforward; the very idea of paying money to a possible conman would stick in Ferguson's throat.

'But look,' Hamish objected, 'if our brand's being faked, it's us that'll suffer – our brand, our markets. That won't be a priority for the police, so it's us that'll have to stop it. Which means we need to get any scrap of information that this chap's got.'

'If he's got it,' Ferguson said quietly. 'Aren't you rather taking that for granted?'

'And if this man *has* got information,' Gosling interjected, 'the Met and I can get it out of him. *If* he has information, it's all the more important to do a proper job on him. And why pay him for his information when the Met'll get it for free?'

'Hamish,' Ferguson said, 'if he was an honest man and he simply wanted to help stop a crime, why couldn't he just hand the information over and be done with it? If he's not an honest man, then why not let the police sort him out?'

There was quiet in the room. Ferguson's short speech rang with heartfelt sincerity. What he said struck a chord with Hamish, in his upbringing, in his conditioned belief in the law which his training had instilled. Remembering how his father had suffered at the hands of a conman. He could understand Ferguson's view so well that it silenced him for a moment.

Gosling purred unctuously into the silent opening. 'Exactly right. And if, on the other hand, he's a conman, it'd be a bit irresponsible not to have him dealt with.'

Ferguson nodded. 'It *is* what the police are there for. This company wasn't set up to chase crooks. Nor was it set up to hand out large slices of cash to anyone who walks in off the street.'

'Except,' Hamish said, irritable at losing, 'that *if* the police cock it up it'll be our department that ends up having to sort it all out.' He could hear petulance creeping into his voice even as he spoke. Ferguson's frown showed he'd made a tactical error.

Gosling waved his hand. 'No time for interdepartmental jealousy, Mallows,' he said patronisingly, barely glancing at Hamish, oozing confidence in his own rightness. 'Just get him in again. Then let the experts do their job. Right?'

'Very well,' Ferguson said. 'That's the way we'll do it.' He stood up. 'I'm sorry,' he added to Hamish, not unkindly, as they moved towards the door. 'But I really do think Phil's right on this one.'

CHAPTER 14

The sun slanted in through Sarah's window, lighting up the busy Lizzie on the shelf beside her desk. She hummed to herself as her fingers flitted over the keyboard, her mind dreaming of last weekend's trip to Scotland with her new man.

Her door burst open, banging against a filing cabinet. She frowned at the noise as Hamish strode moodily in.

'Feeling a little pissed off, are we?'

'Yes, we sodding well are.'

He paused by her desk, his eyes lighting on the coffee bubbling through the electric coffeemaker. 'Bring me a cup, could you?' He stomped into his room without waiting. She let out a little sigh, poured out a mug and took it in.

'That man Gosling,' he expostulated as she crossed the floor towards his desk. 'Christ, he's such an *arsehole.*'

'Your *language,*' she said, voice rising in tandem with her eyebrows, pouting in a mockingly prim fashion and feigning shock. 'It's a *disgrace.*'

'Haven't noticed yours being so fucking pristine,' he retorted.

'You could hardly expect it to be,' she said sweetly, placing the mug on his desk. 'Not after working for you for five years.'

'Typical. If there's a man around, blame him.'

'If you're going to start being sexist, you can make your

own coffee in future.' She stretched out her hand as if to pick his mug up again. He whipped it quickly away from her, spilling coffee on his trousers as he did so.

'*Bugger!*' he exclaimed crossly.

She laughed happily, and perched against the back of a chair, arms folded, watching him scrabbling about in his desk for a tissue. When he had tried all drawers unsuccessfully she tossed her chin with a smile, went out, and came back with a hand towel.

'I mean, talk about life's bullshitters,' Hamish said, mopping at his lap. 'I go down, prepared for a balanced discussion of what to do about this bloke, Robinson, and instead of listening to the pros and cons he leaps straight in with a lot of crap about how the police know best, how well connected he is in the Met, how all his old mates'll fall over backwards to do him a favour, what a wonder he is, blah blah blah.'

She put her head on one side and looked thoughtfully at him.

'He could have a point,' she said slowly. 'Dealing with crooks *is* his business.'

'Oh God, don't *you* start.'

'Well, if it's something he's got experience of…'

'Yeah, but I bet you anything you like he's got bugger-all experience of brand protection. Wouldn't know a trademark from his bootlace.'

*

An hour and a half later, he nipped up to the canteen to grab a sandwich. He came back to find Sarah still sitting at her word processor, a half-eaten apple beside her.

'You missed your friend,' she said, not looking up from her keyboard. 'He rang about a minute ago.'

'What friend?'

'Robinson, or whatever he calls himself.'

'Oh. He did, did he? What did he say?'

'He wanted to speak to you, of course. You don't think anyone in this business is going to speak to a mere secretary, do you?' It was a recurrent complaint of hers.

'Oh God. Not another complaint about male domination. You obviously like it, or you wouldn't work in this industry.'

'Up yours.' She pursed her lips at him. Waited till he was halfway into his room. 'Hey,' she called. He turned and lifted an eyebrow.

'This came,' she said, flicking a disdainful finger at a brown envelope lying on her desk. Red-stamped, *Confidential, open addressee only*.

'What is it?'

'How should I know?' she sniffed.

'Ah. Too important to be opened by a mere secretary, is that what you mean?' he murmured smugly, and nipped quickly into his room to avoid the coffee-stained cloth that she threw at him.

The heavy brown envelope contained a single sheet of A4.

CONFIDENTIAL.

FIRST INTERIM REPORT.

1.   Acting on instructions received from client, a watch was placed on the doorway of client's premises commencing 14.30 on Tuesday 21st instant.

2.   Between 14.30 and 14.50 a number of individuals were noted entering client's premises. At 14.50 an individual, male, white, approx. sixty years of age, dressed in rumpled blue suit that has seen better days, was seen entering said premises. Said individual was subsequently identified as Subject. Subject is height approx. 5'10", of portly girth, hair light brown to grey, florid complexion, weight estimated approx. fifteen stone. Photographs were subsequently taken of Subject and will follow.

3.   At 15.45, in company of client's instructing officer, Subject appeared in doorway and proceeded on foot through Berkeley Square and Berkeley Street to Piccadilly. Subject entered entrance of Underground/subway on north side of Piccadilly and re-emerged on south side. After purchasing newspaper, Subject entered Green Park at 16.00, seated self in deckchair, and commenced perusal of newspaper. Subject made no contact with third parties during this time.

4.   At 16.55 Subject entered Underground and travelled to Brixton, alighting 17.20. Subject made way on foot to 21, Bacon Road, Brixton. On arrival Subject took key from pocket with which he entered said house at 17.40.

5.   Enquiries locally reveal said address occupied by Eleanor Mary O'Flaherty and Patrick Flynn O'Flaherty. Eleanor O'Flaherty lets rooms on bed and breakfast basis.

6.   At 18.15 a white male, approx. fifty years of age, casually dressed, was observed leaving said premises and was followed to public house Magpie and Stoat. Same was engaged in casual conversation in course of which our operative was able to confirm identity as P. O'Flaherty. Further casual conversation revealed one person, male, currently staying in 21, Bacon Road on bed and breakfast basis. O'Flaherty confided said person is colourful individual having spent much time abroad, especially in Far East. O'Flaherty did not volunteer name of said person and no direct enquiry was made in order to avoid arousing suspicion.

Hamish sighed. This didn't sound like someone with half a million pounds' worth of story to tell. Maybe Gosling was right. He hated the thought.

*

Having rung at midday on the dot, Robinson was rather put out at not being able to speak to Hamish. Now he had to think how to kill time. He had rung from a public phone box. It was true that there was a telephone where he was staying, but it was in the hallway, where every word could be heard. He didn't fancy going back to his B&B; it was a sunny day, and he was fed up with being cooped up inside the house with its lingering smell of stale cabbage. He decided to go for a walk.

*

Static. Crackle. Hiss, filling the Escort, broken suddenly by speech.

'Subject leaving phone box, moving west.'

Crackle.

'Subject turning corner into Brixton Hill. Moving towards shops. Window shopping.' Hiss.

'Oh shit, he's going in a bloody department store.'

*

It was twenty minutes later when Robinson got back to the phone box. There was an old woman inside; a black youth

69

lounging about outside, a couple of yards away from the box.

Robinson stood by the door of the box. 'Hey, man,' from the youth.

Robinson looked up, startled. He was a well-travelled man, he was accustomed to the ways of the Chinese, Filipinos, Americans and Japanese. But the black people in Brixton spoke with a rhythm that was new to him. He was hesitant, wary.

'There's a queue, man.'

Robinson relaxed, smiled nervously.

The woman finished her call. The black youth swaggered into the box and fiddled with his coins, his foot drumming a rhythm on the floor. Robinson could see he was taking his time deliberately.

*

'Hamish Mallows.'

'This is Robinson again.'

'Ah. Hello.'

'Now then. You've spoken to your director, have you?'

'I certainly have,' Hamish declared with ringing tones. Might as well enjoy telling the truth while he could.

'And? Is he prepared to do a deal?'

'Well. The thing is this. We're certainly, what shall I say, sensitive to the potential value of the information which you have. However, I need a further discussion with you before we can, ah, come to a final view.'

Just get him in again, Gosling had said. *Get him here and then leave him to me.*

'Further discussion? I thought we'd already discussed everything,' Robinson said impatiently. 'I showed you evidence of what's happening, the ball's in your court. D'you want to deal or not?'

'It's not as clear-cut as that, we don't get your sort of approach every day.' Hamish cursed himself for finding it difficult to come out with the direct lie; bloody legal ethics, why not just say he's got a deal. He cursed Gosling for putting him in this position.

'It's time for some commitment from you,' Robinson said, curtly. 'I've said all I can. I don't see the point of further discussion if you're not interested.'

'Of course we're interested,' Hamish said, anxious now. 'As I told you, I have limited authorisation. I have to abide by my director's instructions.'

'Tell me straight, is your director interested in a deal or not?'

'Yes,' Hamish said, abandoning his attempt to cling to the truth, 'certainly he is. If you can come here for a further meeting I'm sure we can wrap this up.'

There was a pause while Robinson seemed to consider this. 'Very well,' he said. 'When?'

Hamish gripped the telephone and held his breath. 'How about now?' he asked.

*

Hiss, growing and fading, reception not as good as the day before. 'Subject leaving phone box. Walking east.'

Two minutes crackle.

'Subject entering Underground.'

The two men in the front of the Escort looked round at the girl sitting in the back seat. 'Okay, he's gone to his meeting.' She paused before going on; their eyes flicked at each other in the silence.

'Let's do it,' she said softly.

CHAPTER 15

Hamish doodled, unable to concentrate on the work in front of him, thinking of the meeting happening on the floor below, of Robinson bumbling hopefully into the building looking for a deal, only to get Gosling's aggressive hectoring instead. He imagined the systematic way Gosling would bully and cross-examine and sneer, treating Robinson as a police suspect, as a man already condemned. Hamish felt guilty about setting Robinson up with so blatant a lie, instead of trying in good faith to reach a deal. The day he had been called to the Bar, some pompous old judge had got up and spouted about 'fearless integrity'. Some integrity, he thought.

And Robinson sounded like an unusual case. He regretted losing it. He looked down at the paperwork on his desk: a distributorship agreement for the Maldives. Routine legal paperwork; necessary, but boring. It looked even more dreary than usual, as if to punish him.

He went and stood at the window, looking down into the street. As he stood and watched he saw three men cross the road towards a dark blue Granada. Robinson in the middle, closely flanked by two men, one in a suit, the other in a bomber jacket. Plain-clothes officers, he thought.

Poor old bugger.

*

Robinson had run across a wide variety of policemen during his life, mostly in developing countries which had not yet acquired a habit of suavity in dealing with suspected criminals. The treatment he had received had not always been of the kindest. He was far from being intimidated by the polite and urbane officers of Kensington and Chelsea. When he arrived at the station he was booked in at the desk, relieved of his watch, wallet, diary, loose change and room key, and shown into an interview room. He stayed there for forty minutes on his own, contemplating a crack across the ceiling.

At last, the door opened and a man in a suit walked in. He was tall, straight, grey-haired and introduced himself as a chief inspector. Robinson's eyebrows rose in surprise. He was not usually dealt with by so high a rank. He guessed, rightly, that the tribute was to Gosling's influence, not to him.

A detective constable followed, sat at one side of the chief inspector, pulled out a notebook and raised a pen. The chief inspector threw out one question after another. Robinson made no reply to any of them. He had experience of this sort of thing. Silence had sometimes earned him a beating-up, heavy boots in his stomach as he lay in a filthy cell, but he knew enough about the police to distrust the lying suggestions that it would be better for him to cooperate.

Only when the chief inspector had given some explanation of the case against him did Robinson speak. He did so briefly and tersely, saying that he had genuine information about criminal activities which he had been trying, in all good faith, to report to an interested party, pointing out that the activities were taking place entirely abroad, outside the chief inspector's jurisdiction, and that he had no intention of giving the information to the chief inspector or anyone else. After which he sat back in his chair, pink in the face and breathing heavily, refusing to answer any further questions.

After another half an hour of questioning, the chief inspector got up and left the room.

*

'Look.' Gosling protested. 'The man had a forgery in his possession, he's clearly a villain. How can you even consider…'

'*You* look, Phil,' said the chief inspector, beginning to lose patience. 'It's no offence to possess a forged trademark unless he intends to put it on something. You yourself told me that he had it in order to give to you.'

'In order to defraud us, you mean.'

'It isn't fraud if the information's genuine. For all I know it might be. You certainly can't prove it isn't.'

'But he's done nothing to prove that it is!'

'Phil, you know as well as I do that it's for the prosecution to prove the fraud, not for the defence to disprove it.'

'But if he's been party to this faking—'

'We don't know that he has. He hasn't said so to us, to you, or to your man Mallows. He's not that stupid.'

'But you can't just let him go!'

'I'm *sorry*,' the chief inspector said, his emphasis saying that he wasn't. 'I've already told you, I've done everything for you I can. More than I ought to, I dare say. I've got nothing to hold him on and there's nothing I *can* do but let him go.'

'Shit!' Gosling muttered, pacing about the room. The chief inspector said nothing. Inwardly he sighed. The old, old story. As soon as they leave the force for inflated commercial positions, they lose their grip.

*

Hamish tried to force his mind back to his drafting but it kept drifting, fluttering like a butterfly from one thought to another. Eventually it settled on the evening ahead. He left his office on the dot of six o'clock, nipping lightly down the main stairway, humming, almost cheerful. As he rounded the landing of the first floor he saw Gosling approaching along the corridor.

His heart sank, anticipating a smirk of triumph. To his surprise, Gosling's face stayed blank and stony. Hamish sensed a chink at which to probe, slowed, and hailed him in a hearty voice, borrowing the loud bonhomie of the commercial reps.

'Hello, Phil,' he called, 'all well? Got our friend all wrapped up for the night?'

Gosling glowered and strode on, intending to pass without answering. Hamish stepped sideways into his path.

'All went according to plan, did it?' he asked.

'I met him,' Gosling said, forced to a halt. 'The police arrested him, as I said they would, took him down the nick.'

'And? Did they get the information from him?'

'He didn't have any,' Gosling said, truculently. 'It was obvious. I told you he wouldn't.'

'Oh? He confessed, you mean?'

'Not in so many words…'

'So now what? They going to charge him with fraud?'

Gosling shifted slightly to one side. 'I don't remember being accountable to you, Mallows,' he said irritably, 'and now *if* you'll excuse me…' He placed a hand on Hamish's arm to move past him. It was a mannerism Hamish loathed, invariably it triggered a surge of irritation.

'I'd like to *know… Phil*,' he snapped. 'Is he being charged or is he not?'

Gosling looked at him in silent truculence before giving a grudging answer.

'No. As it happens, the police don't feel it appropriate.'

'Ohhhh,' Hamish said, the long syllable rising, curving in an arc like a leaping fish, grabbing enlightenment in midair and falling back down. 'You mean he didn't tell them anything, he didn't co-operate *at all*?'

Gosling stayed silent. Hamish's irritation was replaced by a cold knot of apprehension.

'But, does that mean they're not holding him?'

'If you don't mind, I'm on my way to a meeting. We can discuss this some other—'

'They've let him go, haven't they?' he asked softly.

He got his answer from the look in Gosling's eye as he pushed past.

*

He stood alone on the landing as the swing door Gosling had gone through flopped gently to and fro.

'Shit,' he murmured. He spun on his heel, ran back upstairs, threw himself into a chair, grabbed the telephone and punched the buttons. Looked anxiously at his watch, counted the hollow ringing. He had nearly given up when there was a click at the other end.

'Hamish Mallows. Is that Arthur?'

'Yep.'

'The whole thing's been a fuck-up. They've let him go.'

'Jesus.'

'Can you get the team back on him?' There was a pause, then a small sigh. 'Sorry, Hamish, not till tomorrow.'

'Oh Christ. Are you sure? Isn't there anyone?'

'No. You said pull them off when the police took him, so that's what I did. They're out on another job. I've no one else.'

Shit. Now what do I do?

CHAPTER 16

Thirty minutes later Hamish nosed his Golf south over Chelsea Bridge, bumper to bumper in the rush-hour queue, a sodden blanket of drizzle over the river turning the autumn evening into a dark grey mess. As he came level with Battersea Park, a dirty Renault van in the inside lane pulled out in front of him. He swerved sideways, nearly hitting a bus coming the other way, and slammed his hand on the horn. A hand emerged from the window of the van and stuck two fingers in the air.

Accelerate, brake, start, stop, into the packed roundabout, through the traffic lights, jockeying to pass a telecom lorry parked by the kerb, inching round the long curving bend underneath the grimy brick of the railway bridge. Train thundering overhead, the whole neighbourhood shaking.

Along the Victorian brick of Queenstown Road, houses of dull yellow, sooty red and grey; up the hill to the T-junction at Clapham Common, headlights picking out joggers panting in the dark. *Which way now* – Hamish twisted to look at the map on the seat beside him – *shit, I should have gone left after the railway bridge.* Left now, then, along the common, half peering at the map, Brixton to the right, road sign saying no right turn. *That's where I want to go, shit, shit, shit. Try a U-turn.* Solid traffic the other way, no one going to let him in, traffic piling up now, hooting and a scream of abuse from the car behind. He looked at the line in front of him; finally a car stopped and waved him on, luminous maroon Escort with fat tyres, tinted glass, full-volume rap, grin from the driver with long Rasta dreadlocks. Hamish waved his thanks, swung the car round, road sign saying ahead only. *What the hell, give it a go.* Accelerated left round the corner and nearly hit the back of another queue.

Twenty minutes later, threading through the warren of Victorian terraces with his map in one hand he found Bacon Road. Coasted cautiously along – 186, 174, 162. Other side of the road – 97, 63, 49. *Must be soon – 17, 15 – that makes 21, two doors back.* Drove to the next corner and stopped. *No good parked like that, Hamish, you idiot, you're looking the wrong way.* Reversed round the corner – *shit, mind the boy on the skateboard* – angry thump on his roof as the boy swept past. Parked again, felt the whole of the empty street was looking at him. God, is this what those investigator chaps do for a living?

Hamish was already feeling self-conscious. After twenty minutes he felt he was sticking out like a man waving a flag. Looked ostentatiously at his map. *I'm really just lost, my goodness would I be doing surveillance on anybody, who, me, do I look the type?*

Forty-five minutes and Hamish was squirming in his seat and feeling a fool.

Well, now what? Suppose he's already in there? Suppose he comes out and walks down the street? What do you do, do you gun the engine and stop with a squeal of brakes, what d'you think this is, television? What if he isn't in and walks up to the door, do you yell at him, go and knock on his door; what?

Along the pavement towards him came two youths, sauntering, taking their time, looking around. Looking through the windscreen as they passed, staring into the car; Hamish buried himself in his map.

I don't know, he told himself. All I know is that ass

Gosling's gone and fucked it, I should have stopped him, don't know how though – all I know is, if this bloke had any information we've lost it. No idea how to play it now, coming here was all I could think of.

There was a soft bump against the rear wing of his car, a man swaying along the pavement, middle-aged, scruffy and drunk. Stopped by his window, knocked on it. Hamish ignored him. The man bent down to peer inside, knocked again. Hamish wound down the window and got a slurred imprecation in a blast of beer fumes. Hurriedly Hamish searched his pockets for a coin, anything to get him to go away, pushed it into the man's palm. The man stared at him and leant against the car, his hand still outstretched, not wanting to lose an easy prey. Hamish wound his window up, the man knocked again.

Hamish had forgotten to concentrate on the street. Out of the corner of his eye he saw a movement on the pavement opposite. As he looked across the street, he saw Robinson walking slowly up the front path to the house. Immediately Hamish pushed the car door open, the inebriated tramp staggering across the pavement and cursing fluently, loudly, incomprehensibly.

Hamish got to the gate just as Robinson was opening the door.

'Mr. Robinson...' he called.

Robinson looked round, surprised at hearing his name called, astonished when he saw who called it.

Hamish hurried up the path.

'Mr. Robinson. Look, I must talk to you.' Robinson's face began to show hostility. 'I'm sorry about this afternoon, it wasn't my idea, it was taken out of my hands, I didn't—'

'Well, you can bugger off for a start.'

'Look, I—'

'I never heard of such a thing. I come to you in perfect good faith, I offer my services to help you out, and the next thing that happens I'm hauled off by some blasted policeman.'

'I—'

'If that's how you do business I'm glad I found out before I told you anything. If you're here looking for my help, you can sod off.'

'*It wasn't me.* You've got to believe me. It was the security man, the man you met, it was his idea to bring the police in.'

Rain was plastering Hamish's hair to his head, dripping down over his ears, running down his face. 'Look, can we talk?' he pleaded. 'In the pub or something? I'll buy you a drink…' Hamish heard the words come out of his mouth; how weak they sounded.

'A drink? You shop me to the police and you want to buy me a drink?'

'I…'

'Look, I don't know what you're playing at and I don't know what your company's playing at. Is this another setup?'

'No, it—'

'Has your board told you to come and do a deal, then?'

'Well, not exactly, but I—'

'No, of course it hasn't. Your board shops me to the police – of course they don't want to do a deal. So you can tell your board to stuff it.'

The door opened behind Robinson and Hamish saw a thin-faced woman, pointed chin, grey-streaked brown hair, her eyebrows raised in surprise. Robinson took a firm step through the doorway and turned with a baleful look at Hamish.

'And the same goes for you. So bugger off.'

He pushed the woman into the hall and slammed the door behind him.

As Hamish turned away he saw the drunk crossing the road to meet him.

CHAPTER 17

The next day, the rain had disappeared as if it had never been. In the communal garden behind Hamish's flat a blackbird fluttered through the bushes, *chuck chuck chuck*, under a sky blue from one horizon to the other; the sun shone with a clear brilliance, pushing its way past Hamish's curtains and into his bedroom, where he lay with his duvet pulled over his head to shut the light out. Lay with his head throbbing, not wanting to move, wanting to stay cocooned all day, with scarcely the strength to curse the noise of the bird outside.

An electronic whine exploded into his hangover. In reflex he jerked out his hand, smacked the alarm to turn off the source of this new pain, groaned at the sudden movement. Fifteen minutes later when the throbbing had lessened, he raised his head cautiously from the pillow; moving slowly he levered himself upright and shuffled to a sitting position on the side of the bed.

He staggered into the kitchen, on automatic pilot, towards the fridge. Opened the door, fumbled for the orange juice, a pint bottle. *Oh God, please let it be full.* Half an inch left in the bottom and starting to curdle. Slowly he groped for the milk, assembled a bowl of Shreddies, chewed his way through them, trying to sneak some gentle jaw movements past the growling watchdog in his brain.

It was ten o'clock when he slunk into the office. His spirits rose slightly at the thought of the coffee Sarah would have made. He gently opened the door to her room, anticipating a cackle of ribald abuse. To his surprise the room was empty, silent, the lights off, the plastic cover still over her keyboard. There was a yellow note stuck to the door of his room.

Hamish. Sarah won't be in today.
She'll call you later. Trish.

Great. That was all he needed. He looked in despair at the coffee machine: clean and dry. His headache thumped in protest.

Wearily he sat down in his chair. Only then did he notice the brown envelope propped up in the centre of his desk.

CONFIDENTIAL.

SECOND INTERIM REPORT.

1.   At 11.45 on Wednesday 22nd instant Subject was observed leaving 21 Bacon Road and was followed to telephone box at Brixton Water Lane. Subject entered same and made one short telephone call. On leaving box Subject hesitated as if considering next move. Subject then moved at leisurely pace through Brixton, pausing outside numerous shops before entering department store. Subject browsed in store without making purchases, left store at 12.20 and retraced steps to telephone box in Brixton Water Lane. Subject waited five minutes for box to be vacated before entering and making one further call. Both calls were subsequently confirmed as coinciding calls received by client. Subject left box at 12.50 and proceeded to Brixton Underground station.

2.   From thence Subject proceeded by Underground and foot to offices of client. Surveillance was maintained outside client's offices until Subject's departure in company of two police officers apparently under arrest.

3.   Acting on a pretext, access was gained to 21 Bacon Road during absence of Subject. Casual conversation with Mrs O'Flaherty suggested she has no information regarding antecedents of Subject.

4.   Access was gained to room occupied by Subject. Suitcase in cupboard contained British passport in name of William Michael Seymour, bearing photograph recognisable as that of Subject. Details of passport were photographed and will follow. Suitcase also contained pocket diary which was also photographed. No airline tickets or other travel documents were apparent, but suitcase bore luggage tags issued by Philippine Airlines and TAP. No further information discovered in room in brief time available.

5.   It was observed said passport contains a number of entry and exit stamps for Philippines, most recent being exit stamp for June 3rd. No exit or entry stamps for Portugal or other European countries were apparent, but as client will no doubt know such stamps are no longer in common use within European countries for European nationals.

Wearily he tossed it to one side. Robinson, or Seymour, or whatever he called himself, would be long gone by now. He wondered vacantly whether he had really had anything of value to tell. Unless the investigators came up with some bright idea, he'd never know.

CHAPTER 18

Jo Derby sat in front of her bedroom mirror and stared into her eyes, asking herself where she went wrong.

She picked up the gold earrings from her dressing table and watched herself, head on one side, as she fixed one into place. They were a source of comfort, Aunt Elizabeth's earrings; she had been especially fond of Aunt Elizabeth. Tonight she could use a bit of moral support.

She looked down at the gold watch lying beside her jewellery box and pursed her lips. This was another matter. She'd worn it with delight every day since Alan had given it to her six months ago. Now the pleasure was soured by regret, tightness in her stomach instead of lightness in the heart.

It would seem odd to leave it off now. Wounding, perhaps; she had often seen his glance flicker to her wrist. But then… it might seem tactless to flaunt it. She sighed, unable to decide.

What was it, she thought, looking back at her calm hazel-green eyes in the mirror, what was it about her that attracted the wrong sort of man? Why did she do it? She wasn't stupid, she knew herself to be bright, switched-on, streetwise. She knew perfectly well that married men were not a good idea, why had she let it happen?

She pursed her lips and looked down again at the watch, took a decision, strapped it on. Alan would be hurt enough anyway. She would try to soften what she had to say but she had to say it anyway. It wasn't right for her. Wasn't right full stop, she supposed, but certainly not for her.

She stood up, smoothed her dress down and picked up her bag. What a way to spend a Sunday evening, when most of her friends were curled up with husbands, out with lovers or nattering to their girlfriends. Oh no, not you, she said to her reflection, you have to be going out to some bloody hotel to have a weepy scene.

*

She got back to her Baron's Court flat just before midnight. It had been a depressing evening. Alan had been more upset than she had expected, made a fuss, made all sorts of promises, made it more difficult for her to do what she'd decided to do. She'd almost wavered.

But only almost. When she decided to do something, it got done.

When Monday morning came the watch stayed on her dressing table for the first time in six months.

*

A gust of wind tugged at her skirt as she walked across the open square in front of Westminster Cathedral. She glanced fleetingly up at its red and white stripes of brick and stone. Privately she thought it grotesque, like a large liquorice all-sort. She'd been inside once, couldn't get over the contrast between the gold and ornate opulence at ground level and the starkness of the dingy, unfinished-looking brickwork above.

Ran out of money. Probably conned by the builder, she'd muttered: as always, scenting a crime.

Despite the gust of wind her walk stayed neat and poised as always, her feet clicking precisely along the paving, her body slim and upright. Five minutes later she pushed open the door of Farthingdale's office, swerved round a potted plant and headed for her desk.

*

An hour and a half later a blast of wind scudded down the street, catching Hamish as he stepped out of the taxi, rattling a 'To Let' sign and blowing a discarded plastic bag past his ankles while he fumbled in his wallet to pay the cabby.

He spoke into a grille outside the door, pushed through double mahogany doors, ignored the lift with its ageing brass cage and walked up the red-carpeted communal stairs.

In the second-floor reception the carpet cooled to steel-grey beneath stark white walls, carefully designed to give an impression of clinical efficiency. Arthur Farthingdale came down the corridor, smooth forty-year-old face smiling blandly beneath his straight, fair hair, exuding an air that was slightly too sleek for Hamish's taste, smacking a little of the salesman.

As Hamish was ushered into the firm's one meeting room he saw that there was a girl already there. She was standing by the window, looking out at the wind, her oatmeal blouse standing out against the dull blue-grey sky beyond the glass.

Hamish put out a hand as Arthur introduced them to each other and ran an appreciative eye over her. Freckled, heart-shaped face. Neat body, upright, composed. Watchful eyes below short brown hair. Late twenties, okay on age but not really Hamish's type. Worth a two-second glance in the street but not someone you'd crane your neck at, he thought.

They sat round the table and Arthur flexed his shoulders, squared up the pad of paper in front of him and looked purposefully at Hamish.

'Jo led the team that was on your friend, Seymour,' he

explained. 'The morning after you rang, she tried to get back onto him but he'd gone.'

Hamish turned his head towards Jo, silently, his mind going off at a tangent as he thought of his futile last-ditch attempt, driving to Clapham to speak to Seymour and being told to bugger off. His glance lingered, turned into a blank stare which Jo mistook for criticism.

'Don't look at me,' she said: cool, aggressive voice. 'It wasn't me decided to get him nicked. Christ, talk about a fuck-up.'

Arthur sat back in his chair, a subdued smile at one corner of his mouth: referee moving to one side.

'I didn't say you did,' Hamish said, taken aback by her unprovoked hostility. 'And if it comes to that, it wasn't me either.'

'It was your bloody company though, wasn't it?' she rasped, thinking angrily of the time she had spent in Seymour's room while Ron distracted Mrs O'Flaherty downstairs: adrenalin pumping through her as she searched the luggage, laid Seymour's stuff on the bed, worked the camera; twitching every time there was a noise from the stairs, and all for nothing. 'I bust my arse on that bloke – we all did, me and the whole team, and then you lot go and screw the bloody case up.'

Hamish gave an exaggerated sigh. 'I didn't come here for a post-mortem. I came to see if we can retrieve the situation.'

'Oh yeah? How?' She laughed sarcastically. 'The man's gone. What you want us to do, advertise for him?'

'No. I mean, can we check up on what he said?'

'Oh, brilliant. Twenty-four hours ago you think he's a bullshitting con artist. Now you come along and say you think he's for real. After you've got him nicked. Bit late in the day to change your mind, isn't it?'

'I'm not changing my mind,' Hamish retorted, flushing a little. 'I said at the time I believed him. I still do.'

'You do?' she said, scepticism and disbelief ringing in her voice. 'Why?'

Hamish frowned and raised a hand to his forehead, brushing aside a curly wave of his brown hair, a gesture to sweep aside her scepticism. 'To be honest it's difficult to put my finger on exactly why I believe him. Sort of… instinct, if you like. Okay, he was beat up, and a bit of a bullshit merchant maybe, but there was something about him which… I don't know – I felt he had conviction in what he was saying.'

She raised a questioning eyebrow. *Instinct,* she was thinking, the man's a lawyer and he says he's got *instinct?*

'And there was the label, too,' he added. He pulled out a calfskin wallet, took the label from it and laid it on the table. 'Arthur's already seen it. It's a bloody good copy, I expect he told you.'

She picked it up and held it at arm's length, gave it a quick glance, and then returned to looking at him, green eyes calm, assessing, silent for perhaps half a minute.

'So?' she said at last, one eyebrow raised a little further.

'So I want to find where the bloody thing came from,' he said, tersely.

'Well, then,' she said, face expressionless, voice soft and gentle now, the deliberate gentleness which shows infinite feminine patience for male stupidity. 'You should have asked the man when you had the chance, shouldn't you?'

'Look,' Hamish said angrily, leaning forward, one elbow on the table. 'I've *told* you, I didn't come here to—'

'I mean,' she persisted, 'there's no point in hiring us if you don't let us get on with it. If you want the police to mess it up for you, you don't need us. It's a pain for us and a waste of money for you. Got it?'

'Are you saying you don't want our business?' Hamish asked frostily, leaning back in his chair, and looking supercilious.

Quickly Arthur put a hand on Jo's pale forearm, anxious now to soothe the client. Smoothly he launched into a salesman's eulogy, a plummy tribute to Jo's abilities as an investigator, her commitment, her professionalism. Earnestly he explained her reaction, how she disliked not getting a result. How, of course, Farthingdale's fully appreciated the business of so substantial a client as Grand McCowrie.

Hamish listened, detached, quietly amused by Arthur's concern to retain a client's goodwill. He wondered how the girl would have put it. Probably tell him to take his case and stuff it.

'So what d'you recommend?' Hamish asked, not looking at Jo.

'Well…' Arthur paused, reluctant to turn away business, but stumped for an answer. 'Of course, there's a report outstanding from our Hong Kong office. Maybe they'll turn something up. But that apart—' He spread his hands, eloquently expressing the difficulty they faced.

The same message flashed more bluntly from Jo's eyes. *Okay smartarse, can* you *think of anything we can do?*

*

Oh, very well, Hamish thought as he said a rather curt goodbye, I'll forget the bloody man. He trotted down the stairs and into the street, leaving thoughts of Robinson behind him, upstairs with the potted plant, in the plastic air of their sterile office.

He stretched his arms behind him, limbering up, wanting air in his lungs, and set off to walk through the streets to Buckingham Palace and across Green Park. The wind whipped the branches of the plane trees, blew leaves across the paths, pulled at his hair and caught the umbrellas of a few bedraggled tourists. He left the tarmac and set off over the turf, striding uncaring through the wet grass that swished water over his shoes and darkened the ends of his trouser legs.

Back to dictation and drafting, he thought as he marched up the steps of Grand McCowrie's front door, back to regulations on distillation and maturation, to structuring joint ventures, to faxing foreign lawyers. Back to sidestepping the Mexican Government's latest prejudice against foreign multinationals. Back to persuading commercial directors to accept the correctness of laws they thought idiotic.

Back to being a lawyer.

CHAPTER 19

Seymour spent a fitful night in his dingy B&B. As he awoke, there was a moment in which his mind was empty. Then he remembered. It made him feel unwell, it gave him a bitter feeling in his stomach. It was like the feeling he had when he was so desperate to get out of Manila, but worse. At least then, when Raul came along, a spark of hope appeared. Now that spark had been extinguished. His clever plan, or what he had told himself was a clever plan, was gone. For good. It was what he had been pinning his hopes on, why he had suggested the counterfeiting in the first place. Now the plan had failed. It was dead. What should he do? Where could he go?

He heaved himself out of his uncomfortable bed, looked out of the window in Brixton, at the grey streets, the rain falling, people scurrying about under their umbrellas. He had forgotten how dreary the English summer can be. He felt no connection with anything he saw.

He sat on his bed and tried to think. At least in Portugal there was sun. At least he could hide from his failure of yesterday. No one in Portugal would know about what he had been up to. Thank God. Or maybe thank his own planning; at least that bit worked. And maybe, maybe, if those fools at Grand McCowrie were so incompetent, then maybe the counterfeiting would succeed, it would make money, and he would get a share of it. He thought of the sun again and stirred himself. Took a deep breath, and started to pull on his clothes, readying himself for the trek to Heathrow Airport.

*

When he arrived in Lisbon, it was sunny, hot, and he started to feel reinvigorated. He had not realised: after all those years in Manila he had got used to the heat, and England had seemed almost alien. Well, he thought, perhaps that's what being an expat was all about. Bit late to find that out. Maybe he was better off here in Portugal anyway. And by tomorrow, by the time he next saw Raul, he would be feeling stronger, would be back to his old self, spinning them a yarn about how useful his trip to Scotland had been. And no, of course he did not bother to go to London, why on earth would he have done that?

CHAPTER 20

Sarah stalked silently into Hamish's room and dropped a brown envelope on his desk with a thud, scattering half a dozen sheets of his scribbling. Hamish looked up and gave her a sigh.

Half an hour later, when he had finished what he was drafting, he opened the envelope. It was the outstanding report.

CONFIDENTIAL.

THIRD INTERIM REPORT.

1.   In accordance with instructions from client, enquiries have been instituted in Manila through our Hong Kong associates. Enquiries reveal address of Subject on file with Phil. immigration service given as 1053 Ave del Pilar. Confidential photocopy of entry on immigration file attached (Annex 5).

2.   Visit made to said address revealed no information on Subject. Person at said address claimed no knowledge of Subject.

3.   Enquiries with Phil. banks revealed bank account in name of Subject with Bank of Luzon. Account closed June 2nd. Bank indicates financial status of Subject is low. Confidential photocopy bank statement for last three months of account (Annex 6) shows balance fluctuates between nil and 37,192 pesos (approx. £825). Subject did not hold any

external account in US dollars or other currency at bank.
Bank not aware of such account elsewhere.

4.   Records of Bank of Luzon indicate address of Subject
as from eleven months ago as follows:

983 Avenue Villar,

Pasay,

Manila.

Enquiries continue.

He pursed his lips. Typical investigator's stuff, scurrying around in the dirt, scraping the barrel for any bit of background that they could write down on a report. It was no bloody use, that was obvious. Which wouldn't stop them putting in a bill for it.

He tossed the report dismissively back on the desk. He had more pressing things to think about.

CHAPTER 21

Soft, night-warm Philippines.

Smelling of the heavy, damp, musky scent of the tropics. In downtown Manila, smelling of fragrant scents, of flowers, of rich women stepping out of limousines.

In the Avenue Villar, smelling of dogshit and urine. Of rotting rubbish by the side of the road, strewn in the dirt of the vacant lots, chewed by the dogs padding about in the daytime, crawling with cockroaches at night.

Through the shadows of Avenue Villar, down the uneven track, stepping carefully round the potholes and the tin cans and the piles of dogshit, stepping slowly because the road is dark — who is going to bribe municipal officers to put lighting down *here?* — a figure is walking alone, scarcely visible, dressed in black tee shirt, shorts and sneakers.

After five minutes he arrives at the house he wants, the house he has been watching for two days. He knows exactly where the door is, where the windows are, where the locks are. He knows which of them Rosita locks and which she forgets about when she goes out.

In less than a minute he is inside the house.

He turns on his torch and shines its beam around the ground floor: the one square room, sparsely furnished, with a kitchenette at the back. Cockroaches scuttle into the crevices, disturbed by the light. Two of them stay, fighting over a piece of onion in the middle of the floor.

The torch picks out a door at the back of the kitchenette. The intruder looks briefly through it. A tap high up in the wall drips water onto the concrete floor of a makeshift shower.

Back in the room there is nowhere much to look for anything hidden, the only furniture being a few chairs, a rough table and a rickety sideboard, faced in plastic. This holds an assortment of glasses, most of them obviously stolen from one bar or another. There are some plates and a bowl, an empty box of Filipino cheroots, an aluminium ashtray and some tattered books. He leafs through the books, finds nothing, goes upstairs.

Upstairs is also one room, a bedroom, more promising.

No jewellery, but there might be something under the mattress.

He is right, there is a wad of notes, though these are not what he is looking for.

There is a cupboard at one side of the room. He thinks this might be a possibility, but there is only Rosita's shoes and dresses and jeans, all dishevelled and pushed in anyhow.

It is the three cardboard boxes on the floor near the window that he thinks will be the most promising. A quick flick through them shows papers, notebooks, hotel stationery and a passport, out of date. It will take all night to look through this lot, he will have to take them away. He picks up two of the boxes and carries them downstairs, leaves them by the door, comes back upstairs for the third.

Suddenly there is a shuffling noise coming from outside the house

There is a click from the front door opening. A pause. A creak as the mosquito screen is pushed open.

He stands poised, silent.

'Rosita?' a voice calls, nasal, half-muted, half-shrill. The screen groans as it swings slowly shut.

'Rosita?' It is an old voice.

He does not move.

Nothing happens for a moment. Then there is a click. Light floods into the space downstairs, washes up the stairs, spills dimly into the bedroom.

Footsteps shuffle across the floor and stop at the bottom of the stairs. 'Rosita?' the voice calls again, insistent, querulous.

His eyes flick around the room; there is nowhere to hide. Silently his rubber-shod feet take him to the corner by the cupboard. From his waistband he pulls a short, thick, wooden stick, holds it beside him in readiness.

Slowly the footsteps start to shuffle up the stairs. They are the footsteps of an old person, an old woman, he detects from the voice. She stops on the step below the bedroom.

He can see the shadow of the figure, shifting uncertainly. He can hear her breathing. No doubt another slut like Rosita; if only she will go away, and he will leave her in peace.

He wills her to go away.

From where she is standing she can see the bed, can see the mess of the tangled, dirty sheets, can see Rosita is not there.

As he grips his stick more tightly, he curses her.

Still, she hesitates, unaware, poised to step into the darkened room.

CHAPTER 22

Next day the English summer edged a tremulous step forward, one degree warmer and more confident, one degree less frightened of being dragged back into a cold, wet spring. Hamish stood at an open window, refusing the sterility of air-conditioning, his nostrils twitching at the scent of outdoors. He sighed as he turned back to his desk, cluttered with letters and contracts and memoranda, and thought of sunshine on the grass.

Nestling among the scattered papers was another brown envelope.

CONFIDENTIAL.

FOURTH INTERIM REPORT.

1.   A visit has been made to 983 Avenue Villar, the last known address of Subject. It is understood that one person now lives at said address, a Rosita Concepcion, who is understood to have cohabited with Subject. Enquiries reveal said Concepcion to be an erstwhile prostitute who has recently returned to the profession.

2.   Said Concepcion had a number of papers in her possession belonging to Subject, and these being no longer of use to her she has relinquished same. Our Far East correspondent indicates few of these appear likely to be of use but they are enclosed, for what they are worth. These include an address book: most names therein appear to be names common in Philippines.

As Hamish opened the book he saw that it was a mess. The ruled lines printed in the book had been ignored. Names were scrawled all over the place, sideways, diagonally, even one or two upside down. Some of the names had no addresses at all, only numbers, telephone or telex, hastily scribbled beside them. Even where there were addresses, just street names were visible, the town and country left blank.

He read half a dozen pages and then his reading sped up, flicking quickly through the rest of the book. None of the names meant anything to him; he might as well have been reading a Mongolian telephone directory. It would take an hour or more to make any order of this; there was little promise that it would repay the effort. He chucked it to one side. Time for lunch, fresh air, sandwiches in the park.

As he walked down the stairs to the ground floor, Spicer was standing in the hall, poised to go out for an expensive lunch, Freeman fawning at his heels. Someone out in the street called a loud greeting, and Gosling's face appeared in the doorway as he stumped up the front steps.

They saw Hamish as he stepped into the hall and half-turned towards him, murmuring conspiratorially to each other out of the corners of their mouths, watching him as he crossed the hall towards them. Gosling rocked on his feet, bumptious and cocky; Spicer and Freeman contented themselves with predatory smiles.

Three school bullies, Hamish thought. His stomach tightened and he forced a thin smile as he passed them.

'Afternoon, Mallows,' Gosling called.

Hamish's stomach tightened, and he kept his insincere

smile in place as he walked up to them.

'Off out to the bank, then?' Gosling asked as Hamish was about to step past him. ''Nother little half-million handout to the criminal classes?'

Hamish stopped and gave the man a look of distaste.

'Better than giving handouts to the police,' he said coolly. 'Better chance of getting something in return, too.'

Gosling went a shade of red, and a muscle in his neck twitched. 'What the hell d'you mean by that?' he demanded.

'I should have thought that was obvious,' Hamish retorted. 'You only have to read the papers. Another case of police corruption every week.'

'That's a bloody libel,' Gosling snarled. 'I'll bloody do you for that.'

'No more defamatory than what you just said to me.'

'Pah. That man you wanted to pay was a sodding crook. Anyone except a bloody lawyer could have seen that.'

'Balls,' Hamish drawled. 'You just jumped to conclusions. He came to us with information, and you went and blew it.'

'He never had no information. You saying I don't know my job? You want to watch what you're saying, my lad.'

'Too true,' Spicer said coldly. 'We can do without company lawyers, of all people, criticising fellow employees in public.'

'Well, perhaps we might not,' Hamish said hotly, 'if we didn't have to go round clearing up the messes other people make. Which is most of the time.'

Freeman gave a soft low whistle in mock amazement. Spicer looked at Hamish silently for a long moment, pale, ice-blue eyes narrowing coldly.

'Meaning what?' he asked.

Meaning Spain, shot through Hamish's brain. He bit his lips together to stop himself saying the words aloud. The look in Spicer's eyes showed he'd read Hamish's mind.

Oh God, Hamish thought, *why did I get into this?*

Spicer gave him a smile of predatory relish. 'Well, then,' he said softly, 'we won't be expecting *you* to make any mistakes, then, will we?'

He widened his smile towards Freeman and Gosling. Pleasure spread over their faces.

'Just see that you don't, Mallows,' Spicer said, tapping Hamish squarely on the chest. 'Just see that you don't.'

As he walked down the steps he heard a brief murmur behind him, followed by a stifled laugh. What a trio of shits. The thought stayed with him all through his lunch hour, spoiling the freshness of the grass and the warm sun.

*

Hamish spent all afternoon in the City, closeted with accountants, numbing his brain with figures. He came back at quarter past five, to find Sarah's room abandoned for the night and the lights off. Outside it had started to rain and the room was grey and dark. He ignored the light switch and slumped in his chair. He stared out of the window at the heavy graphite-coloured clouds that were drifting wetly past, closed his eyes and raised one hand to cover them up in retreat from the world. The grey and the dark matched the mood that had been building up in him throughout the afternoon.

You clot, he thought. Alec goes out of his way to tell you about Spicer, he gives you as clear a warning as you'll ever get and you have to run straight out and stir the bugger up. Fool, dolt, *idiot.*

103

Bloody Spicer. And Gosling, particularly. Spicer's protégé, damn it; Spicer had recruited him as part of his new management drive. And in one short week Hamish had managed to put both their backs up.

He opened his eyes slowly and looked at his desk. Letters, faxes, memoranda, all still there, all waiting to be dealt with, all mocking him silently. *Come on, lawyer, here's a mess, clear us up.*

He let his gaze wander; it stopped at last on Seymour's address book at one corner of the desk. He picked it up and considered it idly. At least Seymour had managed to stuff Gosling. He smiled at the thought. That bloke must have been all right if he could do that, and his spirits lifted a little.

He opened the address book at random. Realtime Investments S.A., Rick, Ricardo, Raul, Steve M., Steve R., Sam, Sing Chai Mong, Sue A, Susie, P. Saretski, Sally's Bar, Tim, Trevor, Terence, Tai Koo Chak.

96-30-11, 405.7894, 27841, (221) 983 4986, 0832 468739, 47.95.10.12.

He flipped back towards the beginning. Briginshaw, Cardoso, Chiu-lin, Carrera, Charlie, De Souza. What a muddle.

His thoughts went back to Alec's warning: *Don't get in Adrian Spicer's way.* He was going to have to watch his step there. But it was Gosling that really irritated him.

He ran a finger over Seymour's diary. Now here might be a chance to prove him wrong. Bugger you, Gosling, he thought. Crass oaf.

Tuesday: Charlie, Mandarin, 5.15. Wednesday: blank. Thursday: bank, 900 pesos. Friday: R, Manila Hotel, lunch. Saturday: Sally's, 8.00. Sunday: blank. Monday, Tuesday: blank. Wednesday: Quibilan Escort Agency, 6.00. Thursday, Friday: blank. Saturday: 756392. Tuesday, 610203.

Well, there was a Charlie in the diary and one in the address book. Perhaps the two tied up. Perhaps if he read them more closely he'd get some sort of a clue. He turned the page. A whole week blank, then a few initials next to a number. He turned to the last entry: only six weeks ago, and just a six-digit number, nothing to say what it meant. No notes to explain the entries. Blast it, why did the man have to use abbreviations all the time? So infuriating, all these entries, so meaningful to the man who'd written them, so uncommunicative to him. His brain was tired and he felt frustrated at being unable to get any solid deductions out of what was in front of him

He turned back to the address book, hoping he'd spot some of the numbers that were in the diary. He tried for five minutes but it was hopeless, each number just hung precariously in his mind until it was superseded by the next, then dropped off, like drops of water clinging to the underside of a kitchen sieve.

Something more systematic was needed. He walked to Sarah's desk, his eye half-flicking over the cartoons she had pinned above the mirror, sat down in front of the keyboard and pushed off its plastic shroud. Flicked the switch of the computer and waited as its orange screen hummed into life. Slowly, with the clumsiness of unfamiliarity, he started to tap numbers onto the screen, sorting them into numerical order as he went.

An hour and a half later his eyes were starting to ache from squinting at the screen, his head was starting to thump and he needed a drink. He looked at his watch. It was half-past eight. Time to knock off.

*

He'd planned on finishing the task the next morning, but Sarah adamantly refused to let him use the computer, protesting volubly about the amount of typing he'd given her to do. He was unable to shift her except by promising to take her out to lunch. With a pretence of reluctance, she went off down the corridor to have a cheerful natter with the other secretaries.

By eleven o'clock he had a computerised copy of the address book. By using the computer's search function he could cross-reference each number in the diary. Sally's Bar came up three times. The Manila Hotel once. And about a dozen individuals. Irritatingly, only four of these had addresses; for the rest, the address book gave the phone number alone, without even any indication of what country they lived in.

He gave up at midday and took Sarah out to lunch. They went to a bistro in Shepherd Market, tables outside for the early arrivals to sit in the sun and watch the world go by. Sarah leaned back on the folding metal chair, stretching like a cat, closed her eyes and turned her face upwards. Tourists wandered vaguely around, the office dwellers strode busily out of their grey caverns, purposeful-looking girls stalked along the pavements.

A wine list came, brought by a clumping Australian waitress. A minute after taking Hamish's order she was back with a bottle, dumping wine brusquely into their glasses.

'Just the stuff for sitting in the sun with,' he said.

Sarah stretched out a blonde arm, twisted the bottle and squinted at the label, sun bouncing off her tawny hair, lighting up the freckles on her cheeks. Two junior executives at the next table sat watching her. Really, Hamish thought, it's an awful pity one has to be platonic with one's secretary.

'*Gatão?*' she read. 'What's that? Some sort of cake?'

'It means cat. The bottles I remember had a moggy on the label. Strolling along with a walking stick. And boots. Bit like the ones you like wearing, actually. Which I suppose makes you Puss in Boots, too.'

She laughed richly; the junior executives pricked up their ears, shifted regretfully in their seats.

'So why no cat on this label?'

'Dunno. Suppose they feel that the sophisticated English consumer – you, for example – might be offended.' He bit into an olive. 'Little chance with a raunchy mind like yours, but they're not to know that.'

She put on her sunglasses, gave him a severe look, and lifted her face to the sun again.

He turned to watch the passers-by and lifted his glass. As he sipped the light, not-quite-fizzy wine and recalled his holiday in Portugal, a switch flicked in his brain and he remembered the luggage tab on Seymour's suitcase.

CHAPTER 23

Hamish had been looking forward to telling Arthur of his discovery. He counted on Arthur to show a proper respect for the fee-paying client. Unlike that pert little bitch, he thought.

When the receptionist squawked that Mr. Farthingdale was away for the day and would he like to speak to Miss Derby, he nearly hung up. But he had to get things moving; it was Jo or nothing. And at least, slightly to his surprise, she made no complaint about being asked to come to his office.

*

Jo arrived in Mayfair fifty-five minutes after he called, dressed in jeans and white tee shirt under a black leather jacket, driving the Kawasaki which had tailed Seymour. She pulled off her bright red crash helmet, shook her short hair, flexed her back, and stepped neatly past the bemused doorman into Grand McCowrie's elegant Georgian reception. She refused the seat the receptionist offered her and stood by the central table, flicking disparagingly through the fashion magazines lying on it as she waited, helmet swinging to and fro, wrinkling her nose in scorn at the pictures of debutante girls in *Country Life*.

She looked up as she heard high heels clicking down the stone staircase and gave a quiet sniff of amusement at seeing Sarah's swept-back blonde hair and tartan skirt, straight off the page lying open on the table. Sarah lifted her chin in disdain as she saw the pert girl in jeans. They looked coolly at each other, two women about to indulge themselves in the feminine art of mutual dislike.

Jo followed Sarah silently to Hamish's room, crash helmet looped elegantly over one arm, flaunted in parody of a Gucci handbag. Hamish welcomed her aloofly, cut-glass thank-you-so-much-for-coming routine of conventional politeness, courteously took her helmet and waved her to a seat.

'That airline tag on Seymour's luggage,' he said, and stopped. He ran a hand through the wave of hair that fell on his forehead, a small gesture of self-doubt; if he'd got it wrong this stroppy bitch would jump straight down his throat. 'It was the only one, I take it?'

'If there'd been others I'd have put it in my report.' Her voice was cool, crisp, an air of answering a stupid question.

'Quite,' he said flatly, pursing his lips. 'So,' he continued, his hands toying with a gold propelling pencil on the table, 'unless he flew TAP from Manila—'

'TAP doesn't fly out of Manila,' she interrupted. 'I checked.'

'Oh, did you?' he said, in slight surprise. 'Well, then… if he flew a Portuguese airline it's quite likely—'

'…that he went to Portugal?' she cut in. 'Yeah. It is a bit, isn't it? It's why I put it in the report.' She spoke in a bright tone which floated ambiguously between sarcasm and agreement. Stupid man, she was thinking, dragging me round to his office and telling me about information we gave him in the first place.

Hamish flushed slightly. 'Well, can you check if he actually did? I suppose the airline'll have a record, you could—'

'Forget it,' she said. *Why do bloody clients insist on making half-*

baked suggestions? 'Airlines scrub their passenger lists as soon as a plane's safely on the ground.'

'Oh,' he said.

Sarah came through the door, two cups in hand, best china, from which came the dubious smell of company caterers' dishwater tea. She banged them both on the table just heavily enough to get a little into each saucer, wrinkled her nose and stalked out. Jo flashed her a tight smile, on-off, fast and insincere.

Hamish frowned at the smell of tea; usually Sarah made Earl Grey. 'Well, anyway…' he continued, 'if that's where he went to there's a good chance that's where he was six weeks ago, right? We know he wasn't in Manila.' He paused. 'Thanks to your enquiries,' he added, in a voice of scrupulous politeness.

'Yep,' she said, confidently, she knew that already.

'Right then.' Hamish rose and moved towards his desk, three long-legged cricketing strides, confident once more; swung into his chair and pulled open a desk drawer. He returned with the Seymour reports, riffled through the diary and pointed. 'Look. This six-digit number here. The very last entry just before he came here. Could just be relevant.' Then he grabbed the address book, turned to a page marked with a self-adhesive yellow tag and pointed again. 'Here it is again, the same number. Someone called Cardoso. Doesn't say what country, but if Seymour was in Portugal it could be there.'

She raised her eyebrows at Hamish, surprised that he'd made the effort of cross-referencing Seymour's papers. The sort of thing clients usually didn't bother with. Nice to see this one start to do something sensible for a change.

'I know,' she said. 'I read them too.' Her voice was a little softer this time, she even gave him a hint of a smile. 'That what you called me round to tell me?'

'Well, yes, actually.' He kept the disappointment from his voice, he'd already known he wouldn't get any appreciation from this pert little piece. 'That, and to ask you to follow it up.'

'I see.' She picked up her teacup, sniffed it, took a small doubting sip, wrinkled her forehead and put it down. Pushed it away, dismissively.

'Well, now. Let's see what we might do,' she said. 'First, enquiries in Portugal, to see if the number ties up there. If it doesn't, maybe we'll think about trying other countries. Secondly, if it does, you'll want us to investigate it. Is that what you have in mind?'

'Yes.'

'Background in depth, full enquiries into every lead we can find, in the hope that we might get to this fake label of yours. A full investigation, in other words, going on until we get a result. Is that it?'

'Yes,' he said calmly.

'You're sure? It'll involve a lot of running around. Us, local agents. Heavy expenses. Once we start it'll be open-ended. That sort of thing costs. That okay with you?'

'Yes. Of course, we'll have to keep it under review as we go along, naturally; but in principle—'

'Well,' she snapped, 'let's get the *principle* straight first. If we go ahead, I want to be sure that you're prepared to see this thing through. I want to know that you'll give us your full backing, that your company won't suddenly ditch the whole thing in the middle, like you did before. Right?'

'Yes,' he said coldly. 'That wasn't my doing, I told you that the other day. You made your views perfectly clear then.'

'Great,' she said, an ironic lift to her voice. 'Just checking.'

She swung her green canvas shoulder bag onto her lap, pulled out a sheet of paper and skidded it across the table to him. 'In that case you'll want to see this.'

It was a fax from Hong Kong.

> *Discreet enquiries conducted of Philippine Immigration Bureau have verified one Raul Cardoso, Portuguese citizen, arrived Ninoy Aquino International Airport May 13 and departed May 26. Purpose of visit declared 'business'. Address in R.P. declared as Manila Hotel, Manila.*
>
> *Discreet enquiries at aforementioned hotel confirm Raul Cardoso guest there between above dates. Paid bill using American Express card, photocopy bill to follow. Discreet enquiries of hotel staff have been unable to elicit further information regarding Cardoso's activities.*

Below was a note in a neat feminine hand:

> *Directory enquiries Portugal confirm Raul Cardoso for diary number. Address following from our Portuguese associates.*

She watched Hamish read it. He frowned, irritation dawning as he realised that she'd been stringing him along, testing him out. 'Tell me. Is this how you usually report to your clients?' he asked.

She smiled sweetly, irony in her eyes. 'Only got the result of the check this morning. Came straight round the moment you phoned.'

'Well, that's good,' he said drily. 'But since you want to get principles straight, let's chuck in another one. If I'm going to back you, I want you to consult me in advance about what you're doing. not rush off and present me with a fait accompli. Right?'

Her eyebrows lifted. 'Is that all the thanks I get?'

Hamish leaned back, flexed his shoulders, linked his hands behind his neck and studied her. 'Well, now,' he said. 'That rather depends on you.'

'Meaning?'

'Meaning Arthur said you're keen on getting a result. Okay.' He smiled. 'Now go and get one.'

CHAPTER 24

Lisbon Airport. Pale, dirty-grey luggage hall, smeared with the scuffing of a million passing tourists, smelling of travel-stained bodies, stale heat, aviation fuel.

Jo sat on the edge of a luggage carousel, trying to ignore the mewling baby thirty yards away, willing the battered, black rubber conveyor to get moving, to give some small hint of disgorging just some of the luggage from her flight. She yawned, hating the captivity of being a passenger. Morosely she gazed at a Portuguese phrasebook she had found in the back of a drawer in her flat, and flipped through the handy sections for the traveller.

Viagem de Avião. I feel sick. Have you some cotton wool for my ears? Cotton wool, I should be so lucky, she thought, wincing as the baby drew breath and screamed.

On the boat. A deckchair in the shade. At the customs, na alfandega. I cannot open this case, não posso abrir esta valisa.

At the hotel. On arrival, a chegada. Bom dia. O meu name e, I have been stranded here, I wish to stay the night...

Great. What about how to get to the bloody hotel, how to deal with an offhand Portuguese taxi driver? *Will you drive as quickly as you can, I must catch the train to Oporto. That seems a lot to pay for so short a distance, this is all I have, keep the change. Help, it is urgent, many people have been injured. Danger! Look out! Fire! She has fainted, ela desmaiou.*

She shuddered. Great sense of humour, whoever wrote

this.

The luggage carousel creaked and started to move. She looked at its bare surface rolling out, devoid of suitcases, and curled her lip in disgust. Limply she stood up, dropping the phrasebook into her bag.

It was another twenty minutes before she trailed her case down the ramp, one of a crowd of fretful travellers making their escape. She went through the door and stopped dead as she smacked into the sun, a great warm blanket pouring over her like hot cream.

It took her five minutes to get a taxi, cutting the queue ahead of a bothered English father of two with an insipid twittering wife. Her driver was large, fat, in a grey-blue nylon shirt – *nylon in this heat, yee-ik*. Muttering something, he lifted her case slowly into the boot and slumped into the driver's seat. *Now's your chance,* she thought as she slid into the back – *Bom dia, lleve-me a, please drive as slowly as possible I do not trust your driving/insurance/hospitals.*

'Sheraton Hotel.'

'Sheratão?'

'Si.'

*

At half-past seven the next morning she is sitting in a van in a small, quiet, village street. This alone is an achievement. Only when she went to Gonçalves' office the previous afternoon did she discover he had no van of his own, that she had to bully him into hiring one. *Shit,* she'd thought, *all that crap about his surveillance capabilities and he hasn't even got an observation van. Bloody local associates, every bloody country you go to they're the bloody same, long on bullshit, short on ability. Should have driven the van out from London.*

115

She looks at the house fifty yards down. Small stone house, rather shabby, last painted about ten years ago, paint flaking now. Not the house of a big earner.

At eight o'clock a man steps through the doorway. Dark hair, tanned complexion. *Him and fifty million other Portuguese,* she thinks. Fawn blazer, dark trousers, blue shirt. *Christ, these continentals, someone should tell them bright blue doesn't go with fawn.* Briefcase in hand, he gets into a Renault; the car is grey, looks about six years old.

It has to be Cardoso. Late thirties, the age is right from the passport details copied by the Manila Hotel. Either that or his wife has a lover, and from Gonçalves' preliminary report she does not sound like a woman who would have a lover.

Jo has decided the first day will be low-key, warming up. She wants to test Gonçalves' men as much as check Cardoso. She takes some photos as he gets into the car and they follow Cardoso to Vinhos Felgueiras where he works. Then they sit outside all day, baking in the heat. Jo is wearing a tee shirt, even so she is sweating well before midday, the car is a mobile oven.

Jo is wary of Gonçalves' men. 'I will put my best men on it,' he said. *Yeah, I've heard that one, we all use that line.* Armando in the van is all right but the other two are overconfident, over-casual, pretending they do big jobs for multinationals all the time. Which is bullshit. Their English is basic, halting. Henrique, in particular, is a shit, she spotted him as a chauvinist pig in five seconds. Overweight, too. He is not going to like taking orders from a woman. *He better start getting used to it.*

On day two, Cardoso goes to his office at Vinhos Felgueiras again. Jo is in the car with Henrique, and she tells him to park in the position she wants. It is the obvious place but Henrique kicks up a fuss just because she suggested it.

They are in a street in the town looking down a slight slope to a T-junction onto a broad dusty road. On the other side of the dusty road is a twelve-foot whitewashed wall, the whitewash turned to dull cream with age and flaking off in patches, showing ochre-grey stone underneath. It runs right across their vision, extending maybe a hundred yards in each direction along the edge of the road, growing straight out of the tarmac, a few clumps of drying grass straggling at its base.

As soon as they got in position Jo checks on the rest of the team. She cannot see the observation van.

'Where's the fucking van?' she snaps at Henrique.

'Oh, we leave that up road from his house. Is there for when he goes home,' he mutters. 'Well, sodding well go and get it!'

She frets irritably until it arrives. It is just in time, five minutes later Cardoso goes out and they just get him with the camera from the back of the van. He drives for ten minutes and goes into the office of a supermarket chain. He stays there two hours then goes out to lunch with three men from the office.

'Did you get photographs of the men from the supermarket?'

'Well, not yet, but…'

'Why not? What d'you think the bloody van's for? Get it in place, get them when they come out of the restaurant.'

Jesus.

Back to Cardoso's office after lunch. Home again at seven. He doesn't stir all evening. At midnight they call it off. Gonçalves' men go to bed with the satisfaction of a job well done: six hours' overtime for the multinational client.

Jo goes to bed depressed. *If he's involved in anything our chance of sticking to him's no better than fifty-fifty, not with this lot. And the chance of getting clocked by the opposition's about 3 to 1 on.*

If there is any opposition. If this Cardoso isn't simply what he seems, just a middle-ranking executive in a wine company, trudging drearily from home to office every day to scratch an unexciting living in a dull and ordinary life. If he isn't simply a bloke that Seymour chatted up in a bar, a rep on expenses handing out a drink to a sponger.

*

Day three, and she was getting to know the outside of Vinhos Felgueiras so well it bored her to sleep.

Down the slope below her there was a ten-yard gap in the wall, the only entrance. Through it she could see a scruffy, potholed dirt yard. In the middle of the yard was an office block, two stories of 1960s grey breezeblock with plate glass windows. Casual snooping had revealed that there were a couple of warehouse-shaped buildings round the back. Mechanical noises reached the street, rattling, growling, clinking, and every so often lorries laden with bottles clanked out of the yard.

The street she was parked in had a cafe, two vegetable shops spilling out onto the pavement, a shop selling old clothes. Jo's glance flicked at the shoppers, making a note of what they were wearing, soaking up the local colour. Out-of-date clothes for the women, casual shirts, jeans and slacks for the men. One old boy had been sitting at a table in the cafe almost as long as Jo and the team had been there, nursing a solitary cup of coffee, moving as little as they did. *Perhaps we can recruit him onto the team*, she thought in a bored moment.

Cardoso went into his office in the morning and stayed there all day. They saw him in the morning, they saw him in

118

the evening. In between they sat and gazed at the outside of the dreary factory where he worked. This had been their routine, all of two and a half days and it was beginning to seem like a month.

In the middle of the third afternoon there was a commotion by one of the vegetable shops as a boy cycled along the pavement, weaving in and out of pedestrians. He cycled past a pretty girl, turned his head to ogle her and came to grief in a pile of watermelons. He got screamed at by a plump woman in black wearing a headscarf.

They watched with amusement, even Henrique smiled. It was the only incident that had happened all day.

Their smiles faded into vacant boredom as they resumed their watch. With a guilty start, Jo realised they had taken their eyes off the front door of the office block while the boy was messing about. She snapped at Henrique, managing to get a flurry of anxiety going as they used the radio to check with the other watchers.

By four they were half asleep. Cardoso was going to stay in the office until it was time for him to go home; they knew this with a dull certainty.

A container lorry slowed down in front of the gateway, then stopped. They paid it no special attention, it was the seventh one to arrive that day. They squinted through half-closed eyes as it moved slowly into the yard, halting so that its driver could talk to someone. After a minute it moved on, grinding slowly through the yard. They could see the top of the container over the wall as it came to rest at the back of the compound.

As the lorry moved across the front door of the office it blocked their view so that they did not see Cardoso coming out and trotting down the steps. He walked over to his car, which was hidden by the wall.

Suddenly a car nosed out through the gateway. It was Cardoso's Renault.

'Shit! Go!'

Henrique fired the engine, accelerated into the street. When they reached the road Cardoso was sixty yards in front, overtaking a green truck belching exhaust fumes. Henrique swung out, only to see cars coming towards him. He could not follow, he was stuck behind the truck, cursing.

Jo looked round for Armando on the motor scooter. He was twenty yards behind them, gaining fast. Overtaking them, he hesitated behind the rear quarter of the truck and squeezed past, inches from the oncoming cars.

The truck slowed, squeaked to a halt: there is a traffic light, red. Still there was no room to pass. Ahead, the scooter disappeared into the distance.

The lights changed. The truck lumbered slowly forward, Henrique accelerated, swerving past it, nearly hitting an oncoming van. Jo shut her eyes, let out a hiss of breath.

The radio squawked. Henrique picked up the handset and acknowledged; there was a flood of Portuguese.

Five miles on they saw the other car, parked by the side of the road.

Henrique slowed, intending to stop and talk, but Jo waved him on, she did not want to create a roadside conference for the whole world to listen to.

Fifty yards past the car was a track, leading up to a white house. Beyond the next bend they found the motor scooter.

Henrique stopped. Armando spoke volubly to him, then haltingly to Jo. Cardoso had driven up to the house. He stayed in it for forty-five minutes. Then they followed him home. They did a check on the house the next day.

It belonged to Cardoso's aunt.

*

Next day was the fourth day and at the end of it they still had nothing.

The team was getting better; Jo had given them a hard time whenever they didn't come up to the mark. But however much they improved, everything depended on what Cardoso did, they could only wait for him to make a move.

And he went nowhere. His routine was exemplary, he was the perfectly disciplined husband and employee, always at his desk on time, always home to the wife in the evening. He did nothing to excite suspicion. He looked clean. Jo's mind started to nag that he *was* clean. She began to doubt the deduction she had made in London. It seemed irrelevant, a distant memory, a half-forgotten thought that had come to her on a dull grey, rainy day in a city far away. Here she was bombarded by a bright sun and it was hot, hot, *hot*; bright light beating down and washing thought out of her mind.

There was nothing to exercise her brain, to give her something to work on. Nothing happened to suggest their time was being well spent. There was nothing to while the time away, no jokes for her to share with Gonçalves' men, there was little conversation between her and them. Their English was not up to amusing chitchat.

They had nothing to do but sit and roast in their cars in the sun. They shifted the cars occasionally: to park in the same position all day long attracts attention. It did little to relieve either the boredom or the heat. There was still no action to watch and although the air drifted through the cars when they moved, it was hot and sluggish, it taunted them by reminding them what a real breeze might be like.

Even though they changed places from time to time, people were starting to notice them. The old man peered at the van as he hobbled into the cafe; at lunchtime the woman in the vegetable shop took a dustpan out of the shop to shake it into the gutter, then stood for a few seconds longer than she needed, gazing blankly at the car parked ten yards up the pavement. It was inevitable, Jo knew this, you cannot do a static surveillance indefinitely and hope not to be noticed. They would have to limit the time they spent on this – if they had not scored by the end of the week, they must think again.

It was depressing to risk being noticed for someone so unrewarding. Jo started to form a dislike for the factory wall, the blank grubby cream wall off which the sun shimmered, the nondescript grey building behind it. She tried not to let her dislike influence her judgement but it was impossible, there was nothing to reinforce her belief in what she was doing. A feeling grew on her that they were wasting their time. It combined with the tedium and the heat and was close to overwhelming her. There was a hollowness near her stomach as she contemplated the inevitability of failure.

*

In London the rain was dark and heavy, slanting down onto the black of the tarmac. Victoria Street was a gloomy canyon of concrete and brick down which the rain poured endlessly. Cars had been using their sidelights all day, lights were on in the offices, it could be winter now.

Arthur stood by a potted plant, a wild verdant jungle creature sold into captivity and branded by an M&S label round its neck. He stared gloomily at the rain bouncing and spraying on the window ledge beyond the darkened window, wondering whether to go home now, out into the yuck out there, whether to wait for a while in the hope that it would ease. His hand reached out automatically when the telephone trilled.

'Hi, Arthur,' she said, weariness in her voice.

'Hi. How you getting on?'

'Bugger all. There's no connection so far, and he's acting like he's legit.'

'Doesn't surprise me. It was a bit of a shot in the dark to begin with.'

'I'm starting to wonder how long it's worth persevering.'

'You know my views. I think it's a waste of the client's money being there to start with. It's up to you, but…'

There was a silence. From anyone else he would expect a sigh. He knew that she never liked backing down, never liked being wrong, never liked giving up. 'I'll give it another day,' she said. 'Tomorrow's Friday, if we've drawn a blank by the end of the week… I'll come home.'

'Good.' He smiled. 'See you Monday, then.'

Another small silence. 'Yeah. See you Monday.'

CHAPTER 25

Unlucky. So unlucky. But that is so often the way of surveillance, she would have been the first to agree.

It was unlucky that she was not there the week before to watch Raul and Seymour as they drove to the centre of Lisbon. Unlucky that she could not have followed them as they walked up the white marble steps of the Ritz into its cool old-fashioned interior, stood at the enquiry desk, surveyed the lobby. Unlucky that she had no chance to photograph the Chinese man who rose from the armchair to shake their hands.

He was from Singapore, the Chinese, and he was a trader. He did not care what he traded in. Arms or flak jackets, Land Rovers, scent, cigarettes or whisky, it was all one to him as long as there was a profit to be made from it. If he avoided selling drugs it was not from moral scruple but because there was a penalty for getting caught. Why let a nagging worry spoil the pleasure to be made in amassing profit?

Of course, even when trading in branded goods there were certain precautions to be observed. His speciality was undercutting distributors, and that made him a thorn in the side of the large corporations. Their executives raged with frustration every time they found their goods diverted to the wrong market and would have given much to know his chain of supply. He took care that they should not find out, which was the main reason why Morato had suggested him.

'We will be selling into Japan,' Cheng said. This was neither a surprise nor a secret. As Miguel had remarked, the whole whisky business knew of the profits to be made from the parallel trade to Japan.

'There is one problem emerging there,' he went on. 'As you know, for many years the Japanese authorities take an, ah, enlightened view that attempts by brand companies to stop parallel trading is an unlawful restraint on trade competition.'

Seymour nodded knowledgeably, gave Raul an 'I told you so' look.

'Now, however, we find that the companies have filled the ears of these same authorities with scaremongering stories about the dangers of importations of counterfeit whisky.'

Cheng looked intently at both of them to see what reaction this produced. Raul succeeded in looking mildly surprised, as if this was something he had never heard of.

Naturally they had not told Cheng that the whisky was fake. Not from fear that he might refuse to buy; he would have been only too happy. Indeed, one of his companies had a steady business supplying watch movements, made in Hong Kong, to Switzerland, there to be turned into fakes of well-known Swiss watches and re-exported to the Far East. But selling the whisky as fake would have brought a sharp drop in the price.

Cheng continued to probe. 'So, the authorities are now insisting on certificates of origin, from UK customs. I need to have one from you.'

Raul frowned and tut-tutted, as if shocked about the perfidy of government organisations who put obstacles in the way of free trade. He stroked his chin, frowning a little, as if considering a problem. 'Of course,' he said, 'not all of our suppliers can present us with a certificate of origin. As you know, the producer only supplies them for certain markets.'

Cheng's face took on an expression of superiority.

'But if the original buyer contacts UK customs, he can get a certificate issued for a particular cargo.'

Raul looked surprised. 'Oh?' he said. 'I've never thought of doing that.'

This was perfectly true. The idea of getting genuine certificates had not crossed his mind; he intended to have them forged.

'Well,' he went on slowly, pretending to mull the matter over, 'if what you say is correct, that should present no problem.'

'Good,' said Cheng.

Five minutes later they had struck the first deal. Five thousand cases a month for the next three months. Sixty-three dollars per case, f.o.b. Rotterdam. Three hundred and fifteen thousand dollars for each consignment, nine hundred and forty-five thousand dollars in all. Delivery of the first consignment to take place in the next four weeks.

Seymour and Raul shook hands with Stanley Cheng in the lobby of the Ritz and said goodbye. It was the only time they would meet. From now on, all contact would be on the telex or through their banks.

The two smiled at each other as they got into the car and drove away.

'Well,' said Seymour, 'I told you it would be a good way to go!'

'You did,' said Raul happily. Really, it was all turning out so easy. As Miguel had said, there could be no problem.

CHAPTER 26

They have been in the car since nine o'clock, three hours. Cardoso is in his office as he has been all this week, the heat in the car gets worse every day and today it is unbearable. Jo is feeling sleepier by the minute.

'This is a bloody waste of time,' she mutters. Henrique raises an eyebrow, tries to question her in his halting English, so strongly accented she has difficulty following him. 'Nothing,' she shrugs.

A truck comes noisily down the street, old and clapped out, its exhaust smoking, clinking and rattling with a load of crates of empty bottles. With a belch of exhaust it changes gear, crawls through the gate in the dirty whitewashed wall in front of them, and stops in the warehouse yard, its front half out of sight, its tailgate blocking off their sight of the office.

Thinking of the way the container lorry blocked off their view the previous day, Jo gets out and wanders down the street to where she can see the front door, looks resentfully at the building. She wills Cardoso to come out and give them something to do, anything, even if he is just buying a packet of cigarettes.

After five minutes the lorry goes, a cloud of exhaust as it starts up, reverses clinking and rattling out into the street and away. She walks back to the car.

Another fifteen minutes pass.

She looks at her watch, thirsty. *Twenty past twelve, that*

makes, what, two hundred minutes since this morning, another five and I'll have a swig of orangeade. Two hundred minutes, what's that in seconds? Sixty times two is a hundred and twenty, another yawn ooooaaaahhhh, add two noughts, is…

She tails off her calculation, bored with its pointlessness. Sits forward in the car seat, reaches round behind her to pull the damp tee shirt from her back. Puts an elbow on one knee – she learned days ago to keep her arms off the hot metal of the car door. Props her neat little chin on her small fist, stares gloomily through the windscreen.

Hey. Look, there he is. Coming down the steps. Carrying his briefcase, as always. A minute later his Renault turns down the street in the direction the lorry came from.

He is not in a hurry, he is just a man looking for his lunch. Jo suspects he is not on his way to anything important, that he is going to do nothing significant, that she might as well go home. She tries to ignore the thought, tells herself it is only her subconscious, whingeing for an excuse to go home.

Ten minutes later Cardoso slows, starts looking about him. On the left is a restaurant, blue tiles round the doorway, dark blue awning over the street to keep the sun off the windows. *This must be where he plans to have his lunch, he's looking for a parking space.*

The street they are on is packed with cars, there is nowhere to park. Cardoso goes round the block and they follow, slowly, keeping well back. After a minute or two they are all in front of the restaurant again.

His Renault goes on for a quarter of a mile, turns left across the road and disappears into a small gap between a hardware shop and a bar. When they reach where he has gone, they see he has gone up a side street which is small, narrow, the houses crowding in towards each other. There is scarcely room to drive up it, let alone park.

Henrique is about to turn into the street but she signals to him to wait; if they follow immediately, he will see them. They stop at the end of the street and look up. The back of the Renault crawls uphill, then goes out of sight as the street curves and dips away at the top.

'Back to the restaurant. Quick!' An instinctive decision. Could be wrong, could lose him.

'But…' Henrique has still not taken to being ordered about by a woman, a girl.

'Back to the bloody restaurant! Come *on!*'

The restaurant is on a corner, there is a little alley going up the side of it. Jo makes Henrique stop, double-parked. The alley is empty, Henrique starts to complain: 'I told you we should have followed him…'

It looks like a fish restaurant. The blue azulejo tiles each side of the doorway depict lobsters, swordfish, clams. Jo can dimly see the motif repeated inside. It looks cool and inviting; she longs to go and have a long lunch in there, out of this heat, out of the fumes and the noise of the traffic. She licks her lips, tongue feeling how rough and dry they are. *Hey ho.* Cardoso appears, walking down the side street towards them. He crosses the street, heads for the door of the restaurant.

I wonder who he's meeting, she thinks.

There is something about him that puzzles her, but she feels sleepy and can't think what it is for a moment. He was swinging his arms, bit energetic for this heat, he doesn't usually walk like that. His form dims as he enters, is greeted by a waiter, is taken into the invisible interior. She thinks of him swinging his arms. Both arms. Both of them, swinging free. No briefcase. For once he didn't have his briefcase.

Oh God, come on, you stupid bitch, you're getting slow, wake up.

He's left his briefcase in his car.

She cannot see if he has met someone or is by himself. She picks up the handset of the radio, thrusts it at Henrique, tells him to tell the others to watch the restaurant door.

'Come on.' She points back up the street, in the direction they had followed the Renault.

Henrique moves off, puzzled a little. Out of sight of the restaurant he does a U-turn, there is protesting from the other traffic. He slows down as they get to the azulejo tiles – *No,* *keep* *going.* They go on until they come to the mouth of the little street Cardoso's car disappeared into.

"Up here!"

Light dawns on his face and he twists the wheel. Up they go, onto the narrow pavement to avoid a motor tricycle, sniffing for the Renault.

On the right is an alley, only twenty yards long. Empty.

Their little street goes on, curves left and dips; this is the point where Cardoso's car went out of sight.

The houses are old: soft, flaking stone, paintwork flaking to match. There is a smell of rubbish. No one is out of doors in this little street. But for a radio blaring from an upstairs window the whole place could be deserted.

To the left, another alley, too narrow for a car.

To the right a lane curves up, twisting immediately back parallel to the street they have come. There is a big red no-entry sign; they drive past.

'Wait a minute.' She put her hand on Henrique's arm. He stops.

She turns and looks back towards the lane. The crumbling stone of the house on the corner comes right out to the edge of the tarmac, blocking her view.

'Back up.' Whine from the transmission as he reverses.

There it is. The Renault, Cardoso must have backed it up there. She sits and thinks for a moment.

'Go on. Go down to the end, past the restaurant. Slowly.'

She hopes the lane they are in is the one that comes out beside the restaurant. She winds up her window – the restaurant will be on her side of the car, the pane of glass should lessen the chance of Cardoso noticing her if he happens to be looking.

The lane curls down past the restaurant, as she hoped. She keeps her head as much to the front as possible, lets her eyes swivel into the restaurant as they pass the window. *Shit, it all looks different from this angle, where is the bastard? Oh, come on, where... Got him, still at his table, still by himself.*

She thinks again, considers the distances. The Renault is a bit too close to the restaurant for comfort, it is only a hundred yards, maybe less. The street is one way; for Henrique to drive back to the Renault he must make the circuit again. He will have to position himself between the Renault and the restaurant so he can warn her if Cardoso comes out while they are there.

Two minutes later the car has circled round and up the lane again, and parks where she wants it. She gets out and slowly, casually, she wanders back up to the corner with the no-entry sign.

She has a camera in her hand, loiters like a tourist. The sun beats down, deep purple shadows from the houses on her right, bright, bright white off the flaky stone on her left, blinding glare from the Renault's windscreen, *why couldn't the silly bastard park it in the shade?*

The radio is still blaring further along the street, a wail of Fado – *Why can't they turn it down, tuneless rubbish. If anyone walks along the street I won't hear their footsteps till it's too late.*

The windows of the houses are all closed against the heat, wooden shutters giving them a dead look. From behind a shutter she is walking past comes a soft clink of glass and cutlery, a desultory murmur of conversation, appetising sounds of lunch. A bottle glugs into a glass; vinho verde maybe, or bottled water. The thought makes her throat feel hot and dry.

The Renault is three yards away.

She drops a coin, stoops to pick it up and uses the opportunity to look behind her.

Christ, I hope I can do this one, I'm out of practice – haven't done a car for six months, hell of a time for a revision course.

She leans against the car.

Fifteen seconds can be a long time, each one hot and slow; a tightness in the throat, a prayer that she will do it right, a prayer that no one will come.

There is a click, the lock opens.

She takes a breath, looks briefly up and over her shoulder.

Into the car, leaving the door open so she can hear; she tenses as she hears a car horn, thinking for a second it is Henrique's signal. No, it is only the traffic in the main street. *Can I trust that stupid bastard to do a signal if he has to, if he hasn't gone to sleep? No, he'd probably land me in the shit deliberately, chauvinist sod.*

There is nothing under the driver's seat, nor the passenger's seat, nor the seats behind, it must be in the boot.

She releases the lever inside which unlocks the boot, steps outside, goes round the back, lifts the lid.

There it is, lying beside an old polythene bag.

Be nice to take it away somewhere and fiddle with it privately. Oh, wouldn't it? Stop whingeing and get on with it.

It is a leather briefcase, standard issue to businessmen, two combination locks, three digits each lock. *Do the stupid bastards who use these think it makes them thiefproof?* 999 possible combinations, even a child can try them all at one a second which is sixteen minutes for each lock, half an hour for the pair, but she does not have thirty minutes to waste.

It takes her ninety seconds, ears straining to concentrate.

She makes a mental note of the numbers for future reference, opens the lid. What has he got here, will it be just a diary and an old sandwich, or…?

Oh.

Wow.

CHAPTER 27

Gravel spat at the underside of the car as the wheels scrabbled at the corners, the open-topped Golf twisting through the dark shadows of the wooded valley side that hung over the narrow Devon lane, like a fish flitting through the dark patches of a sunlit riverbed.

Hamish blinked as the road curled out into the open glare of the sun, bright and blinding for five seconds. Then the lane curved under a solid canopy of branches at the wood's edge, their green broken only by small scraps of light torn out of the sky and littered among the leaves.

Below and to the right, light flickered off the river, peat-brown water, oily black between the trees. Hamish's lips tightened in regret; this was exactly the stretch of river he'd planned to fish today, the pools deeper and fuller than those he'd fished yesterday.

His mind lingered on the image of the thin, dark pencil shape of an underwater trout, gently undulating, lifting occasionally to swirl and pluck at a fly on the surface. Instead of a steering wheel his hands ached for the feel of the rod in his hand; his imagination sparkled with the lift of his heart as the fish took, line tightening and slicing through the water, until the quarry was finally subdued and guided over the net.

Damnation, he thought, as he throttled down a rare straight in the winding lane. The fishing season will be ending soon, this was probably his last visit to the river before it did.

Why couldn't the girl have waited till Monday?

*

As he sat in the characterless cocoon of his airline seat, he tried to cling to a lingering vision of the river, white and frothing as it tumbled over the rocky pools, brown and clear as it swirled smoothly beneath the alders. It faded as the plane landed, evaporated as he waited in the luggage hall at Lisbon Airport, then seemed from another world as he walked down the exit ramp into the hammering heat. Noise and fumes blew through the window of his taxi, his nostrils twitched as he started to absorb the new smells and light of a foreign place.

The battered Mercedes taxi shuddered as it swung in front of the Sheraton doors and squeaked to a halt. He stepped out, shook himself and walked inside. He was swallowed by air-conditioned coolness, artificial, so different from the fresh, leafy cool of the English countryside. Crossly he announced himself to the receptionist, filled in the chit she pushed towards him.

When she gave him back his passport there was a slip of paper with it.

Hamish. May be out when you arrive. If you stay in the hotel I'll find you. Jo.

Oh, bloody hell, he thought. If she was going to drag him away from his fishing, drag him all the way to Lisbon on a Sunday, the least she could do was meet him when he got there.

*

Three hours later Jo found him by the pool, lying on a reclining chair, basking warm in the sun, a book propped up in front of him, outwardly the picture of relaxation, no sign of his inner crossness and boredom.

She walked across the tiles towards him, hot and sweaty in her jeans and faded khaki blouse, damp and crumpled. She had spent the last seven hours roasting in a car, watching the banal inactivity of Cardoso's weekend. She longed for five minutes in the pool to wash away the heat of the day; the thought had been in her mind for the last two hours. At the sight of Hamish taking it easy in his swimming trunks she felt a small twinge of irritation.

He looked up as her shadow fell over his book.

'Ah,' he drawled, deliberately offhand, 'so *there* you are.'

His slow drawling voice increased her irritation. 'Yup.' Terse, staccato. 'Got it in one.'

He pushed himself up on one elbow and brushed a floppy lock of hair out of his eyes, squinting up at her.

'Arthur's message said you wanted to talk to me urgently. Having spent the last three hours twiddling my toes, I rather assume he got it wrong.'

'He didn't.' She flicked her glance sideways at the other people lounging round the pool. 'You want to come up to my room? We can talk there.'

'I don't see—'

'2041,' she said. 'See you there.' Without waiting she turned and threaded her way back through the oiled, basking bodies.

∗

Jo was leaning against the wide plate glass window, buttocks perched on the grey ledge of the air-conditioner, her chin back and a can of Coke at her mouth. She watched Hamish over the rim of the can as he pushed the door open, and waved him casually to the one armchair. As he sat she picked a brown envelope off the ledge beside her, spun it onto the coffee table beside the glossy Sheraton brochure about Lisbon, and took another gulp of her Coke.

He picked the envelope off the table, opened it, and held it upside down to get its contents out. A small piece of paper slid out and fluttered onto his lap. As it fell it caught the late afternoon sun, blazed with bright metallic gold, green and vivid orange. Hamish stared at it, flicked his eyes to her face, then back to the label lying in his lap.

'Bloody hell. Where on earth did you get this?' he asked.

'Cardoso.'

'Cardoso? You mean you've spoken to him?'

She snorted. 'No. Don't be daft. Nicked it off him.'

'I hope you don't mean that,' he muttered, frowning.

She ignored his frown. 'He had telexes too,' she said. 'Offers of your brand. 30,000 cases each at sixty dollars a case. Didn't think it a good idea to nick those, thought he might notice. Took some photos instead. They're in there too.'

He pulled them out and read them. 'So… he was right. Seymour, I mean.'

'Yep. Looks like it.'

'Tell me how you got these.'

She told him, in short, curt sentences, about her week's observation, of the frustration of getting nowhere, of the triumph on Friday.

'So,' he mused slowly, when she had finished. 'Someone *is* faking our brand, and this Cardoso *is* involved in it.'

'Right,' she said with a tight, satisfied smile, raising her can for another drink.

'Well,' he said slowly. 'On the one hand, well done. But

on the other hand… what are you suggesting I do with this stuff?'

'Well, it's over to you now. You're the lawyer. You wanted evidence, now you've got it.'

'Evidence? No we haven't. Not evidence we can use. You broke into his car, broke into his briefcase and stole a label. That's illegal, and it probably means the evidence isn't legal either.'

Jo gripped her cola tin tightly and stared at him.

'Plus,' Hamish went on, 'there's an angle you haven't thought of. We're a public company, a market leader. I'm a lawyer, I spend half my life making sure the company complies with regulations in every country we trade with. We can't afford not to. The one thing we don't need is trouble with foreign authorities, them getting the idea that we come into their countries and break their laws.'

'Well thanks a bunch!' Jo pushed herself off the ledge and stood with her legs apart, looking down at him. 'I've been sweating my guts out after this bastard Cardoso, *literally* sweating, spending all day in a baking bloody car in the middle of bloody Portugal. A chance comes up, I take it and I get information which you wouldn't have got in a month. Then *you* come swanning out here—'

'I don't come *swanning* out here,' he snapped, 'I come out because Arthur rings me and says you need me out here urgently.'

'Plus,' she went on as if he hadn't spoken, 'you don't seem to realise how lucky we've been,' she said.

'*Lucky?*'

'Yeah. Another day and I'd have said he was clean, called it off, gone back home. End of investigation, end of case.'

He looked up at her, half wishing that had happened so

that he needn't have spoiled his weekend.

'Well?' she probed, seeing him hesitate. 'Is that what you want? If you do, say so – I can be on a plane in the morning.'

He stayed silent, hamstrung by a sense of duty, of expediency. If she went back he'd have to employ someone else. Delay, expense while they started from scratch, with no guarantee of a better result. He could feel the tightness of the muscles in his forehead, it seemed to have tightened into a knot ever since she'd arrived. On the other hand, he thought grudgingly, it was she who'd made the breakthrough, got the proof that the faking was happening.

'No,' he said at last.

She smiled wryly. 'Wow, what a vote of confidence. Anyway, now you're here, let me spell out what we don't know. We don't know who Cardoso's working with, we don't know where their factory is, we don't know where they're selling. All we know is he had a label. But we don't know who printed it, who's making the caps or any of the other components. We've had a lucky break, but we've only just started.'

'Go on.'

'What we need is information, intelligence. We've been trying to get it by surveillance, it's given us a breakthrough, but it's left all these questions unanswered, so…'

'So?'

'I've been giving it a lot of thought,' she said, tensely. 'There's only one way.'

'And what is that?'

'We have to penetrate his communications.'

'What?' he asked, not comprehending.

'His phone,' she said, leaning forward towards him, eyes urgent. 'You can see the wire from the street. He'll phone his associates, he's bound to. That'll tell us who they are, where they are. Plus, somewhere he's got a telex. Shouldn't be difficult to find it. If we can intercept his messages that'll tell us where he's sending it.'

'Are you…?' Hamish tailed off and looked at her blankly for a moment, as if not understanding what she had said. 'Oh Jesus.' He went to her minibar and took out a can of tonic water, peeled the tab off, poured it into a glass, took a swig. 'You're not suggesting we bug his phone, are you?'

'It's the best way,' she urged. 'Surveillance isn't. Every day we sit there it goes on costing you. And every day we sit there increases the chance of our getting spotted. Technical surveillance is the best answer, believe me.'

Hamish looked coldly at her. 'Is that speaking from experience?'

'Yeah, of course.'

'Well then. In your *experience*, is it legal?'

'We-ell…'

'It's not legal in England, is it?'

'Umm…' She gave him a wry smile, a hint of humour creeping into the corners of her eyes. 'Not very.'

'Do you *do* it in England?'

She looked at him, smile fading, eyes opaque, not liking being cross-questioned, silence giving him his answer.

'And I don't suppose it's legal here, either,' he said. 'It's not likely to be, is it?'

She shrugged.

'For God's sake!' he exclaimed, annoyance surging into irritation. 'I've told you what our policy is. We don't break the law and that's that. Don't you *listen*?'

She bit her lower lip in vexation. 'You're very *keen* on the law, aren't you? It's great at getting in the way. But I haven't noticed you saying what the hell it's going to do to help.'

'Well,' Hamish said, with a lift of his chin. 'We'll just have to see, won't we?'

CHAPTER 28

At ten o'clock Hamish's black and green Lisbon Mercedes taxi pulled up in front of Correia, Guimaraes & Teixeira, lawyers to a long list of multinational clients. As he stepped through their door he felt at home. Soft carpeting, smoothly dressed secretaries bustling demurely hither and yon, papers rustling, fluttering, piling into stacks. Here was wooden panelling, here were bookshelves, row upon row of textbooks, law reports, statutes, so reassuring to the barrister; leather bindings, smell of calfskin, nostalgic testimony to the international solidarity of brother practitioners in the law.

A crisply bloused receptionist greeted him deferentially, waved him to a flaxen armchair, reached for the polished plastic of the phone. Dr. Vasconcelos appeared in less than a minute, smartly suited, hand outstretched, crinkly haired, urbanely smiling, early thirties like Hamish. Vasconcelos ushered him suavely down a corridor into a meeting room. An older man, the Guimaraes of the partnership, materialised softly behind them. Much shaking of hands, offering of coffee, pampering the client from the big London company. Hamish relaxed, on familiar ground for the first time since he'd arrived.

Papers were flourished, dry reminiscences of whisky paraded, all to show the client's affairs were uppermost in their minds. The two lawyers listened to Hamish's brief outline of the problem and nodded serenely. Yes, they said, switching into gear, counterfeiting was strictly dealt with under Portuguese law. They made portentous pronouncements: 'fraudulous copying', serious offence, substantial penalties, fines, imprisonment. Copies of the penal code were produced, international conventions, textbooks, law reports, all in Portuguese, English translations for Hamish's benefit. Secretaries summoned to photocopy for Hamish's files. Successful cases quoted, decisions of tribunals, appeal courts, supreme court. Yes, there was no doubt but that the law frowned severely on such matters.

Excellent, thought Hamish, now we're getting somewhere, it's all clear, it's all just as I thought it would be. The lawyers sensed he was content and smiled benevolently, poured him more coffee, pressed him with sugar and cream.

And of course, he asked, of course the police will investigate such cases?

The elder lawyer coughed discreetly. Of course, he did not himself make it a practice to work with police, that was not quite, not really, how should he put it, not the function of a lawyer here in Portugal. The function of a lawyer was to deal with the administering of the law, with jurisprudence, with the courts. But his colleague – an elderly liver-spotted hand made an elegant turning movement in the direction of young Vasconcelos – had some experience of such matters. He sat back in his chair, as if to indicate that he would take no further part in the conversation until it returned to more seemly topics.

Yes, Vasconcelos said, the law was most certainly enforced: there was a special branch of the police to deal with economic crimes, the Direccão-Geral da Fiscalizaçao Económica; there was the Polícia Judiciária for the more straightforward case. Yes, as a matter of routine they took action on complaints from the owner of the rights infringed.

'And, of course, this action will include investigations?'

The lawyer looked blank, as if he did not know quite what Hamish meant. 'Why, yes,' he said, 'of course the police will investigate the strength of a case when a complaint is made.'

'No, no,' Hamish said. 'I mean preliminary investigations, to discover the facts. To discover who is doing the counterfeiting, to trace their activities.'

Vasconcelos was puzzled. 'You mean you do not have this information now?'

'No,' said Hamish. 'That's why I want to know if the police will investigate.'

The elder lawyer, the distinguished Guimaraes, shifted in his chair. How messy this was, not what he had expected, it was to avoid exactly this sort of discussion that he confined his career to jurisprudence.

Vasconcelos spread his hands apologetically. 'If you do not have the evidence, it will be difficult to get the police to take action on your case.'

'But—'

'You see,' the lawyer went on, 'the police handle many complaints. They are frankly overburdened. The complainant is expected to come with evidence showing a need for action, evidence of the offence and who has committed it. If he cannot, pfff...' He shrugged again, a fluid continental shrug.

Hamish was silent.

'And even when there is evidence,' the lawyer added, 'there is a backlog of cases, the complaint cannot be acted on immediately.'

'How long does it take them?' Hamish asked.

'From the time of filing a complaint... say, well, at the

moment, say… about twelve months.'

Hamish blinked. The lawyers' English was so fluent and polished, surely it could not have slipped; but… *how* long?

'Twelve months. Sometimes a little less, maybe even as little as nine or ten.'

Hamish sat astonished.

Senhor Mallows must appreciate, the police have many cases and there are so many crimes more serious: rape, murder, burglary, theft.

Hamish's mind was stuck in neutral, numbed by this unexpected turn, unable to think of what to ask next.

In the silence the lawyers looked at their watches, exclaimed about the nearness of the lunch hour, pressed Hamish to eat with them. In silence he acquiesced.

The lunch was delightful, they were charming and attentive hosts, but by the time they left the restaurant at a quarter past three Hamish was resigned to the inevitable.

There was nothing they could do to help, there was no solution that the law could offer.

*

The next day he took a taxi to the top end of the Rua São Domingos à Lapa. Got out, stretched in the sun before walking slowly on down towards the embassy, drinking in the soft pinks and ochres of the houses, the green of the gardens, the splashes of colour from the flowers. He walked into the British Embassy lobby at twenty-five past two, five minutes ahead of the time arranged, and found himself in a small piece of dingy Whitehall decorated with dog-eared leaflets from the DTI about trading with Britain. At three o'clock, his bottom aching after half an hour on the hard chair he had been given to wait on, he was shown into the office of the commercial secretary, a harassed-looking man with orange hair and a short-sleeved shirt who half rose from behind his desk to give Hamish's hand a perfunctory shake. He had the manner of an overworked doctor on the National Health who has five minutes to hear symptoms, come to a diagnosis and write out a prescription.

Hamish's frustration had been building since his meeting with the lawyers; it had not lessened while he was kept waiting. He let some of it out by expressing himself in less than diplomatic language about the Portuguese legal system.

The commercial secretary knew little of the law and privately cared less, but he cared a great deal about British subjects who complained about the Portuguese system and threatened a disruption to the smooth waters of diplomatic life. He shrugged in an abrupt Anglo-Saxon way quite different from that of the charming lawyers.

'What we invariably suggest,' he said, 'is that, if you have a legal problem, you use legal channels to resolve it. That must be your first port of call.'

Seeing Hamish was about to speak, he held up his hand.

'If you find they don't work, of course,' he said with a tone that he hoped sounded reassuring but which sounded to Hamish like condescension, 'then that's another matter. We could certainly raise it in one of our meetings with the Minister.'

'But if we try it and it doesn't work, it'll be too late!'

The commercial secretary shrugged again, dismissively this time, and pointed out that Hamish was by no means alone in his predicament. A number of other British companies had experienced the same problem, he said, implying that this was an excellent reason for Hamish to be content with his lot. Hamish retorted that surely this gave the British

Embassy all the more reason to – he was about to say, 'get its finger out', but changed it at the last moment to 'assist a major British exporter'. The commercial secretary launched into five minutes of civil service platitudes ending with an assurance that he was only too sorry to be unable to be of help on the present occasion, glanced at his watch and pleaded a meeting with the ambassador.

Hamish left in a barely disguised temper.

CHAPTER 29

'Bloody law, it's useless,' Hamish said moodily, pulling his tie off and flinging it at his dressing table.

'Just what I've always thought,' she said sardonically, arms crossed, from her perch by the window.

'*Portuguese* law, I mean!' He flung himself into an armchair and threw his legs into a sprawl. 'You'd think the bloody police would do *something*.'

'God. An optimist,' she muttered.

'And as for that bloody prat in the embassy… Jesus!' He kicked at the table in frustration.

'Well then,' putting on a voice of sweet feminine reason, a smile of charm on her elfin face, 'if we want something done, we'll have to do it ourselves, right?'

'Oh, sure.' Tone of cynical disbelief.

'Come on. I don't see what your problem is. If the police won't do the investigation we do it ourselves. It's what I spend my life on.'

'Well fine,' he said, with an edge of exasperation. 'Perhaps you'll be good enough to tell me what we can do, then.'

'I already have. Technical surveillance.'

'Oh God, not that again.' He sprang to his feet and stared at her. 'I've already *told* you, we are *not* going to break the law.'

She looked down at her nails, thoughtful expression on her face. 'Why not?' she asked casually.

'*Why not?*' he squawked in astonishment.

'Yeah. Why not?

'What a question! For one thing the company simply can't take the risk. I spelt that out the other day. If it comes out that we—'

'Oh for God's sake. If I get caught breaking the law, it's *my* neck. Mine, not yours. D'you think I'd drop you in it? Is that what you think?'

'Well, I—'

'Sod it, you do, don't you? Well, you've obviously got one or two basics to learn too. Like we don't drop our clients in the shit. If we get caught, *we* carry the can. Right?'

'That's not the point, the point is—'

'And,' she persisted, her voice rising, 'I can't see why you're so fussed about the bloody law! It's not doing a bloody thing to help, is it? Is it? You've said as much yourself.'

He said nothing, gave her a cold look.

She sat on the armchair he'd vacated and gazed up at him.

'Look,' she said, 'what's more important? Droning on about the law? Or do you actually want to catch this bloke?'

'Of course I want to catch him! What d'you think I'm out here for?'

'Well, I'm beginning to wonder. Maybe it's time you got to see what it's like at the sharp end. Stop swanning around in offices, come and take a look on the ground. See what the problem actually *looks* like.'

'You want me to come and stare at his house?' Hamish gave her a patronising smile.

'And why not? Get you away from your law books, give you a taste of what it's like in the real world.'

His smile faded. Being called a book-reading lawyer hit a nerve: it was to get away from that that he'd left the Bar.

He thought of his evening in London, driving down to

Clapham, sitting outside Seymour's house. God he'd *tasted* how that felt, tasted sitting in a car feeling foolish, tasted despair afterwards.

'Well?' she demanded.

He looked at her with narrowing eyes.

'Very well,' he said at last. 'If it gets you off my back.'

CHAPTER 30

A thin, black mongrel, tongue lolling from its mouth, padded a few steps along the sun-bright paving and flopped in the shade of a doorway. A shutter banged in an upstairs window, pulled to by an unseen hand.

Two, old, black-dressed widows, pausing in the plastic strips of a shop door, stopped their conversation to watch the Fiat as it passed, turned slowly into a small square and stopped. Nothing else in the square moved, except the air shimmering with heat and a fountain dribbling feebly from a niche in the wall of a building.

'It's a bitch of a place to do surveillance,' she murmured. 'You start sticking out ten seconds before you arrive.'

She turned the wheel and the car drifted out of the square down a gentle slope. The right-hand half of the street before them was dark, shadowed, sullen grey-green ochre-coloured stone massed on the black of tarmac. On the left the sun dazzled the same stone into a brilliant sandy off-white, a light dusty grey washing across the road up to the thick line of the shade.

'It's on the right, about fifty yards,' she said.

He craned his head forward to look up at the wrought iron balcony, the teasing half-open shutters with a glimpse of a deeper dark beyond. He thought he caught a hint of a movement inside but could not be sure.

'That's where he lives,' she said. 'The only one we know

about. What's he doing? What's he thinking about?'

Hamish turned his head to stare as they went past, twisted his neck as the house fell back out of sight.

'Think of him,' she told him. 'He'll be there this evening, hidden in his house, waiting for his wife to dish up the salt cod or whatever crap she gives him, scribbling a thought on a piece of paper, telephoning his mates. Get in there, get the paper he scribbles on, you might have something. Out here in the sun' – she waved a hand at the heat bouncing off the tarmac and half-turned to look at him – 'out here where we are – zilch.'

Hamish grunted. She accelerated out of the village and drove on.

She parked the car outside Vinhos Felgueiras. They sat in the sun staring at the long white wall, tantalising him with the sense of the office beyond.

'He's in there now,' she said softly. 'Doing something. Maybe selling wine, maybe planning what he's going to do with your fake whisky. God knows what.'

They continued to sit there as the sun climbed higher and the shadows shortened. The temperature in the car rose steadily, the sweat started to gather on their foreheads and their throats dried. Deliberately she had brought nothing to drink, she wanted him to feel what it was like to be in a baking car all day, sitting, watching, waiting. Thinking of the hours ahead of mind-numbing boredom. Not knowing where the hub of their problem lay, not knowing how to get at it; knowing only the need to find a way and the frustration of seeing none.

She stared ahead in silence, occasionally sneaking a glance at Hamish, until she reckoned he'd got the idea. Then she drove him off for lunch, a quick snack in a restaurant, dull fish, overcooked, but his mind wasn't on the food.

'Well, okay,' he said, 'so now what are we—'

'Not in here,' she interrupted, an artificial smile fixed on her face for anyone who might be looking. 'If you're going to talk, talk about the local architecture or something.'

'Oh, come on, I mean it's not as if they're going to understand what we—'

'No,' she hissed, '*later.*'

'Come off it, they're all Portuguese, they—'

'I don't care if they're Ethiopian,' she growled at him, 'if you're ever planning on sitting around in public talking about a job, do it on a job I'm not involved in. Right? Why d'you think we've been talking in a hotel bedroom, you think it was 'cos I like to get cosy with my clients?'

Hamish went slightly pink, pursed his lips and stared at her for a moment, then silently concentrated on his fish.

*

They'd left the Fiat in the shade of a tree, its shadow growing in a circle on the pavement, but on their return the sun had moved and as they opened the doors a cushion of hot air rose up to buffet them.

She slammed the door after her, started to put one hand on the wheel and quickly took it off again, stung by its heat.

'Okay,' she said, 'you've seen what it's like. It's not easy. And right now, like I said, we're not getting any leads.'

'No.'

He looked away from her, through the windscreen. A cultivator sputtered past, pulling a small trailer with half a dozen melons on it.

'What's it been costing us, this investigation?' he asked, thoughtfully.

She gave him a quick sideways look, her lips slightly pursed; the investigator in her disliked talking finance, knowing the way it could deflect clients from operational planning.

'Quite a bit,' she said. 'There's me, for a start. Then the surveillance team back in London, while we were tracking your Mr. Seymour. Then the surveillance team out here.'

'And how many of those?'

'Well… on the surveillance we had last week, three operatives, four sometimes. Plus me.'

'Four? D'you really need that many?'

'That *many*? That's a third of what I'd like. To do a proper job you need about a dozen.' She let out a sarcastic sniff, wrinkling her nose at him. 'That'd really cost you.'

'A dozen? In shifts?'

'No, I mean all at once.'

'You're joking,' he said, his head drawing back in disbelief. 'I mean all the stories you read, there's just one bloke.'

She raised her eyes to the roof of the car. Put one freckled elbow on the steering wheel, leaned her chin on her fist and turned to gaze at him.

'Oh dear,' she said in a mock-sad tone of voice. 'Don't tell me. No hired Fiat for our hero, he gets in his Aston Martin, sits two cars behind the villain and half an hour later they pitch up at some darkened warehouse where all is revealed.'

He gave an amused snort, laughing at himself.

'Something like that.'

'You ever tried it?'

'No, of course not!'

'I see,' she said primly. *Of course not, lawyers don't stoop to that sort of thing. Supercilious bastard.* 'Well, look, one day when you've got nothing better to do, take a drive into central London, pick out a car in front of you and follow it. See how long it is before you lose him at a traffic light.'

'Hmm.' He stroked his chin, imagining the traffic round Hyde Park Corner, surging in a thick mass.

'And that's without him suddenly getting out of the car, walking up a one-way street, through a department store, down the Underground and taking a taxi at the other end.'

'Yes, all right, I take your point. But it sounds an expensive way to find out that someone goes to the office at nine and comes back at seven every night.'

'It is. It paid off once by getting us that label, but that wasn't what it was intended for. The surveillance was meant to find out who his contacts are and it hasn't done that. It's not the answer.'

'So what is?' he asked, not thinking. As he saw the corners of her eyes light up, he realised that the question was one she'd been leading him into asking.

'I've told you that already,' she said. Her voice surprisingly sweet, soft. Almost seductive.

'No,' he said decisively, looking at her eyes, noticing for the first time how the green contrasted with the suntan on her cheekbones. 'Find some other way.'

She shrugged, gave a small twitch of the lips and started the engine. 'You're the boss.'

CHAPTER 31

She knew she was scratching at the surface, but half-hoped they might get lucky. She sat with Gonçalves for an hour, then with two of his men, Ricardo and Mario.

Both dark and swarthy, with the almost oriental tan of so many Portuguese. If she stretched her imagination and made sure they wore the right clothes she could just see them as minor businessmen.

For twenty minutes they played with names until they found one they liked: Eurimpex. They thought it had a good sound, international, unspecific, slightly shady. She checked the phone book – could be awkward if there was a real company with the same name – no, they were in luck. Ricardo went off to a back room, returned with an address: not easy to do on the spur of the moment; luckily Gonçalves kept some addresses in reserve for just this sort of thing. All that remained were names for themselves.

She left them to organise the business cards, easily done at the print shop on the corner, fifty per cent extra on the bill to get it done in a rush, and there they were, businessmen with credentials, businessmen about to look for a dodgy printer to help them out.

They kicked ideas around for a spiel, a little introductory piece about their company and some products they could pretend to deal in: wine, spirits, cigarettes and so forth. A little discussion about printing labels for the drinks trade.

Then, a proud announcement: they were importing a well-known brand of gin from the UK, bottling it here in Portugal, and of course they needed labels printed. Labels like this one, they would say, producing a label – one which she'd soaked off a bottle, but they wouldn't say that – can you copy this…? Hinting the while of substantial business, promise of useful profit to come. Then, when that had been absorbed they would add a proviso: of course, discretion was needed, business confidentiality was paramount; they did not want their competitors to be alerted. This was when their eyes would hint at other reasons in the background, looking for an answering flash of understanding. They would ask the printer about his previous work, give him a chance to boast about what he'd done, see if he talked of things which were a bit away from the straight and narrow. See if he'd be likely to go for something a bit dodgy.

By lunchtime the ploy was ready to go.

*

Lunchtime brought a new customer to the cafe near the factory gates. Not that anyone noticed: rough blue shirt, dark jeans, heavy shoes, a day's stubble, typical of the workers who wandered in and out. He drifted in a little past midday, stood sipping a bagaço at the bar, looking around him with a casual eye at the bright neon interior. There were a few tourists at the sun-bleached tables outside on the pavement, but it was not them he was interested in.

At half-past twelve the drift out through the factory gates started and the population of the cafe swelled. Some silent, some noisy. One noisier than the rest: a garrulous type who liked his lunchtime drink, had running conversations with anyone near him, friend or stranger.

Like the stranger waiting at the bar.

It took only five minutes to strike up a conversation, ten more to get the conversation to the point the stranger had been aiming at. The casual statement that he was looking for work, did the factory happen, by any chance, to need additional workers?

'Why, yes,' said the man. 'Why not come back after lunch? Come with me, I will introduce you to the foreman.'

*

'No,' the first printer had said, 'we do not copy other people's labels.' A look of hauteur, dismissal, firmly showing Ricardo and Mario to the door.

The second had been more obliging, scratching his head thinking of the technicalities: a five-colour printing job, it will be important to get it exactly in register; see this coat of arms at the top? If not done carefully, it will look wrong. And the paper… he ran his fingers over the thick heavy gloss, pursed his lips at the quality. Frankly, no, it is not quite in our line, food labels on thin matt paper are what we do.

It had not been until the sixth that they met enthusiasm, a man who had all the techniques, all the equipment, all the experience. Why, he even had several local liquor companies as clients. Look, here is a portfolio of the labels we do. Certainly, we could produce a label like that.

Only after half an hour had he thrown in an afterthought: by the way, I suppose you have permission from the brand owner, perhaps you can bring a letter from him when you confirm the order…

Two days later, Ricardo and Mario were on the nineteenth printer on their list, and still had not found the one they wanted.

It was the first time he had worked in a wine factory. He was only working as a loader, a fetcher and carrier, a human donkey, but, as he said to his new friend, he liked to take an interest in his surroundings.

'What happens in this?' he asked casually as he passed beside a huge wooden vat, stained and blackened. Half an hour later: 'How does that machine work, the one that puts the labels on?' Waiting for an order near the end of the afternoon: 'How much does the factory bottle each week?'

His workmates smiled, tolerantly, at what they took as simple-minded curiosity. After two days they started to accept him, noticed him less. Little by little he worked over the factory, methodically absorbing the details, working out how to get into the hidden corners.

*

'This could get frustrating,' Hamish said, in a tone of understatement. He'd said it once already in the hotel room. Then he'd insisted on getting out of the claustrophobic cage for some fresh air. She'd decided to humour him and together they'd traipsed down to the Castelo de São Jorge, walking up to the ramparts, gazing over the splendid battlements at the roofs of Lisbon and the Tagus estuary.

He twisted his head towards her, waiting for a reaction. She sat quite still, back straight, idly playing with the bracelet round her wrist, sun flashing off the gold and wrapping her forearms in a soft haze.

'It does,' she said, deadpan.

Far beyond her, on the other side of the Tagus, a tiny cloud of steam billowed from a refinery tower. His gaze drifted to the lighthouse below them, a splash of white sticking out into the blue of the river, and then back onto the castle wall.

'Your man in the factory – Vinhos whatever they are – got nowhere. Those two blokes Gonçalves sent out got nowhere.'

'Correction,' she said quietly. 'The man we got into Vinhos Felgueiras did a bloody good job. He went all through the factory, found no trace of whisky, whisky labels, whisky bottles or anything. He even managed to sneak into Cardoso's office after everyone else had gone home – at considerable risk of discovery, as he was quick to point out. No papers to do with whisky, no copies of telexes, nothing. He's eliminated the most obvious possibility.'

'Oh, all right, he has. But it still doesn't tell us where the stuff's being made, does it?'

'Nope.'

Out of the corner of her eye she watched a middle-aged tourist couple fifty yards away looking out over the roofs of the Alfama: red tiles, blue slate, occasional grey concrete; the old houses huddled below them.

'We knew that trying printers out of the blue was going to be a long shot,' she pointed out. 'I told you that before we started.'

Moodily he swung a foot at a stone on the gravel and sent it spinning away. A quiet feline smile twitched at the corners of her mouth as she watched him. He was getting the idea.

CHAPTER 32

Welcome to scruffy Britain.

Welcome to the queue along the M4, fine views of Brentford's factories from the flyover, concrete, glass and grime.

Hamish sat hunched up in the back of his taxi, mouth turned down in gloom, gazing at the greyness of dusk. Mind's eye imprinted with the brightness of Portugal, refusing to accept the dull reality of return.

The taxi shuddered to a halt outside his flat, the diesel clattering, bodywork vibrating. Slowly he pushed himself out of the seat and through the door, scowling as he stood on the pavement, fumbling for English money. The driver sat motionless in his seat, making no effort to help with the suitcase, content to wait for payment and a tip. Hamish added a derisory ten pence to the twenty pound fare and smiled with satisfaction at the stream of muttered abuse.

He lugged his suitcase up the stairs, pushed open the door of his flat and entered a stale, dusty, tomblike silence. A week's mail lay on the parquet. He looked at it tiredly and scuffed at it with his foot, sending the envelopes slithering noisily over each other into a new pattern of disorder. Dropped his suitcase with a bang in the middle of the hall, the sound reverberating bleakly down the corridor: echo dying into the bleak quiet that says, *Here is the empty apartment that you call home.*

*

Cold rain-sodden morning, English summer's *nostalgie d'hiver*, puddles in the paving seeping through the shoe leather, wetly chilling the toes. Crossly Hamish queued for the bus, thrust aside by little old women with umbrellas and sharpened elbows. Workers stared sheeplike through the water-streaked windows inside the number 9 bus, steam rising from their dripping fleece and fogging on the glass. Secretaries drizzled lethargically along the Mayfair pavements, streaming damply down the plugholes of the office doorways, swirling into the apathy of the week ahead.

Avoiding the cattle pen of the office lift, Hamish strode up the cantilevered stairs, along the waking corridor and into the sanctuary of his daytime nest. Sarah had tidied the surface of his desk, pushing his letters and notes and scribbled drafts into stacks, the better to focus his attention on the neat pile of mail that had arrived in his absence. He sighed, knowing it would take him half an hour to rearrange everything into the chaos in which he liked to work. He threw himself into his chair, spun three quarters of a turn, surveyed the stacks, deliberating which one to start on.

There was a muffled bang from Sarah's door as she bustled in, shaking water on the carpet from her umbrella; paused in his doorway, acted a look of incredulity at seeing him there.

'Your friend Adrian's been looking for you,' she said.

As if on cue the telephone rang. The carefree hand which plucked the handset from his rest became rigid as he listened to the angry staccato squawk in his ear.

'Serve you right for sitting in the sun all week,' she gloated, seeing the sour expression on his face as he slammed the handset back down.

'Thanks so much for the welcome,' he retorted, pushing

himself to his feet and heading for the door. There was a sigh of exasperation behind him as he knocked one of Sarah's careful stacks of paper off his desk.

*

Three bottles stood in the middle of the mahogany table, their reflections gleaming darkly on the polished wood, the colours muted by its rich brown tones.

Spicer swivelled gently in his chair, murmuring genially into the phone, his free hand tracing lazy patterns on his blotter with a gold pen.

Hamish stood at the edge of the carpet, waiting, as Spicer's conversation slipped away onto football, Wimbledon, Henley. Resentful at being called down then made to wait, Hamish moved to the centre of the room, picked up the nearest bottle, ran his eye idly over it.

Crisp click of handset smacking back into place. Spicer sat forward, geniality fading from his face.

'Is this the parallel you were talking about?' Hamish asked.

'Well done,' Spicer said, his voice dripping with sarcasm. 'I suppose one can always rely on a lawyer to glimpse the obvious.'

Hamish bit his lip to suppress his irritation. 'Then I take it you wanted advice?'

'Advice? No, I don't want advice, what I want is for you to sort the problem out. Get it the fuck off our market.'

'It's not as simple as all that. As I'm sure you know, Japanese law doesn't allow us to stop parallel, it…'

'If you're sure I know it, why tell me? I don't give a *shit* about Japanese law. What I want *you* to do is jump on the little sods who're supplying from this end. Make sure they stop. You lot drafted our conditions of sale – now get on and enforce them.'

'Well, of course, I'll do my best, I—'

'Never mind your best. Just *do* it.'

Hamish clamped his jaw tight and counted to three. 'Can you tell me where these were bought?'

'Tokyo, for Christ's sake, I've told you that already.'

'I need evidence of purchase. Which shops, what addresses, what dates, who bought them...'

'Oh Christ, ring up Tokyo and ask Shikatura, he bought them. Don't bother me about the details, just get on with it. *Okay?*

Spicer settled himself in his chair, indicating the conversation had ended, picked a letter off his desk and ostentatiously started to read it.

Hamish pursed his lips. Deliberately slowly, he went back to the table and stood in front of it, examining the other bottles.

'If you want to spend all morning gazing at the bloody things, take them away and do it elsewhere,' Spicer snapped from behind his back.

Hamish turned and gave him a level gaze. After several seconds he picked up the bottles and wordlessly marched from the room.

*

Sarah's laugh rang down the corridor, greeting him a good thirty yards before he reached her door. When he pushed it open, he saw Alec Johnston leaning casually against the wall by her desk, smirking at her. There was a self-satisfied look on Alec's face, the look of a man who has managed to catch an attractive secretary in her room without her boss being present. The look evaporated as Alec turned to see who had

come in. Reluctantly Alec prised himself off the wall and followed Hamish into his room. Stood in the middle of the
floor, hitched his bottom onto the edge of Hamish's table
and looked about him with a proprietorial air.

There was a piece of paper in his hand. He peered at it
through his glasses, as if wondering how it had got there.

'I was rather hoping,' he said in a distant voice, 'that you
might be able to tell me what this represents.'

He held it out.

To enquiries in London, Manila and
Portugal,

all as previously reported: £45,000

Hamish's eyes opened in surprise at the baldness of the bill:
no details, no breakdown; silly buggers. He was also surprised
that Alec should have got hold of it before he did.

'Where did you get this?' he asked, playing for time.

'It was lying on Sarah's desk. Is that relevant? Were you
hoping to keep it a secret?'

'No, of course not, I simply—'

'Good. Then perhaps you can tell me what these investigators have achieved.'

*They've burgled a car, stolen a label. Now they're asking me to agree
to a phone being bugged.* The blunt answer shot unbidden into
Hamish's mind and he instantly shied away from it. Alec
wouldn't like it any better than he did. Still less would he like
the idea of paying forty-five thousand pounds for the privilege.

'Well,' Hamish said, playing for time, trying to think how
to soften the blow, 'they've done quite a lot of work. It
doesn't say, but I imagine that it covers the work they did

here, as well as Portugal, so—'

'*Hamish.*' Alec interrupted, his left foot starting to swing to and fro, like the tail of a predatory cat. 'The Finance Department, as you well know, now expects justification for the bills that we pass them. Not imaginings – hard facts. Odious as it is for you as a barrister to subject yourself to the scrutiny of a mere accountant, the company's policy on financial control is quite clear.'

'Yes,' Hamish retorted acidly, 'it is, isn't it? Save the company money, full stop. If the *company* hadn't thrown a potential informant to the police, I wouldn't have to employ enquiry agents to scratch around looking for leads.'

'*Scratch around?* Do I take it that this represents forty-five thousand pounds-worth of *scratching around?* Is there no *result* to show for this?'

Result? Hamish thought. Yes, we've got a result, we've hit a dead end and suspended the investigation. 'Well,' he said defensively, 'it's uphill work, they—'

'*Results,* Hamish. That is what the company is interested in. As this spells out…' He held out another sheet of paper. *Personnel Department* was printed at the top. Automatically Hamish groaned.

'It's been sanctioned by the board,' Alec announced. 'It affects us all, from the chairman down to the chap who opens the door. All of us. Me. You. Read it.'

Hamish pursed his lips and read. Performance Review System, screamed in bold type. The memorandum was full of jargon about setting targets, achieving objectives, maximising performance, striving for excellence.

'This is a lot of bull,' Hamish said. 'Targets, my arse. Salesmen have *targets.* We're professional advisers. What do I do? Write ten extra letters every day?'

'My target,' Alec announced stiffly, not liking the message either but having to pretend that he did, 'will be to ensure that this department delivers the service that management wants. What management wants is results. Your target will be to get them.'

'But for God's sake, we don't need this sort of crap!'

'*But* you've got it. If you can be bothered to read to the bottom of the page, you will see that there are to be annual performance-related salary assessments for all staff. A substantial slice of your salary will be made up of a performance bonus. The bonus will depend on *demonstrable* success in getting *demonstrable* results. So, what I want to know is, what *result* can you demonstrate for this bill?'

'Performance bonus,' Hamish grumbled, ignoring the question. 'Sounds like a bloody success fee.'

'Congratulations. That's the idea.'

'*Oh*. So much for professional ethics, then, is that what you mean? Success fees may still be illegal at the Bar, but never mind that, we're in trade now. Is that it?'

Alec sighed. 'Hamish. If you don't like the idea of a bonus, you can do without it. I, however, intend to take mine, and mine depends on the performance of this department. Which includes you. So I shall expect you to focus on *results*. And I ask again…'

'All *right*. I've got the message. The company wants a result, you want a result. All I can say is that it's too early.' Stirred up by the argument, his voice took on a ring of confidence. 'It's a delicate enquiry, we've made some progress, we've identified a counterfeiter but we still haven't got hard evidence. And I'm not going to say any more, certainly to the Finance Department, because I want to keep the details confidential so no one can wreck it.'

He stood square on to Alec, challenging him.

'Very well,' Alec said. 'I'll accept that for the moment but you'd better make sure the end result justifies what you've spent. I don't want this department to get a reputation for squandering the company's money.'

Hamish grunted.

'So keep your mind focused on that. Your review comes at the end of the month. In the meantime,' Alec went on, frowning, 'I've got my hands full with that claim of Morato's. In two days' time I'm booked on a flight to Madrid. I've got a heavy meeting with our own lawyers and then with the opposition. So I don't need you distracting me with all this stuff. Got that?'

*

A minute after Alec left, Sarah stalked into his room. She stood in front of his desk looking stony-faced. She had had a screaming match with her boyfriend the night before and had been in a resentful mood all day.

'Scotland thinks you're potty,' she announced tersely.

'Oh?' he said, looking up at her.

'I checked the code numbers on those bottles of Adrian's. One of them belongs to a customer we stopped supplying five years ago.'

'Five years? Are you *sure*?'

'Of course I'm sure,' she snorted, tossing her hair in irritation.

'Sorry, I didn't mean… what I meant was, are *they* sure?'

'Sure as they ever are of anything.'

'Did they say who it was?'

'Some outfit in Canada. Went bust.'

'*Canada?* Hmph, that's a bit peculiar. Have you got the bottle there?'

'Of course I have. What do you think I've done, drunk it over lunchtime?'

'Wouldn't surprise me a bit.'

She turned on her heel, flouncing.

Hamish wrinkled his nose, levered himself out of his chair and wandered out to Sarah's anteroom. She was already typing ferociously, pretending to ignore him.

He picked the bottle off her desk, casually flipped it over and peered through the back. On the inside of the label, just visible through the deep amber liquid, he could see the nine-digit number of the code, fuzzy black in rubber-stamped ink. He spun the bottle in his hand, gazed thoughtfully at the label on the front, and slowly the penny dropped.

'Where's the copyright file?' he asked slowly.

She pushed back her chair, marched to a filing cabinet, yanked it open with a metallic clang, pulled out a file and thrust it into his hand.

Slowly he leafed through it. It was a thick collection of labels, starting in 1934 and continuing up to the present. Glossy confections of shiny gold, deep orange, bright grass-green. Each label was stuck on a separate sheet of paper, each annotated with the date of its introduction. Each had changed in some small detail from its predecessor, and neat copperplate notes called attention to the changes.

'I thought so,' he said, slowly. 'The front label was updated three years ago. It can't be five years old.'

She half-frowned, half-shrugged as she typed. Not my fault, her shrug said, that's what they told me.

Puzzled, he stared at the label on the bottle. Gold-embossed head of McCowrie himself. Brand name, descriptive blurb, extra special, blah blah. Alcoholic strength 43%. Contents 0.75 1. Royal warrant, discreet lines round the edge, curlicues at the corner.

Royal warrant. He squinted idly at the coat of arms at the head of the label, bold orange on green background. Ran his finger over it, an unthinking, automatic caress.

His finger glided smoothly over the flat surface of the paper.

He looked again at the file. Flipped back in curiosity to see how long the royal warrant had been there. Granted in 1955, the file told him. It had appeared on every label since then.

And on every label, it was embossed. Every label, except the one on the bottle in his hand.

'Shit,' he muttered, as it dawned on him what that meant.

*

Spicer was standing behind his desk, slipping on the jacket of his pinstriped suit. He looked up with an annoyed frown as Hamish entered.

'I've got an important lunch to get to. What d'you want?'

Hamish sighed in resignation at Spicer's unprovoked rudeness.

'I wondered if I could have a word about that parallel from Japan. There's—'

'You've got cracking on that, I hope you're going to tell me?'

'I've identified two customers. I'll be writing to them, of course—'

'Writing to them? Never mind writing bloody letters! Cut off their supplies. Sue them. Jesus, do I have to tell you everything?'

'There aren't any supplies pending – I checked. And if I don't write first, we don't get the costs of suing them.'

'Christ. Don't come and badger me with the ins and outs of the bloody legal system. Just get on with it!' Spicer eased his way round his desk and made for the door.

'But there is just one problem. I—'

'A problem? Well, sort it out, is that beyond you? For God's sake, I'm late already and my week's short enough as it is.'

Without waiting for a reply Spicer swept out.

*

'That man,' Hamish muttered, 'is *such* a shit.'

Sarah sniffed in disdain. 'So he's a shit, so what? What's new about shitty men?' She thought crossly of her boyfriend. Ex-boyfriend, if he didn't watch out. 'You only get places by being a shit. It's about time you woke up.'

Bloody man, Hamish thought, why on earth do I bother?

When lunchtime came, he mooched out into Hyde Park, gulping in some fresh air, trying to get his thoughts straight. He'd gone to Spicer as soon as he'd seen the bottle's label was fake. He hadn't hesitated, he'd gone as a reflex reaction, automatically wanting to report what he had noticed; however much he disliked the man himself. If there was fake on the Japanese market, Spicer had to know about it. *Had* to know about it, so that he could alert the salesforce, start them investigating...

Christ. What a thought. Bloody salesmen leaping about like startled antelopes, rushing into every shop in Japan. The counterfeiters would get to hear in about ten minutes. The first thing they'd do would be to cover their tracks. Any chance of a discreet investigation would go down the drain.

And as for investigating, the man Spicer would choose would be Gosling, not Hamish. Hamish could just imagine it, he could practically write the script.

'Sound man, Phil Gosling, lot of experience.'

'Well, actually, our department has some experience of its own…'

'We've seen what form that takes, paying money to conmen.' A sneer. 'This is a job for the expert. We'll need the police, and as we all know, going to the police isn't something you're too keen on. Give the whole thing to Phil, whatever you've got.'

And to make it worse, if Spicer told him to tell Gosling everything, that would include the Robinson label, Portugal, Cardoso. And Gosling would take that over as well.

And what would Gosling do? He'd made a balls of it before; he'd make a balls of it again. 'If that idiot gets hold of it,' he muttered to himself, 'he'll go crashing through every bloody door he comes to.' No chance of a discreet investigation; no chance.

Hamish gave a sour laugh. If results were what mattered to the company, he practically owed them a duty to keep Gosling off it.

A duty. The word niggled at him as it pushed himself into his thoughts. It was the one thing that bothered him. The idea that he had some sort of duty to tell Spicer.

After all, Spicer was in the position of his client, and as a lawyer he must have a duty to keep him in the picture. But then again, did he? Who said? He wasn't a solicitor, he was a barrister – well, technically, anyway – and there was nothing in the barristers' handbook of etiquette about feeding information to a client. In fact, it was all the other way about. All those corny cocktail party questions – 'What do you do if you suspect your client's guilty?' You don't act on suspicion, you rely on what your client tells you.

Indeed, now that he thought about it, Hamish remembered, the handbook went even further. Pointed out that it was a barrister's job to rely *only* on instructions, and that it was unprofessional to use information which he'd obtained himself. It was surprisingly stern about it. Quite wrong to put such information before the court. And, he supposed, improper to mention it to the client, too.

Well, that put a different complexion on it. Hamish suddenly felt a whole lot more cheerful.

Indeed, it was no more than Alec had said when he'd joined the company: 'Ours is primarily an advisory department. We are not executives. We advise our commercial colleagues on the problems they put before us.' And no commercial colleague had put the problem to him. Not as counterfeit, that is, only as parallel, and that was quite different. Not for him to go round stirring things up. Especially, he thought, if Spicer was so stupid that he couldn't see it for himself.

And, for that matter, he'd even *tried* to tell Spicer. Not Hamish's fault if Spicer was so ill-mannered that he couldn't be bothered to listen. Serve him right for being an arsehole, he thought with a grin.

And anyway, what was important was getting results. Alec had made that very clear to Hamish. *That was what the company wanted; very well, that's what he'd worry about.*

Delighted by his ability to interpret principles in a way that justified what he wanted to do, Hamish returned to the office, a spring in his step; bounced up through the front door, grinned at the receptionist and returned to work.

CHAPTER 33

It was quarter to eight in the evening before he left the office and he had one more call to make. When he got to the unfamiliar street in Baron's Court he cruised, looking unsuccessfully for a parking space; double-parked.

All the houses had porticos in front of their doors, cream-glossed columns receding down both sides of the street, soot-smudged reminiscence of a more genteel era when all the houses had been kept as houses, before they'd been converted into flats. He found the number he wanted two thirds of the way along, examined the small panel of bell-push buttons, flicked a glance up at the small video lens four feet above. Pushed a bell and waited for the door catch to buzz.

Her flat was up two flights, cornices, mahogany banisters, white walls, carpet the colour of unpeeled almonds. A solid teak door to her flat. It opened exactly as he reached it.

She seemed more tanned than he'd remembered, a healthy glow after the rain-bleached secretaries in the office, freckles coming up on her nose and cheekbones, highlights from the sun still lingering in her hair. Brightly coloured blouse, splashes of yellow and green and red, image of sunshine and heat. He felt suddenly fusty, wreathed in the dankness of his work-tired City suit. He followed slowly as she led the way into her sitting room, glance dropping to the movement of slim buttocks in tight-fitting white corduroy jeans.

She picked a glass of white wine off the mantelpiece,
drank. As an afterthought she handed one to him. Didn't ask
what he'd like, take it or leave it written on her face. Even
that much of a welcome was more than he'd been expecting.
He sipped it gratefully.

'Better than the office tea,' he ventured, with a faint smile
of appeasement.

'Thank God for that,' she said tartly, remembering the
dishwater she'd been given by Sarah.

'No, I didn't mean…'

'No no, it's a real compliment. Don't go and spoil it by
explaining, the way men usually do.' She stood, legs apart,
arms folded, glass in one hand; her head cocked to one side,
a mocking look on her face.

'I'm surprised they get the chance to say anything,' he
said, 'with you around.'

One corner of her mouth lifted into a brief half-smile.
'Well, now I'm giving you the chance, suppose you tell me
what you're so desperate to show me?' she said.

Clumsily he fumbled with his briefcase, trying unsuccessfully to juggle his glass in one hand. Crouched to put glass
and briefcase on the floor, pulled out the bottle and handed
it to her.

'Is this what I think it is?' she asked in surprise.

'Yes.'

'Christ,' she muttered. She turned it this way and that,
held it up to the light, looking critically from every angle.

'Done a good job, haven't they?' she said wryly.

'Too good. The cap's bloody brilliant. Look' — he fished
a small gilt cylinder out of his briefcase — 'one of ours.' He
held it alongside. The two were identical, from the tiny man-
ufacturer's mark to the size of the knurling on the upper rim.

'Trying to spot this stuff on the market's going to be a real bugger.'

She unscrewed the cap and sniffed in curiosity, wrinkled her nose, looked at him with questioning eyebrows.

'It's not too bad,' he admitted. 'I'm sorry to say.'

'How come one of your people spotted it?'

'Pure accident. One of our blokes in Japan thought it was a parallel import. Because of the European label. If they'd been clever enough to use a label with the Jap distributor's name on it there's no way we'd ever have picked it up.'

'So who realised what it was?'

'I did. Only because I was thinking about counterfeit already.'

'And you reckon…' She tailed off, her eyes asking the question for her.

He picked up two labels. Laid one on top of the label on the bottle, showed her how it was half a millimetre longer. 'That's the genuine,' he said, pointing out the embossing on the coat of arms. 'And that,' he said, replacing it with the second label, 'is the one I got from Seymour.'

It fitted exactly, even to a minute nick on one corner from the cutter that had stamped them out.

He did the same with a third label. 'That's the one you, ah – acquired – from Cardoso,' he said, giving her a diffident look. It fitted as exactly as the second.

She sat in a chair, leaned back, looked up at him. 'Surprised you can bear to touch it,' she said derisively. 'Handling stolen goods.'

'Yeah well,' he said, ignoring her jibe, 'it's all getting serious. We didn't know it had gone on sale anywhere – and now we find it in Japan. Japan, of all places. Our third biggest market; it's a potential disaster.'

'So?' She drank from her glass. 'You've found it on sale, that gives you another chance to use the law. It's what you love. Get the police onto it, kick the shit out of the shop where you bought it, should be just up your street.'

'Well, I would. But here's the problem. Japan's highly publicity-sensitive. About the most sensitive market there is. One whiff that there's fake McCowrie on the market would be a disaster. All our hard-won customers will go back to drinking White Horse or Black Label – the news spreads, and our market slumps.'

'So...?' She paused quietly, and looked at him, back straight, hands demurely in her lap. Sensing what was coming, waiting.

He came and stood next to her. 'Action in Japan's not what we need. First, because of the publicity. Second, because we already know where it's come from. So I just want to think through the... er, strategy.'

She looked at him, calm, catlike eyes. *You know what I think. But you made such a bloody fuss about it I'm damned if I'm going to say it again.*

'There's another thing,' he mused. 'The Japanese authorities like parallel imports. They think it increases competition. They think trying to stop it is anti-competitive. In fact, they even passed a law. Taking action to discourage parallel's illegal.'

'Is that so?' she said, looking at her nails, as if bored.

'Yes. It is.' He clasped his wine glass with both hands, thinking, one thumb rubbing over the other. 'And of course the chap who bought this bottle for us, did so we could investigate the parallel.'

She looked at him silently.

'So... technically...' he went on, 'some might say he was

breaking the law.'

She flicked an alert glance at him from under her eyebrows. 'Tut tut. Surprised you can bear to talk about it.'

'Um, well…' He gazed down into his glass, frowned.

She said nothing, waiting, watching him.

'I do sometimes wonder…' he said. He took a sip from his wine. 'I sometimes wonder… if one doesn't, er… make too much fuss about… um' – he stroked his chin – '…legal technicalities.'

There was a slightly glazed expression on his face as he placed his glass on a table, raised his eyes and looked at her.

She crossed one leg over the other, clasped her hands round her knee.

'Let me hear it from you. You want…'

'…to eradicate the problem as discreetly as we can.'

'And when you say eradicate it…?'

'Find the source.'

'Well, now. If that isn't what I was trying to do last week.'

'Things have changed. It's more of a problem now.'

'Well, well, well.' Her hazel-green eyes bored into his, her lips twitched; slowly she stretched out a hand, grasped her wine glass, raised it slowly to her lips. She drank delicately, her gaze steady over the rim of the glass, unblinking, locked into his; the blaze of intensity in her eyes giving him an unexpected churn of the stomach.

CHAPTER 34

A moped sputtered into the village square, exhaust echoing loudly in the shimmering silence of the midday heat. It slowed uncertainly, swung into the shadow beside the trickling fountain and stopped. The rider wiped his brow, twisted round in his saddle to pull a bottle of orangeade from his pannier, drank, wiped his mouth with the back of his hand. He looked about him, took another swig and sat for a moment, resting. Squinted at the light bouncing off the walls opposite, let his gaze travel along the horizontal lines of the balconies, railings, eaves, along the telephone wires looping from house to house.

After a minute he put the bottle back in his pannier and set off, down the street opposite the one he'd come in, coasting gently.

The road passed Cardoso's house, rose slightly, curved gently to the right. Thirty yards after the bend the village stopped, leaving the road to run on alone, a ribbon of grey bordered by scrubby dried-out grass, cutting through the parched ochre of the fields. A line of telegraph poles marched beside the road towards a patch of trees, the only patch of green in the dusty landscape.

As the road reached the trees it curved sharply left and started a gentle drop downwards. The plain beyond shimmered in the heat, chequered with squares of pale fawn.

Halfway down the slope the rider stopped again, turned

and looked back. By now the road had fallen out of sight of the village and all he could see was the brown earth of the field, stretching from the verge beside him to the bright blue sky in the distance. Three feet away from him a telegraph pole pointed up into the sky.

The other side of the pole was a ditch. He smiled, opened up the throttle and went on his way.

*

The next day, a van, battered and coughing, painted in the livery of the Portuguese telephone company, pulled to a stop.

When the engineer climbed to the top of the pole he could just see the roofs of the village, pink and russet and terracotta, a higgledy-piggledy patchwork of geometric shapes, hazy in the heat rising from the fields. He whistled softly under his breath as he worked, his hands making quick neat movements round the cables. After a few minutes he came down again, leading a discreet wire along the back of the pole. He gave a slow look round, then quickly slipped into the ditch, led the wire towards a half-overgrown drain leading under the road, and scrambled out.

From the plain below came a faint buzz. He paused, listening. The buzz grew louder, swelled into the sound of an engine, turned throaty as it met the upward slope.

By the time the car reached him he was sitting in the back of the van, head down, studying a worksheet.

As the car disappeared upwards over the brow of the hill the engineer grabbed a small metal box from inside the van, carried it to the ditch, connected it to the wire and thrust it into the drain. In only a couple of minutes he had buried the wire, brushed the undergrowth over it, hidden the traces of his work.

CHAPTER 35

As Jo came out to her office reception to greet him her face seemed calm and impassive; she managed to suppress a smile but there was a little hint of extra alertness in her eyes, a little extra spring in her walk: hinting at triumph, like her voice when she'd rung to ask him round to their London office. She led him to the meeting room and walked straight to a chair, smooth rhythm in her movements, neatness in her poise as she sat, lifted her chin and looked at him.

'We've scored,' she said, satisfaction in every vowel. 'Cardoso made a phone call the very first day. Here, Gonçalves faxed me a transcript.'

> *'João?'*
>
> *'Yes.'*
>
> *'I've just sent the telex.'*
>
> *'Good.'*
>
> *'There are things we need to discuss. Are you free?'*
>
> *'This evening, no. Maybe tomorrow… yes, tomorrow morning is okay.'*
>
> *'See you then.'*

'What makes you think it's this operation?' Hamish asked,

puzzled. 'It could be anything, it could be just a friend of his, it could—'

Silently she pushed another piece of paper across the table, a light dancing in her eyes.

> *466581 cheng rs*
>
> *631471 exporg p*
>
> *confirm next shipment will be loaded*
> *on schedule ten days from now. our*
> *bank has not yet received l/c from*
> *your bank please expedite regards*
> *Cardoso*

'Bloody hell! How on earth did you get this?'

'How d'you think? He's got a telex in his house. We did that at the same time as his phone.'

'God almighty.' Hamish sat still for ten long seconds, staring down at the two sheets of paper. Then he looked up at her; slowly a smile inched into the corners of his mouth, widened, stretched his face into a grin, broke irresistibly into laughter.

'*That*,' he said, voice ringing round the room, 'is *amazing*!'

She gave a lazy little shrug, contented, like a cat licking its whiskers. 'It's only what I said,' she reminded him. 'Get into their communications and there you are.'

'I know, but all the same… seeing it… sitting there on the table… it's… *brilliant!*'

'Yeah. Not bad, is it? Pity we didn't do it before.'

'Mmm, yes,' Hamish muttered, his smile turning wry. He gave a gruff, throaty grunt, steered his mind away from the thought, back to the contents of the telex.

'Cheng,' he muttered. 'That sod.'

'You know him?'

'Yep. Well, not personally of course. He's one of the main parallelers into the Far East. He's been a pain in the arse for years.'

'Does he supply Japan?'

'God, yes. He sends it all over the place. Africa, South America, even the USA. But Japan most of all. We know damn well it's him doing it, but he's too slippery for us to prove what he gets up to.'

'Well then,' she smiled, 'it's just as well you agreed to send our bloke up the pole then, isn't it?'

'Yes.' His face cleared. 'Well yes, now you put it like that, I suppose it is.' He smiled at her, acknowledging her point. Fingered the transcript again, as if unable to believe the result.

'Who's this bloke he's ringing? Does your interception stuff tell you that?'

'Of course it does,' she said. 'It picks up the number he dials, then you get the subscriber.'

'Thought you couldn't do that.'

'Contacts.' She gave him a slow deliberate blink, catlike, serene. Then opened a notebook on the table in front of her.

'Bloke called João da Silveira,' she read. 'Gonçalves said the name rang a bell. He couldn't think why at first, then did a few discreet enquiries. Five years ago, he was charged with smuggling but got off. Three years before that, he was charged with evading income tax. Again, he got off. No convictions, but the word is he's a highly successful smuggler with some serious criminal connections. If he's involved, we know we've got a problem.'

'Why?'

'One, he's successful, he's made a lot of money out of

what he's done in the past, and any operation he puts together is going to be well thought-out. Two, he's a canny operator, he's never been caught, and he's going to know how to avoid getting caught on this. We're not going to be able to trail round after him like we did after Cardoso. This bloke'll be surveillance-aware, he'll spot that team of Gonçalves in five minutes.'

'Are you sure? After all, you had them on Cardoso for over a week, and he never gave any sign of spotting you.'

'*Listen* to me, will you? Silveira's a completely different ball game. From what we could find out, he's spent his whole life going up and down every side road the whole length of the border, running every bloody kind of contraband you can think of. Checking his back is second nature.'

'So what do we do? The telex says they're loading in ten days, so we've only got ten days to crack it, and now you're telling me there's nothing we can—'

'No, I'm not,' she smiled. 'There is a way. It's just going to cost you a bit, that's all.'

'How much more?'

'Not much. Only thirty thousand a week.'

Hamish thought of his finance director, gave a sigh of gloom, and closed his eyes.

CHAPTER 36

She had the team out from London, ten of them. No expense spared, Hamish had said, through gritted teeth. Four ex-policemen and six ex-soldiers, three of them ex-SAS, trained to adapt to all terrains, happy to get out of the city and relive their service days at commercial rates of pay. Plus one of Gonçalves' team for local knowledge, one only and kept firmly under control. The day they arrived they got straight down to it, checking the ground against the maps, assessing where the roads went, finding the dead ground, the places for observation points, the places to avoid. One of them went on the small hill that overlooked the villa, one hid in the grass at the edge of the opposite field, one in the shade of the derelict wall in the cork wood. The others spread over the roads, ready to put full cover on him whichever way he went. By midday João's house was ringed. The whole of that first afternoon they waited, squinting over the countryside, hour after hour, nothing to watch but the grass wavering and sighing in the breeze, the goats bleating in the far corner of the field, the kite soaring overhead, the slow relentless progression of the shadows as the sun swung overhead.

As evening came the shadows stretched and softened, heat ebbed, sky deepened. But no movement came from the villa. No windows opened to let in the cool evening air, no lights came on indoors. No sound filtered out from within.

There was no noise but the incessant rasp of the crickets

in the grass.

By nightfall, Jo was biting her nails. It was a lot of resources for watching an empty house.

Next morning, she was awake early. She lay in a dark universe, watched the faint, pale yellow crack of light grow slowly, separating blue-grey dark of the sky from the blue-green dark of the earth. She watched it spread across the sky, catching the tops of the hills, picking out the trees, washing away the mists in a slow vast flood of light.

Nothing happened all day.

They watched the stone walls of the villa, willing them to reveal the man who lived inside. The walls basked in the sun, growing hot, glowing with white fire, but refusing their wish, staying solid, impenetrable, secretive and unyielding.

Sun sank, walls grew dim. Night fell.

Suddenly light flared beyond the trees, grew, swung this way and that as the road twisted. Engine growling, light now bursting along the drive and flooding onto the end wall of the house, gravel spitting beneath the tyres. Lights flicked off, dark, sudden blindness, silence. Car door slammed, crunch of feet.

A sigh of relief among the watchers.

He moved after breakfast next morning, into his car and fast down the drive, left at the end, into the lane that led south and west, and curled round towards the highway.

They were dancing all round him all the way to Lisbon. Along the motorway, down the slip roads, cutting through the back streets into the centre of town. Into a shopping area, then a small square, twisting left down an old alley, right again and out into a broad commercial avenue, old Lisbon architecture, offices both sides of the road.

Fifty yards down the avenue he stopped, parked, jumped

from his car and strode off down the pavement.

One car dropped a man on the pavement thirty yards behind him, another car dropped a hundred yards in front, a third did the same round the next corner. The motorbike loitered back down the road.

João walked twenty yards down the street and through a doorway.

The man strolling along the pavement behind could see him clearly through the plate glass, leaning over the counter, talking. He strolled on, glancing at the sign over the window: Fremar Ltda, freight forwarding.

Oh to be in there, to hear him, to know what he was discussing. What freight he was arranging, from where to where, what routes, what ships. When to be loaded, to whom to be delivered.

From the car across the street, Jo looked longingly at the window. Debated whether to send a man in. Reluctantly decided against, a casual enquirer wandering in two minutes after him would ring alarm bells for sure.

Ten minutes later João came out. Into his car and away. Out to the motorway again, back the way he'd come.

Halfway home he took a small turning up the side of a valley, a small one-track road, its edges scattered with earth, that weaved and dipped past fields of maize. After five kilometres he came to a group of houses, half a dozen that straggled out along the side of the road in a half-hearted hamlet. On the far side was a country inn, breezeblock whitewashed years ago and greying, set back from the road behind a dusty parking space beaten out of the dirt. He pulled in beside two local vans, the only vehicles there. A place not designed for tourists; a place where strangers would be noticed.

Lunchtime.

Careful now, she thought, intuition tweaking at her brain. Careful, we're nearly there. Fish still on the line – thinking of Hamish and his fishing weekends – this was something he ought to understand. Gently, he'd say, no sudden movement, don't want to frighten it, it's a light line, it'll break you if you aren't careful. *Bet you never caught a fish this size, Hamish.*

They backed off and waited, thinking of him indoors in the shade, cool glass of wine in his hand, them in their cars down the road, metal boxes getting red-hot in the sun, sandwiches and water long since brought to lukewarm.

Two hours and a quarter. Blast him for his long lunch.

He came out at three. Cruised gently down the road, slowed again after one kilometre. Turned off the road, along a sandy track in an open patch of dusty ground, kicking up a cloud that hung in the still air.

The field beside the track was a half-hearted cork wood, trees well apart, old and straggling. Wide gaps, speaking of neglect, of trees long dead and not replaced.

After a hundred yards the cloud of dust twisted, rose slightly, then dropped out of sight.

Their lead car cruised on past the turning. Jo looked at the cloud of dust and cursed. There was no way a car could follow along the track without screaming its presence. No way they could go on foot, no cover in this sparse apology for a cork wood.

They ringed the area for other approaches and lay up for the afternoon, waiting for the cover of night.

*

It felt like a typical resort pool, tropically hot and humid. Two well-plumped swimmers gasped their way through the crystal

blue water to the row of underwater stools round the sunken
bar, unable to face the five-yard swim to the sides without a
Pina Colada. Pretty oriental girls patrolled the tiled terrace,
carrying drinks to the tables, smiling, bare shoulders showing
off the purple velvet tinge to their brown skin. It was just
what Hamish would have expected to find in the Far East.
He had not been expecting it within half a mile of Heathrow
Airport.

Hamish sat at one of the tables, sipping an orange juice,
his eyes flicking round at the waitresses, at the door, at the
crossword of the paper in front of him.

She walked through the door twenty-five minutes later,
with the shop-soiled feeling all airlines give their passengers
as a souvenir. The usual briskness in her walk had faded a
little and her face had a tired, smudged look.

'Hi,' she said. He could hear triumph in her greeting,
could see it flickering from the corner of her eyes as she sat.
She gave a quick look round, checking that no one was in
earshot, pulling her chair close to his; lowered her voice.

'I think we've found it.' She chucked a bundle of photographs across the table and slumped in a chair, rubbing her
forehead and yawning. He leafed through them; they showed
a wide sand-coloured landscape with nowhere to hide. Down
in a dip was a dull, featureless ash-grey building, corrugated
iron roof on breezeblock.

Out of the corner of his eye, Hamish became aware of a
waitress drifting towards their table. Quickly he turned the
photographs face down.

'Champagne, two glasses please,' he said, decisively. Jo
gave him a tired smile, perking up at the thought.

'Celebration time,' he smiled. As the waitress left, he studied the photographs again. 'Any chance of seeing inside?'

'Not a hope,' she said. 'It's a bloody awful place to do surveillance. It's tight as a mouse's arsehole. Look, you can see.' She pointed to one of the photographs. 'It's only got a couple of windows on each side; they're high up and the glass is frosted. So we can't look from the outside; and we can't get in, there's always someone there. They're working late into the night, and they've got someone on guard all the time.

'Hmm.' He frowned. 'Well, if you can't see inside… what makes you think this is it?'

She wrinkled her nose. 'I thought you'd ask that. It's a fair question. I've been asking myself that too.'

'I mean, if he's a smuggler…'

'…it could be just a warehouse where he keeps contraband. That what you were going to say?'

'Yes.'

'Possible. But I don't think it is. He's about to do a delivery, we know that from the telex. If he goes to the factory it's likely to be now. And this is the only place of any potential he's been to since we started watching him. Plus, yesterday his local man, the wine man, he came out there too.'

'Ahhh.'

'Yeah. I reckon that makes it almost certain.' She leaned her chin on her hands and gazed at him. 'I've got a feeling about it. And besides…'

She was interrupted by a splash from the pool, a businessman doing a bellyflop.

Water spattered over the terrace towards them.

The waitress came back to their table with two glasses of champagne on a silver tray. Smiled coquettishly at them — smile saying as clearly as if she'd spoken that she took them for two lovers meeting for a passionate afternoon.

'How on earth did you find this place?' he asked, as he

raised his glass.

She shrugged. 'It's better than Terminal Two. And I thought the dusky maidens'd be right up your street.'

He gave her a look over his champagne glass. 'Actually, I prefer freckles.'

To the surprise of both of them a hint of a blush crossed her cheeks.

'Keep your mind on the job,' she said, pertly. 'I was trying to tell you something.'

'About maidens?'

'About the factory. Like I said, we can't get close. And right now we've got damn all evidence to send the police in, even if you could persuade them to get off their arse in under a year. But sometime soon the stuff they're making is going to have to move. And in theory, as soon as it comes out, there's your evidence. In theory.'

'In theory? Why "in theory"?'

'Think about it. How does your company ship its brands?'

'In containers.'

'Right. If he's shipping all the way out to the Far East, he's bound to use them too. If it's containerised in the factory we'll never see the cargo itself. All we'll see is the containers.'

'Are you telling me they can just go on sitting in the Portuguese corkwoods churning out their stuff and there's nothing you can do about it?'

'Nope. All we have to do is get the containers inspected by customs. Routine inspection, and there you go.'

'But customs inspect imports, not exports, so we have to know where the bloody stuff's *going*...' He threw one hand out in exasperation, giving his champagne glass a glancing blow, sending it toppling slowly sideways. In a fast reflex he

whipped his hand down and caught it. 'Shit,' he swore, looking sadly into his now half-empty glass.

'Oh dear,' she said, 'didn't I show you this? How silly of
me.' She fished in her bag, slid a piece of paper across the
table.

> *466581 cheng rs*
>
> *631471 exporg p*
>
> *l/c received our bank omits to nomi-*
> *nate port of shipment please ensure*
> *l/c payable on receipt of cargo in*
> *transit Rotterdam as per our agree-*
> *ment regards Cardoso.*

When he looked up at her he saw she was laughing. 'You…'
he exclaimed, leaving a heavy pause biting off the insult on
the end of his tongue, but eyes wide.

'Can't think how I forgot,' she murmured. 'And it's what
I came all the way back to tell you, too.' She grinned happily
at him. 'You've been so keen on the idea of using the flaming
law. Right then – get off your arse and use it.'

CHAPTER 37

Willem Vrijhof cruised his Audi Quattro slowly down the double chevron ranks of parked cars, searching in vain for an empty space. Turned the corner at the end of the block, on to the next corner, did a complete circuit without success.

There was one gap in the street, immediately below a no-parking sign. He looked at it sourly and muttered a Dutch curse. Then a cheerful smile broke across his cragged face. 'If we can't park illegally when we come to see these people, when can we?' he said to Hamish, and thrust his car into the gap.

Hamish looked up the building looming above them: a grey, impersonal 1960s' monolith, blocking out half the sky; the concrete streaked by three decades of pigeons. Rotter-dam, he thought, was a disappointment. He'd been expecting the canals, quaint streets and pretty gables of Amsterdam. He smiled to himself; better not tell Jo that, she'd accuse him of only wanting to see the whores sitting behind their red vel-vet-curtained windows.

Willem leaned behind him to pick his briefcase out of the debris on the back seat: squash racket, balls, towel, trainers, the happy chaos of an unmarried man at odds with the or-derliness of his lawyer's office. He yanked the briefcase round onto his lap, then paused and looked at Hamish.

'Remember, they don't have to help,' he cautioned. 'Don't forget that. I know these people. If they don't feel like it, they don't have to tell anyone anything, even the police. They make their own rules, they won't help unless they want to.'

They crossed the road and walked into a lobby with a grey marble floor and heavy varnished plywood panelling; style and decoration self-consciously dated. After three minutes a nameless functionary appeared, led them to a creaking lift. Fifteen floors up they emerged into a corridor of light-blue eggshell paint, smelling of antiseptic sterility, of the Kafka-esque bleakness of government offices everywhere.

Windows all down one side of the corridor showed a pan-oramic view of Rotterdam, buildings, streets and moving traffic in the foreground, the waterways, ships and cranes in its vast harbour misty in the distance.

The functionary led them down the corridor, knocked on a door at the end, waved them in and disappeared. A tall, heavily built man, curly brown hair and a plump jaw, rose from behind a desk. 'Molijn,' he said, stretching out a meaty hand.

As they shook hands a connecting door opened from the next office and a second man entered. Thin, wiry, with an austere, watchful face. It could have been the face of a priest; but for the shirtsleeves, loosened tie and shoulder holster. He gave their hands a perfunctory shake and leaned back in a chair, looking aloof and non-committal. Hamish was fasci-nated by the holster, tried not to be caught gazing at it; it was the first time he had seen one outside a cinema. How odd, he thought; it looks so ordinary in real life, just like under-wear: it must be seeing them on film that gives them glamour.

Hamish sat back as Willem started talking, looking round at the dull grey metal filing cabinets, metal desks, telephones, the snowfall of papers. For an instant he felt the sharp con-trast between the sterile office around him and the real world of movement and colour in the panorama beyond the window: the real world which held the sand and the cork wood and the factory.

He came back to the present as Willem started to spin his spiel. He spoke with the easy familiarity of a salesman, no lawyer-like formality. And how else to start but with a bottle of Grand McCowrie drawn from his briefcase? It drew involuntary smiles from the two officers, as he had known that it would – who in the world doesn't smile at a bottle of Scotch? Not hard-worked customs officers. 'Maybe we have a tasting, American is okay but Scotch is the best, *ja*?'

Delicately he unfolded the story of Hamish's investigation, talking with casual understatement of villains and informants as if they were things that Hamish dealt with every day, as if he were simply plying the same trade as the officers in this room: creating the aura of fellow professionals come to swap notes, rather than supplicants for official help.

Delicately he laid the label Jo had stolen from Cardoso on the desk, glossing over how they'd got it. Watched them as they picked up the label and the bottle and compared them, waited till they were ripe for the punchline.

'Rotterdam?' they said, their tone rising. 'It comes *here*? Pffuughhhh. We don't want this stuff on sale here, ha?'

Hamish and Willem half-looked towards each other, so far so good, but we still have the biggest hurdle to jump… They stayed silent while the two officers murmured to each other.

When they looked up, Hamish spoke.

'If it comes here, you can take action?'

'Of course,' Molijn said, tone rising to say the answer was obvious. 'We make a seizure, no question.'

'And then we… we can work together on this?'

Molijn gave him a solemn look. 'Customs information is confidential – you must understand that. We cannot break that confidentiality. The only people we can tell are another customs service. The law is strict on this.'

'Of course, we understand that perfectly.'

'But, if we make a seizure, naturally we need confirmation that the goods are not genuine.' His face stayed straight but his eyes showed the hint of a smile. 'And naturally we come to you for this. And you will need a sample before you can tell, no? Also, maybe we will have to ask if the shipper is a regular distributor. So then you will know all about it.'

'And then,' Willem said, turning to Hamish, 'I can apply to the civil court, and we can see the documents officially.'

'Excellent,' Hamish said, beaming with pleasure. 'Excellent.'

Throughout this exchange the second officer had said nothing. He was leaning forward toward the desk, quietly examining the bottle and the label. Now he looked up, frowning as if in doubt.

'This label,' he said, holding the fake between forefinger and thumb. 'It's not the same as the one we see in the Netherlands.'

Molijn looked questioningly at his colleague.

'Look, it does not give the name of a distributor. I drink Scotch at home, always the label gives the name of the distributor here in the Netherlands. That's usual, no?'

'For most markets,' Hamish acknowledged.

'So why do they make this label different?'

'It's what we call a general export label,' Hamish explained. 'We use it ourselves, in a number of countries for which we don't have a special label.'

'But you do not use it in Holland. If *you* don't use it in

Holland, why should they?'

Willem shrugged, deliberately casual. 'You know, we don't have as many details of their plans as we would like. Investigation is difficult, especially for our client, operating in a foreign country.' He gave a nod of acknowledgement towards Hamish. 'We don't know which country they want to sell to first. It is a bit like drugs, not so harmful of course…' Careful not to overplay his hand. 'What I mean is they have a product, they sell it where in the world they can make money.'

Nods from the men opposite. They were all too well aware of this.

'Our information is that a consignment will come here, to Rotterdam.' Willem continued. 'Maybe for sale here, at the moment we don't know for sure. When it comes, then it's clear.'

It was the most delicate way he could think of to put it.

A frown came over the austere face. 'Ah,' he said. There was a note of wistfulness, almost of sadness in his voice. 'But maybe it comes in transit. If it comes in transit we can do nothing.'

'Why?' Hamish asked.

'We have no jurisdiction then,' Molijn went on. 'Counterfeit is not a customs offence. To catch counterfeit, we must use the criminal law, and goods in transit are outside the criminal law here in the Netherlands.'

'If we tell you when the goods arrive,' Willem asked, 'you can perhaps find them first and inspect their papers? If they are for the Netherlands there is no problem – if they are in transit, then we discuss what to do, yes?'

'Maybe. But remember this – if the goods are in transit, we can do nothing. No seizure, nothing. Without a seizure we will have no reason to ask you anything, no reason to tell you anything. We would have to keep all information confidential.'

'But if there's no seizure that's a disaster for us!'

Molijn shrugged. 'There is nothing we can do about that. We cannot take action if we have no jurisdiction. You must take action where there is jurisdiction. At the source, in Portugal.'

But we can't, Hamish wanted to scream, *we can't because the system in Portugal's so fucking useless it takes forever, and we can't get any legal evidence unless you help. There's damn all we can do unless you help, don' t tell us what to do, just help us.*

He stirred in frustration on his chair. Willem saw his unease, put a hand gently on his sleeve to restrain him. Hamish swallowed the words, stood silently as the officers got to their feet, summoned up an effusion of thanks, shook their hands with a firm grip and tried to put a smile on his face as they wished him luck.

CHAPTER 38

'Hi there.' Her words resonated down the line, sounding pleased. 'How's the red-light district?'

He gave a distracted grunt, leaning back in Willem's chair. 'How should I know?'

'Oh. That sounded pretty bloody po-faced. Cheer up, we could be in luck. There's only a few ships from here to Rotterdam in the next week. Gonçalves has a man in the port who reckons he can find what cargoes are booked on them. Keep your fingers crossed.'

'Much good that'll do,' Hamish said, his voice dull and gloomy.

'Well, don't sound too enthusiastic, will you?' she said tartly.

'Neither would you if you were here,' he said. 'It's bloody hopeless. If the stuff's in transit when it gets here there's nothing they can do.'

'Why on earth not?' she said, not comprehending.

'They've got no jurisdiction.'

'What you mean, jurisdiction? Jurisdiction means their country, right? The stuff's in Holland – or it will be when it gets there – they're Dutch, so what's the fucking problem?'

'Jurisdiction isn't as simple as that. It's about where the law operates. Counterfeiting's an offence under the *criminal* law, a police offence, but stuff in transit's outside the jurisdiction of the ordinary criminal law. And it's not a *customs* offence. That's what the law says.'

'Well then, the law's a fucking nutter. And this wonderful law stuff, this is the law you're so keen not to break?'

'Come on, give me a break…'

'Huh. If you so much as *think* of getting on the wrong side of it you get your knickers in a twist, and if you stay on the right side of it, it does bugger all to help you.'

'Look, there's a perfectly logical basis to it. Many countries don't apply their own criminal law to goods in transit, in case they're legal where they came from or where they're going.'

'Ah. I see. What you mean is, the Dutch won't seize fake whisky because it might be legal in Singapore or Japan or wherever?'

'Roughly, yes.'

'For God's sake. Is fake legal in Japan?'

'No, but—'

'Or anywhere else?'

'Well, perhaps not. At least not in practice. But in theory, you see—'

'Bugger theory. If the stuff's not legal why won't they nick it?'

Hamish sighed. 'Because their law doesn't let them. I was just trying to explain what—'

'Oh, I've got it,' she said. 'I've always wondered what's odd about lawyers, it's bugged me for years. I keep wondering what turns you on, now I know. You're masochists. You're all into bondage, mental bondage – you worship a set of rules that won't flaming help you when you've got a problem, and you can't break free because you love it so much.'

'For goodness' *sake*, Jo, I want to stop this stuff as much as you do.'

'Yeah, okay… Well, what I called to say is, there's been a development out here.'

'What's that?'

'Best not to speak about it on the phone. Anyway… it sounds like you've run out of options where you are. So catch a flight out here, and I'll tell you.'

CHAPTER 39

Willem drove Hamish to Schiphol; he caught the last flight to Lisbon with ten minutes to spare. It was nine in the evening by the time he arrived at the Sheraton, feeling wrung out. He went straight up to Jo's room, knocked, walked in, flopped in an armchair, and looked at her.

She was wearing a tee shirt that left her arms and shoulders bare: slim, smooth, brown, freckled. He thought of her lying in the sand of the cork woods, watching, waiting. For a moment his imagination switched her to the sand of a beach, playing with seashells, wearing a lime-green bikini. Sun bouncing off her hair, calves speckled with wet sand.

'So tell me the news,' he said.

'Which do you want first? Good news or bad?'

'I could do with some good.'

'Right. I told you Gonçalves has a man in the docks? He managed to get a look at the cargo bookings on ships to Rotterdam. There's a whole lot of wine, port, and stuff. But get this – one booking agent, name of Fremar, is shipping five containers of alcohol.'

'Not whisky?'

'No. But they're not going to call it whisky on the shipping documents, are they? Only draw attention to themselves.'

'Maybe.'

'Of course they aren't. It's got to be their stuff. Because –

and here's the really good bit – the night before last we clocked five containers going to the factory. We clocked them out again last night – they went straight to the port. We followed them to the dock gate.'

'You mean they're down on the docks now?'

'Yep,' she said, in quiet triumph. 'Think about it, Hamish, they're about a mile away from where we are now.'

He looked intently at her. Suddenly his lethargy vanished, replaced by a surge of energy. 'At last!' he exclaimed, springing to his feet. 'So now we can—'

'Wait!' she interrupted. 'You haven't heard the bad bit.'

He stopped in mid-stride and looked at her.

'It's Silveira. I told Gonçalves to find out a bit more about him. You remember I told you he has a record? Gonçalves got it from an old mate of his in the police. It's how he usually gets records.'

From an old mate, Hamish thought, is that how you do it?

'Well,' she went on, 'usually this bloke hands him out whatever he wants, no bother. But this time it was like there was something on his mind. Something he half wanted to say, half didn't. So, a few days later Gonçalves tried someone else.'

'Another... old mate?'

'Yep. And he got the same reaction. So he tried higher up. Yesterday he got an answer.'

'And?'

'There's a feeling Silveira has friends he didn't ought to have. Like in his local police. And particularly in the customs. That could explain a lot. Like how he's been smuggling all his life without having been put away.'

'Oh great,' Hamish said sarcastically. 'So not only is the

law here bloody inefficient, it's corrupt as well.' He went silent for a moment, thinking. 'Hmm. All we need is an honest customs man to open up the containers. Surely to God—'

'They've been sealed,' she countered. 'With a customs seal. It must mean they've got a tame customs officer. No one's going to open up a sealed container without a reason. Plus, there's the danger anyone we talk to will be a friend of his.'

'Oh *God*,' he cried, 'it's so bloody *frustrating*. The stuff's sitting there and you're saying there's damn all we can do about it?'

'Not necessarily,' she said, softly.

She looked at him, green eyes assessing his readiness for what she had in mind. A tension in her stomach; the fisherwoman who sees the fish through the water, who casts the fly, who waits for the take.

'Well sod it,' he said. 'We've got to do *something*. I'll try the embassy again. Surely to God they can have a discreet word with someone, someone high up in the ministry of whatever. Damn it, it's what they're there for.'

She said nothing. *Good luck with that.* She smiled inwardly. Her fly had drifted on down river, unnoticed. No matter: she would cast it again tomorrow.

CHAPTER 40

Hamish looked irritably round the gloomy room in the embassy, the small dowdy patch of Whitehall protected from the Portuguese sun by heavy wooden shutters. He tried not to fidget, fighting down his rising impatience as he listened to the man behind the desk. You really *are* the last resort of the desperate, he thought, come *on*.

The commercial secretary uttered one last blandishment into the telephone, replaced the handset, swung round in his chair to face Hamish once more, and pressed his pink fingertips together again.

'I'm *so* sorry,' he said. 'A *most* important call, do forgive me. Now, where were we?'

Hamish swallowed a sigh.

'I was speaking about evidence we have found since my last visit, evidence that the counterfeiters here are exporting their product onto the world market.'

'Ah, yes, of course.'

'Specifically, exporting it to Japan, which, as I'm sure you know, is one of our industry's most important export markets.'

'Quite.' The civil servant nodded, a sage expression on his plump face.

'Now. Our… what shall I call it: intelligence… which we believe to be reliable… indicates that, at this very moment, five containers of counterfeit are in Lisbon docks awaiting shipment. Which is why I've come to you now.'

'Ah. And you have evidence linking the counterfeit in Japan back to Portugal?'

'Pretty well. We face difficulties of course' – *like the fact that all our evidence is illegal* – 'because of the essentially clandestine habits of counterfeiters. But we're doing our best to overcome this problem.'

'Ye-es.' The commercial secretary thoughtfully stroked his chin. 'But to the extent that the law requires evidence of counterfeiting, presumably that is provided by the counterfeit goods themselves?'

'Yes, absolutely. So—'

'So,' the commercial secretary interrupted, 'the best place to take action – I am no lawyer, of course,' he said, his hand turning outwards, with a dismissive gesture '—the best place to take action would presumably be the country where you have found them; in other words, Japan?' He sat back in his chair, pleased at the thought of shifting the scene of action elsewhere.

Silly bugger, Hamish thought, gritting his teeth, if he's not a lawyer, what the hell does he think he's doing suggesting solutions?

'Yes indeed,' Hamish said urbanely. 'But we found them here and that is why we want to take action against the cargo here. This is our most urgent concern, because we need to act swiftly to stop the current shipment getting out. Once it leaves here, it could go anywhere.'

'Ah. You don't, um, know where it might be destined for?' he asked, hopefully.

'No,' Hamish said flatly. *Concentrate the bugger's mind. No point in telling him about Holland, he'll only tell us to go and try there.*

The commercial secretary fiddled with a paperknife:

imitation Georgian, silver-plated, administrative staff for the use of. From outside came the gentle hum of Lisbon, dozing in the afternoon heat.

At last, a reluctant sigh came from behind the desk. 'So what, er, what were you hoping I might do for you?'

Hamish felt a faint stirring of hope. He leaned forward eagerly.

'If action's going to work it needs to be taken fast. That means bypassing normal procedures. The government could achieve that by opening an official investigation. I'm not in a position to persuade them to do that, but you could, by official contact at a high level.'

The diplomat looked doubtful.

'Also,' Hamish urged, 'it would enable us to overcome another, rather delicate, aspect of the problem.'

'Oh?' There was a frisson of alarm behind the desk. In the commercial secretary's experience, non-diplomats do not properly understand the concept of delicacy. *Delicate* in their mouths usually means something to be steered well clear of.

'Our investigations here have recently revealed that the counterfeiting ring includes a man thought to have a long history of smuggling, a practised criminal.'

The commercial secretary shifted uncomfortably in his chair.

'He has apparently been a difficult man to catch,' Hamish went on. 'He has been charged with criminal offences on at least two occasions but has evaded conviction. There is a strong suggestion that this is because he has, how shall I put it, links, with members of the police and/or customs. In effect, that he benefits from their protection.'

The commercial secretary's eyebrows rose. He gave his paperknife a thoughtful twirl, so that it rotated slowly like a needle in a compass.

'You are suggesting that this man has corrupted the police, and possibly the customs?'

'I'm afraid so.'

'Or, to put it from a slightly different angle, that the authorities here are corrupt?'

'Unfortunately, that would seem to follow.'

'Do you have any evidence to prove this?' His voice was flat, colourless.

'No. Evidence on a thing like this would be very difficult for us to get.'

'I see. You have no evidence.' He made it sound like an accusation of criminal neglect. He stilled the paperknife and laid it, with the precision of finality, in the centre of his blotter. He moved his discreet paunch forward in his seat, poising himself, Buddha-like, to pronounce.

'This would be an extremely – to use your word – *delicate* matter to raise,' he said crisply. 'Even with proof. Without it, without evidence of the *most compelling* kind, there is simply no way in which this embassy can go to the government here and make that sort of accusation.' There was distaste in his voice at the very prospect.

'But…' Hamish said, taken aback, '…but the point is, that *if* the allegation is true, it means that any approach we make to the police through ordinary channels is bound to fail. The *only* way we can succeed is by a special approach, through you. If, on the other hand, the allegation is untrue, no harm will have been done.'

'No harm? You are missing the point. You are asking me to associate myself, to associate the *embassy*, with a most disagreeable allegation. One which, as you yourself acknowledge, is virtually impossible to substantiate. There is simply no way that we could embark on such a course.' He raised his hands from his lap, and laid them palm down on the desk, with an air of finality.

'But surely…' Hamish pressed, '…surely you could raise it, er, diplomatically. As I say, if it turns out not to be true, no harm would be done.'

'On the contrary. It would seriously embarrass a friendly European government. Portugal, in case you have forgotten, is Britain's oldest ally. It is also one of Britain's oldest trading partners. We here in the embassy are charged with cementing that relationship, not with prejudicing it. Certainly not with making unwarranted slurs on the authorities here.'

Hamish felt dismay at the flat refusal to help. Then he felt anger. Anger against the civil service mentality, anger against himself: he had so nearly enlisted the man's support: unintentionally he had given him a chance to escape.

'Oh,' he said tersely, unable to keep his feelings out of his voice. 'I see. I had thought that you in this embassy were charged with protecting British interests.'

The man's mouth formed into a prim pout.

'That was precisely the point that I was seeking to make.'

'Surely that includes the interests of individual exporters?'

'It is the *totality* of British interests which I am charged to protect. There are wider issues at stake than the problems of a single company.'

'So you won't help us on this?'

'I am only too sorry.' Unctuously spoken, clearly untrue: he was only too relieved. 'I was, as you will be aware, trying to approach the matter in the most sympathetic possible way. I am afraid that this latest complication renders it far more difficult. Should you get hard evidence of your allegation, we would naturally review the matter.'

They looked at each other in silence for a moment, and then the commercial secretary rose to his feet. Slowly Hamish followed suit.

The commercial secretary ushered him through the door of his office, along the corridor, and down the stairs, striding vigorously along with an air of satisfaction. Something accomplished: the quiet waters of diplomatic life protected from the rough intrusion of those who failed to understand the political niceties. He came to a halt in the lobby and stuck out a stiff hand of farewell.

*

'God, it really pisses me off,' Hamish exploded, kicking again at the leg of the coffee table. 'Every damn thing we try we get baulked. It's either inefficiency, or it's some bloody technicality, and now its corruption. The bloody embassy's the last straw. They're supposed to bloody well help, who do they think pays their bloody salaries? Instead of which all they do is sit on their arse for fear of rocking the bloody boat.'

A corner of Jo's mouth twitched inscrutably.

'We've tried *everything*,' he said, standing in the middle of the floor, looking at her, wide-eyed, appealing to her to agree with him. 'And we're so *close*. But once that stuff goes we'll lose it, I can just see it happening. It'll go halfway across the world and we'll lose it.'

'Probably,' she said, coolly.

'Oh Christ,' he sighed, sinking tiredly into a chair. 'We've spent a fucking fortune on this. And damn-all result to show for it. I tell you, when your next bill hits my desk the Finance Department's going to go ape. To say nothing of what happens if five containers of fake end up in Japan.'

She stared at him, green eyes fathomless.

'I'll probably be out of a job,' he muttered.

'Well then,' she said lightly, 'you can always go back to the Bar. Back to life in an ivory tower. At least no one's going to ask you to break the law there.'

He smiled ruefully at her. 'That's the least of my worries.'

'Oh?' she probed. 'That technical surveillance on his phone… it doesn't worry you any more?'

He stared back at her. 'No,' he said, in a tone of surprise. 'No. I hadn't thought of it lately, but… no, oddly enough, it doesn't.'

'Hmm. I wonder why.'

He laughed mirthlessly. 'Probably because it worked. It's about the only thing in this country that has.'

'Yeah. And maybe because the worries you had never materialised.'

'Maybe.'

'You see,' she said, gently, softly, 'I told you it'd be all right.'

He looked sharply at her to see if she was trying to score a point. Saw only calmness. Sympathy, even.

'Yes, you did,' he admitted. 'Okay, you were right.'

She toyed with her glass of orange juice, pushing it idly to and fro on the arm of her chair.

'Remember when you first came out here? And I got pissed off because you didn't trust me?'

He grunted, thoughts elsewhere, still wrestling with the problem he faced.

'D'you trust me now?' she asked, looking levelly into his eyes.

He paused, surprised by the direct question. 'Well… yes, of course I do,' he said, automatically.

She said nothing, tightened her lips at the politeness in his tone. He looked at her in silence, looking at her neat, well-trimmed figure, the straightness of her back, her alertness, her poise. Her cool eyes, smooth freckled face. As he did so he realised his words were a simple truth, that he trusted her competence, trusted her drive towards a goal.

'Yes,' he said again, more deliberately, more slowly. 'Yes, I do.'

'Good,' she said. She looked down into her lap, thoughtfully swirling her glass. 'So, tell me. If I thought of a way to get this stuff seized, would you back it?'

'Christ, you haven't, have you?' he asked eagerly.

'You haven't answered the question.'

'Try me.'

She looked at him. This wasn't how she'd planned to tell him. She'd planned to relax him first, maybe a swim, maybe a few more drinks, maybe dinner; maybe more. Soften him up, put him in a good mood.

She took a deep breath. Relaxation could come later. The moment to tell him was now.

CHAPTER 41

'Oh God,' Hamish said five minutes later, resignation in his voice. 'I should have known any idea of yours would be illegal.'

'Well, all the legal ideas haven't worked too well, have they?' she said.

'You'll get me disbarred.' he grumbled.

'That'd be doing you a favour,' she murmured.

'Look,' he said, voice rising in protest, 'what is this constant anti-lawyer stuff?'

She shrugged, holding herself in, wanting to avoid an argument.

'Suppose you just like an easy target,' he said grumpily.

'That's rich, coming from you lot!' she flared; it was her special pride that she would take on any target, however difficult. 'You *really* want to know what pisses me off? It's the way you lot run and hide behind the law when life gets too difficult. Like hiding behind nanny's skirt.'

'Bollocks! You think it's easy, trying to think of a legal solution? We've been trying for the last fortnight and it's bloody well impossible!'

'Well, do something about it, then!' she snapped, and turned away toward the window.

They sank into uneasy silence. He unable to think of an answer, she staring angrily out at the heat-hazed urban landscape. She cursed herself for provoking him. It was the last thing she wanted to do right now.

After a moment she sighed heavily.

'I...' she started, trying to force the words out; drying up. She took a deep breath. 'Look, I'm sorry,' she said, surprising him with the uncharacteristic apology.

'I just wish to God we could find some other way,' he said.

'There isn't one,' she said.

She let the silence hang in the air. 'Look,' she urged softly, 'at least we can get Antonio started. It doesn't commit us to anything, he doesn't know what my plan is. Neither does Gonçalves, for that matter.'

He grunted noncommittally.

'Time's short,' she said, looking pointedly at her watch.

As if to underline her point, the telephone rang. She picked it up, listened for a moment. Covered the mouthpiece with her hand and looked at Hamish.

'It's Gonçalves,' she whispered. 'The containers were loaded this morning. The ship sails in three days' time.'

'Oh shit.' He sank his head and clasped his forehead.

'So what do we do?' she persisted. 'Does he send Antonio out or not?'

He gave her an agonised look.

'Yes or no?' she hissed.

'Oh, Christ.' He sat back in his chair, let out a deep breath. Stared at her wide-eyed. 'All right then. Yes.'

Oh God, he thought, what the hell am I getting into?

*

Antonio sat in front of Gonçalves' rosewood desk, listening to his instructions, watching his boss light up a cheroot from the box on his desk. He knew immediately that the part

214

would suit him. He had always fancied himself as an export-import agent, an international wheeler and dealer, moving commodities around the world. Diamonds here, cement there, flak jackets, whisky, cigarettes.

He was somewhat put out when Gonçalves told him he would be dealing in waste cardboard.

'Why waste cardboard? Why not machine parts?' *I would like to act the part of an arms dealer, everyone knows machine parts are a cover for arms.*

'Machine parts,' said Gonçalves with a sigh, 'are heavy. So is whisky, so is wine. Shipping is paid for by the kilo. Do you want our clients to pay for you to indulge your fantasies?'

'Cardboard is heavy too, so why—'

'Not the way you will pack it, they will be empty cardboard boxes.'

'But surely—'

'Look,' Gonçalves said, raising his voice, 'all we need to do is to ship a container, it could be empty for all we care. But someone will raise an eyebrow if we simply hire a container and ship it empty, so we need a cargo. Empty boxes are what your cargo will be, so that is what you deal in. Also, my cousin Alfonso is in the waste disposal business, it will be easy for him to supply us with as much as we need.'

'Very well,' Antonio said with a sigh.

*

Three hours later Antonio was starting to get disillusioned with his image as an international dealer. If international dealing consisted of moving cargo from one country to another then you could keep it, he thought. He had been to four offices, asked a variety of questions at each; boring questions about freight rates, insurance, shipping schedules. Got a variety of answers from clerks, made the same tentative freight booking with each.

At least, he thought, as he walked through the door of Fremar's office, now I know the process, know the questions to ask.

He leaned on the varnished pine counter and waited as a girl came towards him, her upraised eyebrows asking what he wanted. His spirits rose. This was more like it. A girl with a smooth oval face, somewhat plain features perhaps, but smooth velvety skin, big dark eyes, long glossy dark hair, soft arms. And a spectacularly buxom figure. Perhaps a little short, but with a figure like that – or what he could see of it above the counter – who cared? As she leaned across the counter, Antonio had difficulty keeping his mind on the booking he was supposed to be making.

Yes, they could provide a container. Yes, they could send it to his address tomorrow morning, she said, licking her lips with a coquettish tongue. Yes of course, she would arrange all the paperwork. Personally, she said.

Paperwork. It was Antonio's cue. Looking at her had almost made him forget this important detail. He gazed deeply into her big dark eyes as he talked about his fascination with paperwork, his love of the shipping business. He would love to learn more about it from her. Perhaps she could give him a demonstration of how the documentation was handled? If she showed him, personally, perhaps afterwards they could – they could have a little drink?

'Of course,' she said, smiling softly. She would make his shipment a special priority. If he liked, he could come with her down to the docks that evening, and she could show him how everything was, ah… handled?

In ten minutes, Antonio's enthusiasm about shipping documents had reached a level he would never have predicted.

*

'So what now?' Hamish asked. He was lying on the bed, staring blankly up at the ceiling. She was perched on the window ledge, looking down at him.

'Today, nothing. We wait for Antonio. If I do it, I'll do it tomorrow night.'

'You? By yourself?'

She shrugged. 'Who else can I use? Gonçalves and his lot aren't bad, but I wouldn't risk bringing them in on something like this.'

'What about your ex-SAS lot?'

'They're only here for the surveillance.' She shifted uneasily from one buttock to the other. 'I shouldn't tell you this, I'm not supposed to let on to our clients, but they're not on our regular staff. They get brought in specially on surveillance jobs. If I involve them, Arthur'll skin me.'

'Ah,' he murmured.

'Plus,' she said, 'if I don't have anyone else it makes it easier for you to say you didn't know.'

'But I do know,' he said quietly.

He stared out of the window, high up over the red-tiled roofs of Lisbon, across to the bay. Unseeing, his mind not in Portugal but in Devon, in the green undulating countryside in which he'd grown up.

'When I was young,' he said slowly, 'we had an old boy on the farm. Used to take me ferreting sometimes. For rabbits. Ever done that?'

'Nope. I'm a city girl.'

'There's a wood behind the house. Mass of brambles on the edge. There were lots of bunnies there then. Still are.' He turned and looked at her. 'Once or twice he took me poaching. In the neighbouring valley, at night. Just for the hell of it.'

'You? Poaching? A lawyer?'

'I wasn't a lawyer then. I was fifteen.' He smiled nostalgically. 'Old Will had done a bit of poaching in his youth. He told me it was always easier with two. Quicker to peg out the nets, quicker to pull the rabbits out, quicker to pack up and be away. He told me he'd almost got caught once, doing it on his own.'

'Sounds a good bloke. Pity he's not here.'

'He died ten years ago.'

He lapsed into silence, remembering. Thinking of the rabbits they'd got, of the skins he'd cured. Even now there was one on the bedside table in his flat in London.

'And – confession time – it's not the only time I've done a bit of poaching. Went up to Scotland, fishing, with an old chum, when we were about nineteen. And I wasn't a lawyer then either, before you ask.'

Jo looked at him wide-eyed. 'Did I hear you right?'

'Mmmm.' Hamish paused. 'It'd be an awful shame if it didn't work because you didn't have anyone with you,' he mused.

She looked at him in silence, in surprise.

He went and sat on the edge of the bed. 'Someone to help you peg out nets, as it were.'

'You're not suggesting that you...?'

'Well, it *is* the only chance we'll get. And it's either that or hide behind your skirts.' He grinned. 'And I'm damned if I'm having you shove that down my throat.'

'Well, well,' she smiled. 'So lawyers have some pride after all.'

A remote look crossed his face, like the shadow of a cloud passing over a field. 'There's just one condition,' he said. 'Just drop this lawyer crap, will you?'

CHAPTER 42

The dark of the tarmac beside him merged into the dark of the night sky overhead, a fragile dark at the mercy of the faint orange of the lights of Lisbon, a dark pierced with small points of light from the ships waiting silently by the quayside a hundred yards away to his right. He crouched on the tarmac, seeking some small reassurance from the brick wall rubbing against his left shoulder, but finding instead that its solidity simply emphasised the emptiness of dark space stretching away to his other side, simply increased his unease.

Memory flicked in his mind, of the times in his youth when he had been out in the countryside, going after rabbits. Sometimes with Old Will. Sometimes by himself at night, a gun in one hand and a torch in the other, a torch which he could switch on to stab the darkness and skewer a rabbit with light, skewer it so that it was helpless however much it leaped and twisted and ran. He shivered, feeling that he knew what it was like to be a rabbit, thinking of the coming of a man with a torch.

Five yards in front of him Jo crouched by the front door of Fremar's office building, just visible to him. She had been there two minutes, her movements imperceptible to him, each second seeming to him like an hour. At last she turned, beckoned with a pale hand, picked up the bag she was carrying, stood up and pushed the door gently open.

He pushed himself slowly to his feet and followed her.

When the door was shut behind them she turned on the torch, swinging its white circle of light from left to right and back. Ahead it picked out the horizontal stripes of a stairway. 'First floor,' Antonio had said. 'The room on the left as you come up the stairs.' When she reached the door she slid a wire tracer around the frame, testing for alarms as she had at the front door; then crouched by the lock. Another minute, the door was unlocked, she turned off the torch and pushed it open. They stood for a moment, waiting for their eyes to get used to the dark. Blacker here than outside, the only light a faint dark glow from the night sky coming in through windows.

Two windows, Antonio had said. 'Okay,' she whispered.

She picked her way slowly forward, gently, cautiously, in the way a blindfolded person would, her feet and hands guiding her path past unseen desks and chairs and filing cabinets, her poised figure dimly outlined against the window she was heading for. He followed in her path, his bundle in his hand, keeping close enough to pass her what she needed. She stopped and her hands went out to explore the desk, starting at the edge, stroking their way slowly across its surface, caressing each strange shape in turn. The hard smoothness of a coffee mug, the metal confetti of a pile of paper clips, the crinkling crispness of a pile of papers. She warily cleared the obstacles aside to give her a clear surface; her hands memorising them all, their location on the desk, and the amount she had to move each of them.

She lifted herself up, gingerly standing upright on the small space she had made, stretched out her hands and explored the rim of the window. He held out the reel of tape. As she tore off the length she needed, the tape screeching through the silence of the room as it stripped from the reel.

Her hands came back to him for the soft roll of material. He passed it to her with its thin strip of wood uppermost. Deftly, her hands feeling their way like a garage mechanic's, she taped the wood to the wall, then loosened the strings so that the blackout material fell softly down into the window space. Felt out with her hands to check it was in place, then taped all round the edges of the fabric.

Slowly she got down from her perch, retreated to the centre of the room; advanced towards the second window.

At the end of twenty minutes the room was pitch black, a darkroom, not even the faintest of glows coming in from outside.

She took a deep breath and switched on the torch. Cupped it cautiously with her hand, checked her work in case she had left any chinks. Added a little more tape in one place, checked one last time, was satisfied. Looked for the light switch and turned it on.

They stood blinking in the harsh white light; stock still for a moment, looking around as the contents of the room flashed onto their retinas.

Three hardwood desks. Two of them in front of the windows she had blacked out. She went straight to them and repositioned the items she had moved, drawing on the memory of how her hands had moved.

Only then did she turn to survey the rest of the room, the bank of four-drawer grey filing cabinets running round two sides of the room, the dark military-green metal cupboard standing in the middle of the floor, the battered Formica flooring.

She peered at the filing cabinets, smiling maliciously at their mass-produced locks. Rummaged in her bag, hovered in front of the first cabinet: a hummingbird dipping a sharp metal proboscis into the flower of the lock. Thirty seconds later there was a click as the lock opened.

It was the best part of an hour before they found the papers they were looking for. 'Score one,' she murmured, pulling out an invoice from a trucking company.

Her fingernails riffled again, paused, slid out the paper they had come for. She gave a quiet sigh of satisfaction as she held it up. A Bill of Lading, typed out in triplicate, each sheet stamped by the forwarding agent, each sheet signed by the captain of the ship to acknowledge the loading of the containers. Each sheet listing the container numbers. 'Rotterdam in transit.' And the destination: Japan.

*

The guard walked along the edge of the dock, looking up at the metal cliffs rising over his head, absorbing the lights on the gangways, the gurgling of the sea, the quiet creaks and hums of the ships. Flashing his torch ahead of him to see the bollards and hawsers, looking for the railway lines on which the cranes ran, checking for obstacles in his path. Checking for anything unusual. Flashing it onto the sides of the ships, and then away out through the emptiness of the dockside.

He too glanced briefly up at the lights of Lisbon, the orange at the edge of the sky, glowing above the roofs of the dockyard offices, the darkened offices a hundred yards away on his left.

*

Rubber bands, pencils, biros, staples, paper clips. Letter heads, invoice forms, packing lists. She grunted to Hamish in impatience as they hunted through the stationery cupboard. TIR carnets, customs forms, petty cash vouchers, Bills of Lading.

She pounced on the stack of blank forms, pulled one out and checked it with the one they had left on the table. Flashed him a tense smile and turned to survey the typewriters.

She pulled a sheet of blank paper out of the cupboard, rolled it into the nearest typewriter, put her finger on the switch to turn it on. The typewriter gave out a low hum. She looked up at Hamish. 'Hold your breath,' she murmured. She typed a few words, getting the feel of the keyboard, and there was a series of sharp smacks as the key hit the paper, breaking the clandestine silence of the room.

She felt him wince beside her and frowned at him. 'Pass the form,' she muttered, holding out her hand.

She pulled out the blank paper, handed it to Hamish, fed in the blank Bill of Lading, and started to type; slowly, deliberately, concentrating over each letter. Each time she touched the keyboard a sound came like a pistol shot, making Hamish wince and clench his nails into the palm of his hand.

*

The far end of the dock was emptier, there were few ships here, little for the guard to check on. He paused, gazing out at the dark of the sea, before turning and starting the landward side of his circuit, the side that would take him down through the warehouses and office buildings.

As he went the guard muttered at the number of containers left out in the open, the lorries parked in the dark. Why could they not be secured in the warehouses? That was what warehouses were for. Warehouses are better security, he said to himself. He shone the torch onto his watch. Quarter to three. Nearly time for a coffee. Do the offices and then coffee.

As he turned the corner of the warehouse his glance flicked out to the pinpoints of light in the ships, still thinking about coffee. His mind slightly off his job, it took him a moment to realise there was a faint noise coming from somewhere. He stopped, paused, moved his head from one side to the other as he tried to identify where the noise was coming from

*

'Shit,' Hamish whispered, 'can't you quieten that thing a bit?'

Her hand, hovering over a key, hesitated, wavered, came down to rest on the desk. 'For Christ's sake,' she snapped, 'you nearly made me hit the wrong key. Stop bloody standing over me. If you're going to fret, go do it in the corridor.'

He pursed his lips and frowned.

'Go on,' she said. 'I can't handle you standing there.'

He exhaled tensely as he strode over to the door and pushed it open. Let it swing shut and sat in the darkened stairwell on a cold step. Flinched as another smack of metal on paper sounded through the door, pushed himself off the stair and padded downstairs.

*

Her finger was poised over the keyboard as Hamish pushed open the door. 'Quiet!' he hissed.

She looked up, eyes flaring at him. She was concentrating hard, in the middle of typing the all-important container numbers: two done, one more to go.

'Guard,' he whispered, 'there's a guard outside.'

'How close?'

'About fifty yards.'

'Did you shut the front door?'

225

'Yeah.'

Wordlessly she stood up, switched off the typewriter. Shut the door of the stationery cupboard, shut the drawers of the filing cabinets, hid the Bill of Lading she was copying, put the cover on the typewriter. Switched off the lights, shut the door. Pulled a small, thin steel plate out of the bag Hamish had brought, placed it carefully into the gap between the door-lock and the latch, then thrust two wedges into the gap between the edge of the door and the frame, one above the lock, one below.

*

This was the office block the noise had come from, the guard thought – he paused and looked up. There was no noise now, and it was dark. Nevertheless…

He went to the entrance and tried the door. Locked. He rattled it softly, testing.

He hesitated.

On the one hand, coffee was calling. On the other hand, this was his job. He pulled out a bunch of keys. Fiddled, selected a key and opened the lock. Took slow steps across the hall, flicked a light switch. Walked slowly up the stairs. Paused on the landing; walked down the short corridor towards the office.

Inside the door, Hamish had one hand on each of the two wedges, leaning against them, his feet firmly planted on the floor. Just in case. He heard the metallic jingle of the keys outside the door as the guard selected a key. Heard the key scratch its way into the lock, eighteen inches from his head. Heard the key try to turn; heard it blocked by the already unlocked bolt; heard it turn the other way, now blocked by the bolt that was held in place by Jo's steel plate. He sensed the thudding of his own heart, the warmth of Jo's body next to his, both silently holding their breath.

He heard a grunt of puzzlement from outside. Hamish heard the key being withdrawn. Then another key being inserted. More scratching.

The door handle turned. Hamish sensed the thudding of his heart as he tightened his muscles, letting the strength flow upwards from feet through legs, torso, arms, to the wedges, focusing his mind on the edge of the door.

The door stayed solid. There was another puzzled grunt from the landing.

A pause.

A shuffle away along the corridor, back towards the stairs.

*

They waited twenty minutes before turning the light on again. Their eyes stretched wide as they looked at each other.

Slowly she got out the Bill of Lading. Gritted her teeth and sat down again. Looked at Hamish again, no irritation in her now, eyes pleading for his support. He felt a surge of affection, smiled and padded wordlessly out and down the stairs.

*

She hissed from the landing two minutes later. When he rejoined her, the new Bill of Lading was lying on the table. Destination Rotterdam, full stop. No transit. Almost a perfect copy, just waiting for the final touch.

They ferreted on the desks among the selection of rubber stamps, trying them all on a piece of scrap paper until they found the right one.

Then the hard part, the signature of the ship's captain on loading.

227

Jo practised for quarter of an hour until she decided she'd got it right, pulled the new Bill of Lading in front of her and looked up at Hamish.

'Here goes,' she murmured. The biro in her hand slowly traced its way across the paper.

So, this is forgery, Hamish thought as he watched her. No longer a heading in a textbook, a history traced through centuries of English law, of ancient felonies, Victorian rigour, twentieth-century statutes. No longer the accumulated pronouncements of ageing judges in flowing robes and grey wigs.

Forgery is an office after dark, with your nerves on edge. Forgery is a girl, her face in shadow from the hair falling over her cheek, screwing up her forehead in concentration as she tries to copy a signature. Forgery is something that you could have stopped at any time over the last twenty-four hours; could still stop, simply, easily, just by saying, 'Wait, we can't do this.'

He stood in silence as he watched her sign.

*

'Jesus,' Hamish said, wiping his forehead. He shut the door of their hotel room behind him, dumped the bag on the floor and stood looking at her. Jo took a shallow breath, her lips just apart. Words drained out of his brain. Washed out in a flood of fear, relief, adrenalin, desire, in the tightening of his muscles around her, in the urgent need of flesh for flesh.

Twenty minutes later, drenched with sweat, she put her hand to his forehead and stroked his hair.

They lay in peace. No words. For the first time, none were needed.

CHAPTER 43

Six days later, Hamish and Willem returned to the Rotterdam customs office. Molijn met them at the entrance and took them up to his room. Roovers was standing by the window, looking out, watching container ships moving through the docks. Contemplating how many of them were carrying contraband.

He turned, his mind only half on the visitors; fake whisky was a minor problem to him. *Not for me to worry about these corporations, the men who work for them probably get paid three times my salary, why lose sleep on their account.*

'Back again?' he said.

'Ja,' Willem replied, with an easy smile. 'We think, maybe you do not get enough whisky salesmen in your office.'

Roovers grunted; his eyebrows lifted sardonically.

'We have brought you some more samples,' Willem said. Roovers peered questioningly at Willem's briefcase. 'Sixty thousand of them.'

'God alive. Sixty thousand bottles?'

'Exactly.' Willem sat back in his chair and waved a spread hand towards Hamish: an M.C. introducing his star turn.

Hamish was suddenly conscious of Molijn and Roovers swivelling their gaze towards him. *Come on, buck up,* he said to himself, *this is you on stage.*

'Yes. Our investigators have made some progress.' He bent down, picked up his briefcase, put it on the table, opened it and pulled out an envelope.

'These are the photographs of containers at Lisbon docks.' He pushed them across the table, dull red-oxide of the containers on the grey of the tarmac. There were close-ups showing the numbers painted on the back of each container.

'These containers are now in Rotterdam,' he said.

Roovers picked up the photographs again, flipped through them and frowned. 'You have evidence of what is inside them?'

'We haven't seen inside them ourselves, naturally.'

'But you have evidence from an informant, then?' Roovers persisted. 'An informant who has seen them loaded?'

'It was an informant who started the investigation. From him we got to the counterfeiters, surveillance on them led us to the containers.'

'Can you prove what's in them? Can you prove where they came from?'

'We've located their factory, we followed the containers from there.'

'You have seen inside the factory?'

'Well, no—'

'So you don't know, for sure, what's in them. You have only a suspicion?' He sat back in his chair, stuck his legs out in front of him, and folded his arms in a gesture of rejection. 'So what can we do?' Nothing, his voice implied.

Willem turned in his chair and looked at Hamish. 'Have your investigators seen the shipping papers? Do you know what the cargo is declared as?'

Hamish turned to Willem, unwilling to face Roovers's direct stare.

'Our investigator has a man in the docks,' he said,

answering obliquely, needing to gear himself up before coming out with a direct answer. 'His information is that it is a cargo of alcohol.'

'So,' Willem said to Roovers, 'if it is alcohol, and if it is being imported here you would inspect them as routine.'

'If,' Roovers said.

'So did he see the papers?' Willem repeated.

'Yes,' he said, looking earnestly at Willem. 'Yes. He saw the papers.' He turned his face towards Roovers and Molijn. 'They are for Holland.'

*

What if, Hamish thought, what if the Portuguese checked the Bill of Lading before sending it off? What if they re-inserted the words we left out? What if the customs make enquiries here and turn up a photocopy of the real one? What if someone realises they've got a forgery? Oh God, why did I agree to Jo's idea?

As he sat in the shadowy Indonesian restaurant where Willem had taken him for lunch, a corner of his mind started to hope that the customs would be unable to find the cargo. Willem took his edginess simply as the tension of waiting, tried to buoy him up with cheerful conversation, but Hamish's anxiety stopped him responding, made him pick half-heartedly at his food.

After lunch Willem took Hamish back to his office, installed him in a spare room with a paper, a stack of *Time* magazines and a cup of coffee, and went away to get on with some other work until the customs rang.

The room was small, not quite square. It had a desk, a telephone, a chair, a window opposite the door, four white-washed walls and an oatmeal carpet. There were no pictures on the walls, nothing to relieve its flat neutrality. There was a dead feeling to the room, a microscopic layer of dust, a stale feeling of not having been used for six months. It had an atmosphere of being set apart from life, as if nothing ever happened in it and never would.

He stared blankly out of the window at a back yard, enclosed by the backs of three other buildings, stucco walls in an unlovely mid-grey. No one came into it, nothing moved but a torn paper bag which fluttered occasionally as the wind found its way into this deserted space; it could have been on a dead planet.

Hamish thought of the past few weeks, in which the case had been a game, an abstract puzzle against a shadowy opposition never clearly seen. Now his opponents' main piece had come to within a mile or two from where he was sitting. Shortly it would be brought into view. *If this goes wrong, I could lose my whole professional career. You idiot, what have you done?* Now he was impotent, nothing he did would have any more significance than the fluttering of the scrap of paper in the yard. For two hours he sat staring blankly out of the window; his mind empty, drained, waiting.

It was five o'clock before Molijn telephoned Willem's office.

'We have taken a sample from the consignment,' he said. 'It looks genuine to us. We would like you to confirm this.'

∗

Hamish's throat tightened as he saw the bottle in Roovers's hand.

This is it. Sudden stage fright. *What if I can't tell the difference?* He saw them looking at him, expecting him to pronounce judgment, felt afraid to take the bottle.

Christ, it looks so good, he thought as Roovers held the bottle out. *What if they've put a layer of genuine into the containers in case of an inspection? The oldest trick in the world and we've fallen for it*, he thought in a moment of panic.

That cap, it could be the real thing. Anxiously he shifted his gaze down to the label, peered closely at the details of the printing, conscious of the three men looking at him, waiting for him to speak: the expressionless faces of Molijn and Roovers, Willem's anxious frown.

Christ, wake up. Must be nerves, making you stupid. Wordlessly he handed the bottle to Willem, fumbled in his pocket for the label Jo had nicked from Cardoso, pulled it out, put it side by side with the label on the bottle.

Let out a long breath and smiled up at them with relief.

*

'He is not a happy man, the forwarding agent,' Roovers said.

'Oh?'

'He has a telex from his associates in Lisbon, telling him to ship the whisky to Tokyo. He has already booked space on a ship that goes next week. He says the whisky is only in transit.'

'Oh.'

'But we tell him the papers are not in order. The Bill of Lading says nothing about the goods being in transit, nor does the T-form. So we make a temporary seizure. He cannot understand it, he says someone in Lisbon must have made a mistake. That is what he says.' Roovers shrugged. 'Maybe he tells the truth. So,' he said, turning to Hamish, 'the sooner you take action in Portugal, the better for you.'

CHAPTER 44

Right, Hamish thought as he strode into the embassy, this time you can bloody well get your finger out.

Tersely he told the commercial secretary about the seizure in Rotterdam of five containers of fake whisky; about the action his lawyers wanted to take, about the help they needed from the embassy.

The commercial secretary saw the look in Hamish's eye, took refuge in the knowledge that government employees, albeit of a foreign country, had seen fit to intervene; bowed to the inevitable and promised the embassy's full support.

That afternoon, Hamish and Vasconcelos were admitted to the offices of the police, to meet a stony-faced colonel. He was clearly aware that political pressure was being put on him and his men, and was clearly not happy about being told what to do. Hamish passed over the investigators' surveillance report. The colonel read it impassively, then picked up his phone, barked into it, and started to leave the office. Hamish moved as if to follow him, extremely keen to accompany him. He was brusquely informed that civilians and their lawyers had no place on a police operation.

*

A convoy of three cars left Lisbon, heading down the highway into the countryside. They slowed at the faded signpost shown in the report, turned onto the sandy track towards the

factory. Winding through the cork trees, over the bumps and
potholes, the dust kicked up by their tyres, drifting away
through the trees. The track led down to a shallow bowl,
where it petered out onto an open patch of ground, con-
creted over to make a farmyard. In the centre of the yard
stood a large barn, crudely made of breeze block. Unpainted,
dirty. Around the barn lay old bits of rusting agricultural machinery, a few bales of straw, broken wooden pallets, and
scatterings of sand. At the front of the barn were two large
sliding doors, corrugated iron, reaching up to the eaves.

They came to a standstill, got out of the cars and stood
for a moment, as the dust from their wheels drifted on ahead
of them and settled in the patches of scrub at the edge of the
bowl. The wind moaned through the fir trees that sur-
rounded the yard. A goat pushed itself to its feet, bleated
complainingly at their intrusion, and ambled off round the
side of the building.

A small single door was set into one of the big sliding
doors. It was locked shut. An officer snapped a command in
Portuguese and a policeman ran forward with a bolt-cutter,
snapped off the padlock in the centre of the door.

Three policemen heaved at the door and it rumbled
slowly to one side, an expanding rectangle of sunlight slicing
across the floor in its wake. The officer walked forward,
paused on the threshold, expecting movement from inside
the building. But they saw none, heard nothing; looked into
the interior as if into a tomb freshly uncovered to the light of
day.

The officer frowned. The barn was big, but almost empty.
In its middle stood a tractor, an old Massey Ferguson, battle-
ship-grey blotched with rust. At one end of the building was
a pile of hay, straggling across the dirty concrete floor. Half

a dozen old tyres of different sizes leaned against the back wall. A pile of discarded wooden crates were in a jumbled heap in one corner.

Of whisky, there was no sign.

*

Hamish was pacing the floor at Vasconcelos' office when the call came, summoning them back to the police building. When they got there, they were ushered into an interview room, a dull brown space with cracked lino flooring, Formica-topped table, red, plastic chairs. They waited in silence for five minutes, until the colonel marched in, a thin sheaf of papers in his hand. He gave Hamish an unfriendly look.

'That building we went to' – he paused accusingly – 'at your request… it was empty. No whisky. Nothing.'

'What? But—' Hamish started.

The colonel held up his hand to silence him. 'This is not surprising. We have made enquiries at the port of Lisbon, regarding the cargo which was seized yesterday by the Customs Police of Rotterdam.' His face settled into a supercilious expression.

Hamish said nothing.

'The transport company has co-operated thoroughly with our enquiries and has made all its papers available to us,' the officer went on, patting the papers in front of him.

Oh God, thought Hamish, here it comes. They've worked out that the Bill of Lading was forged, they've worked out what we did.

'It appears that the cargo was imported into Lisbon last week,' the officer said. 'I have here copies of the relevant transport papers. You may look at them.' He pushed them across to Vasconcelos with an ironic sideways glance at Hamish.

Hamish blinked.

He was unable to absorb what he had heard, felt his mind stick. 'Imported?' he stammered, 'but—'

'Yes, imported,' the colonel repeated. 'From Brazil. Here in Lisbon they were in transit.'

'But that's not possible,' was all Hamish could think to say. 'They must have come from that factory—'

The officer waved his hand dismissively. 'There was no factory. That was clear the moment we arrived there. Today has been a waste of our time.'

'But—'

'Please do not waste our time again. If you wish to make criminal complaints in the future, please make sure that they are based on fact, not fiction.'

The colonel stood. Vasconcelos, who had been looking through the papers, had a sad expression on his face. Rising, he made an elaborate apology in Portuguese, and ushered Hamish from the room.

*

But I saw the bloody papers! Hamish wanted to say. I saw them in the office and there wasn't anything about Brazil there, they've cooked it all up, it's a forgery!

As he thought about it, his initial bewilderment changed to a steadily growing outrage, made worse by the frustration of being unable to speak what he knew to be the truth, unable to speak of the shipping papers he had seen in the dockyard at midnight. Unable to challenge the policeman, unable to confide in his lawyer. Unable to confide in any person but one.

He declined his lawyer's lukewarm offer of a lift and took a taxi back to the Sheraton, staring gloomily out of the taxi window, irritated by the foreignness of everything he saw, wishing he was back in England.

When he arrived, he jumped from the taxi, dumped a sheaf of escudo notes in the taxi- driver's palm and hurried through the glass doors into the lobby of the hotel.

The key for her room was not at the desk and he hurried upstairs. No answer when he banged on the door.

No message from her when he checked back at the desk.

He cursed under his breath in irritation, his frustration mounting. It was only after a couple of minutes that he remembered that she had nothing to do that day, her part was already played out, that she would be killing time waiting for him.

There she was, lying on a sunbed on the other side of the pool enclosure, next to the vine that straggled up the wall, sunglasses over her eyes, paperback in hand, drink at her elbow. He saw her flick idly at a fly that had settled on her thigh, lethargically turn a page.

'Hi,' she said, smiling, glad to see him. 'Success?'

'No such luck. Complete bloody disaster.'

'Oh God.' She sat up. '*Why?*

'Upstairs.'

They went up in the lift, standing mutely beside an ageing American woman whose suntan was falling into dry wrinkles. As soon as they were in her room he burst into his account of the fiasco, pacing fretfully to and fro in front of the dressing table. She sat with arms folded as she listened to Hamish describing the colonel and what he'd said.

'What a bugger,' she said, thoughtfully. She wrinkled her nose. 'Neat trick, though,' she added, in reluctant admiration, 'pretending it's come from Brazil.'

'Neat trick?' he snorted. 'What d'you mean, neat trick? They're bloody *forgeries*! His voice rose to a falsetto. 'It's outrageous!'

Jo looked at him in solemnity for a second, cocked her head on one side with a little questioning frown; then the corner of her mouth twitched, and she laughed.

'What's so bloody funny?' he snapped.

'You,' she said. 'If you could see yourself.'

'What the hell do you mean?' he said, irritated by her lack of sympathy.

'Oh, come on. Bit ironic, isn't it? We forge papers to set the police onto them, they forge papers back to get themselves out of trouble. Score fifteen all. Well, thirty-fifteen to them, I suppose.'

'But damn it, it's perverting the course of justice, it's—'

'Oh, *Hamish*, perverting the course of justice, my arse. You sound like a lawyer.'

'I am a—'

'Oh, give it a rest!' She flicked her hand away, dismissively. 'Okay, it's a pain, but there's no use getting hot under the collar. It's a setback, but you can either sit around whingeing about it or you can find a way to stuff them. Which are you going to do?'

'Setback? It's a bloody disaster! And how can we stuff them? We don't even know where the buggers are right now.'

'Well, we'll just have to find them, won't we?'

'Oh? How? Come to that, why didn't this team of yours check up on this bloody factory? We're paying your outfit a fucking fortune, and just at the crucial moment you lose them.'

She pushed herself off her perch and stood to face him.

'We did bloody check it! We followed the containers to the docks, then we took the surveillance off. At your request, may I remind you. To save the fees. What the hell else do you expect us to do, walk inside and ask what they've got in there?'

He opened his mouth to speak but she carried on, glaring angrily at him.

'Don't bloody well take it out on me,' she said, raising her voice. 'All along it's been me and my *outfit,* as you call it, that's produced the answers. Not you and your precious bloody legal systems, they've been less use than a kick up the arse. Without us you'd have got nowhere.'

He gazed back at her for a moment before his eyes slid sideways in defeat. He sat heavily on the bed; shoulders slumped.

'Okay,' he said with a sigh. 'So where do we go now?'

'Not where,' she said. 'Who.'

CHAPTER 45

Another rustic village. Dust from the fields drifting over the tarmac, off-white paint flaking from the walls of the houses. They drove slowly to the end of the road, parked, walked round to the annex at the back. Knocked on the door and waited. After a moment the door opened, and a portly figure stood there. He gaped at them in surprise.

'Mr. Robinson,' Hamish said. 'Or should I call you Mr. Seymour?'

Seymour stood rigid. He felt as if he was about to have a heart attack.

'We'd very much like a chat,' Hamish went on. 'I think you might prefer one in private. Can we come in?'

Numbly, Seymour let them into a small sitting room, sparsely furnished, untidy.

'So,' Hamish said smoothly, 'I've been wondering what you've been up to since we last met.'

'Have you indeed! That's pretty rich,' Seymour said, frantically trying to think up his story. 'There I was, going all the way to England to try and help you out, and all you did was shop me to the police. So why are you bothering me now?'

'Well, you had some information before – or so you said – so I guess you've still got it.'

'Oh? You mean you want to do a deal?'

'Sort of. But before we get to that… how come you're here?'

'I just thought I'd retire here,' Seymour said. 'Lots of Brits do. Sun, sea, nice vino…'

'Oh really? Nothing to do with whisky, then?'

'No, of course not! I haven't had anything to do with that since before we, er, met in London.'

Hamish turned towards Jo, who had been silently staring at Seymour.

'So,' she said, 'what can you tell us about Raul Cardoso?'

Seymour shifted slightly. 'Not much.' He put his hand to his forehead. 'There was a Raul… what did you say his last name was? When I was in Manila. He introduced me to the people I was going to tell you about. Haven't seen him for a while now.'

'Or had any contact with him?'

'No. No, of course not.'

'So you didn't know he lives in the next village?'

'Er, no, no. Does he?'

'And you haven't spoken to him since… when? Three, four months ago?'

'Yes, that'd be about right.'

The corner of Jo's mouth twitched. 'No it fucking wouldn't. You were on the phone to him just the other day.'

'No, no, that's nonsense!'

Jo didn't say a word. Got out her tape-recorder, pressed play.

> *'Hello, Raul,' a voice said. 'I thought I should touch base about Cheng.'*
>
> *'Why? What is it?'*
>
> *'I've had a call from him. Just wants us to confirm shipping time.'*

*'Come and see me tomorrow. We'll
sort it out then.'*

Seymour looked at her wide-eyed.

'So,' she said. 'You said you wanted to do a deal. Here it is. Two choices. One, you help us. Two, you don't. *If* you don't, we tell your friends that you've led us to their little operation. Which you have, by the way. But for you, we'd never have known about it. Well, I dunno about Raul, but it seems to me João might not like you grassing him up.'

Seymour fell silent. Sweat broke out on his forehead. He could think of nothing to say. For once, his salesman's spiel had run dry.

CHAPTER 46

Raul was humming to himself as he drove along the ridge, more relaxed today, smiling as he thought of the failed police raid. Every few seconds he looked in his rearview mirror, checking the empty road behind, congratulating himself on the way he was falling into the habit of vigilance. Off to the right he could see right across the plain to the hills lit by the sun. In the distance he could just make out the thin ribbon of the highway, with the few spots of colour crawling along it, that he would join in a few minutes.

There was a flicker of movement ahead and above. His eyes caught the kite gliding past. The sight caught his imagination: all day long I have been like that bird, he thought, free, roaming the landscape, while my nest stays hidden.

*

The watcher crouching in the scrub ignored the kite. He was concentrating on the car as it drove towards him along the ridge. He watched it brake as it came to the corner below him; heard the change of gear, spoke quickly into the radio as the car slipped into the little side road which would bring it out on to the highway.

*

When his car was halfway along the country road, Raul saw another vehicle enter it from the other end. A tractor, old and battered, dribbling black exhaust towards the sky. He slowed, mildly put out by the inconvenience, waiting for the tractor to reverse. The tractor rolled steadily towards him, with an agricultural vehicle's typical indifference to traffic.

There were banks rising up all along both sides of the lane. There was nothing remotely like a verge. He looked around for a gateway, a break in the banks into which the tractor could pull. He looked in vain.

The tractor was twenty yards away and still coming. The driver's failure to go back started to irritate him. He muttered to himself, crossly now. *Bloody farm worker — must be an idiot.* He opened the window to gesticulate.

The tractor came to a halt five yards from the front of his car and stopped. What a fool, he thought, and exclaimed in impatience. Hit his horn. Then sighed, angrily; he did not have time to waste with such stupidity. He turned in his seat, looking back over his shoulder to reverse. As he did so he saw a large grey Peugeot pull up behind him.

Excellent, he thought, now there are two of us, now it is the tractor who will have to go back. He flashed his lights, hooted again, leaned out of his window and shouted at the tractor, gesticulating towards the car behind him. The tractor driver made no response.

He scarcely heard the click of his passenger door opening.

Out of the corner of his eye he was aware of movement onto the seat beside him, turned in his seat, was startled to see a solid-looking man getting into the passenger seat. Tall, dark curly hair, wide-shouldered, thick-necked, square-jawed. Smiling unpleasantly.

'Who the hell are *you?*' Eyes wide in astonishment. The man said nothing, went on smiling. 'What the devil are you doing in my car?'

No answer.

Finally, he realised what was happening. In alarm, he pulled the handle of his door to get out, found it blocked by the tractor driver now standing outside.

'Relax,' his passenger grinned, leaning a thick, well-muscled arm on the back of his seat.

'What d'you think you're playing at? Get out! Get out of my car!'

The tractor driver opened the car door, reached in, turned off the ignition. Pulled out the keys and tossed them thoughtfully up and down in one hand.

The rear doors clicked open; two more figures slid onto the back seat. The doors slammed shut.

Raul turned his head back to look over his shoulder, eyes flickering at the intruders. Suddenly something was thrust in front of his face. A bottle. As he flinched away from it, he saw what it was: the familiar green and orange and gold glinting dully in the fading light.

'One of yours,' said a man in the far corner. 'Recognise it?'

'What is this?' he protested. 'I don't know what you...'

'Bollocks.' A second voice, from directly behind him. A woman's voice, low and silky.

He twisted in his seat so he could see her. She had the face of a girl, pretty: green eyes, skin freckled with the sun, framed in short gold-brown hair.

'You know bloody well,' she said. 'You, and your friend João da Silveira, and that factory of yours.'

'Factory? I know nothing of any factory.'

'Bullshit. You've just come from it.'

'From a factory?' he said, starting to recover. 'No. I come from a wine warehouse – you have the wrong man, you—'

'No, we don't, Raul,' she said. 'We've got the right man.

We've been watching you every day this week.'

'Watching me?' He turned in his seat so he could see them. *This is not possible, if they had followed me I would have seen them.* 'Why do you watch me? I am a wine merchant, if you watch me you will know this, I—'

'Why? *Why?* Because of this *shit!*' She spat the last word at him, grabbing at his shirt collar, pushing the bottle into his face again. 'Because of five thousand cases we found in Rotterdam, is why!'

'I know nothing of this!' Raul exclaimed, pushing the bottle away. 'I am a wine merchant. I do not deal in Scotch whisky.'

'You made it, you asshole!'

'This is stupid! I do not make whisky! Wine, yes, but whisky…' A sly look came into his eyes. 'It will be from somewhere else. From Brazil, maybe. Perhaps you should go there.'

'Bullshit, Raul! It's got fuck all to do with Brazil. It's made right here in Portugal, we watched you load the containers for Rotterdam.'

'You are crazy,' he said. 'To do such things is not legal here in Portugal. If I do such a thing the police will make trouble. Maybe you should go to the police,' he laughed, sarcastically, knowing this would irritate them. 'Yes,' he sneered, 'go to the police. Do that – threatening an innocent man is a crime here.'

'We're not threatening you, Raul,' she hissed. 'we're just telling you something. We're telling you to take us to the factory.'

'There is no factory! All I know is a wine warehouse—'

'Then take us there! Mario, get this asshole out of the driving seat and drive the car!'

The tractor driver pulled at Raul's arm. Raul looked up at him in alarm. Then thought, Why not? They will see nothing. He got out of the car, and allowed himself to be led round to the passenger seat. Mario got out of the passenger seat, took the keys from the tractor driver, got into the driving seat. The grey Peugeot behind backed out of the lane, and Mario reversed after it, until they could turn. They drove back along the ridge, back the way he had come.

As they drove, Raul looked cautiously at the man behind the driver on the back seat. Younger than he had thought at first. A well-bred look about him, nothing like the thickset thug, Mario. You will be in for a surprise, he thought, and settled into the corner of his seat with an air of quiet confidence.

After two kilometres in the open they came to a double line of poplar trees. As they emerged from the far end of the trees Mario slowed, turned down a sandy track, down through the cork trees, to the dusty farmyard with its dirty barn.

Mario parked close to the wall, Jo got out, opened the back door and yanked Raul out of the car. Gripped his wrists tightly behind his back, pushed him towards the building.

'Open up,' she ordered.

'I cannot, it is locked, you—'

Impatiently she shoved him forward, thrusting him hard against the concrete wall, pain banging at his head.

'…you have the keys,' he gasped.

Hamish took the keys from the car, put them into Raul's hand. Propelled him towards the door, a small metal door set in a wide metal shutter. Clumsily Raul fumbled with the keys to a new-looking padlock. As it opened, Jo stepped inside; Hamish pushed Raul roughly through after her.

There was a click as she found the light switch. A pause, a flicker, then a dull glow of flickering neon as the lights caught.

It was exactly as the police had described it. An old tractor, some wooden boxes, a pile of hay.

Hamish turned to Raul. 'So what's all this?' he demanded. 'Bit odd for a wine merchant?'

'It is nothing to do with me,' Raul said. 'It is a farm building – you can see that.'

'To which you happen to have the key,' Jo said.

'He… I… it is to do him a favour…' Raul gabbled.

Hamish walked around the barn and stopped by the pile of old wooden crates. In one of them he saw half a dozen bottles of wine, covered in dust. He pulled one out. A dark green bottle of red wine, with a label showing a picture of the vineyard outside and the hills behind.

'Ah. This yours? Looks delicious,' he said sarcastically. 'Funny place to store your wine, though…'

Raul shrugged. 'We gave some to the farmer. As I said, I bring him some, as a favour, he is a friend, he—'

'Oh really? And I suppose you bring him whisky too.'

Raul put on an ingratiating smile. 'I told you before. I have nothing to do with whisky.'

'Yeah, well, I don't buy that. *So where is it?*

'We have nothing to do with whisky, yours or any other. I let you bring me here to prove it.' He spoke expansively, as if the visit had been his own idea, his own generosity, and swept one hand round in a showman's gesture. 'To let you see for yourself.'

Hamish stood in the middle of the floor, hands on his hips, and stared at the empty space, slowly sweeping his gaze around the walls.

There were no doors but the one they had come in. No staircase up or down. No cupboards, no side rooms.

Raul walked slowly to the tractor, leaned against it. 'Go on, take a look,' he said, looking sarcastically from Hamish to Jo. 'You can see what is here.'

Hamish looked at Jo. 'What do you think?' he muttered.

She was leaning against the wall, green eyes opaque, head on one side, fiddling with the keys. A car key. And two others, looped separately together. The key for the padlock, and a small double-edged chrome key.

'Hmm,' she said. 'I wonder what this one's for…' She looked at Hamish. 'Try outside,' she suggested.

He went out and worked slowly round the outside of the building. There was no annexe, no other door, no steps down to a basement. Nothing.

Nothing but the sandy ground, the irregular patches of cork trees, the surrounding hills. The blank concrete walls of the building, looming over him, blotting out the sky.

He came back into the building, his face blank.

'I told you,' Raul said, in quiet triumph. 'I told you, but you would not believe me.'

Together she and Hamish looked for anything the key might fit. Maybe a burglar alarm; but there was no sign of one. Nothing.

They padded silently round the outside of the floor, looking at the walls. Nothing.

They came to a halt by the small stack of wooden boxes Hamish had fished the bottle of wine out of. Jo stood with her back to Raul, looking at Hamish. Pursed her lips, mouthed a word at him. Hamish kicked at the heap of cases, making the few bottles inside rattle. Pulled out a second bottle, tossed it from one hand to the other, as if thinking.

Let it fall. It shattered, and the wine flooded out over the dusty concrete of the floor, forming a pool. A pool which spread to a straight edge, then went no further. Hamish looked down.

There was a crack in the concrete floor. The wine on the floor did not run across it, but seeped down into it, running away.

Hamish bent and looked at the crack. It was thin and straight, running at right angles out from the wall, then passing under the edge of the pile of boxes.

He moved slowly along the crack, scuffing the dust away with one foot, until it made a right angle, running back to the end wall.

A foot away from where the crack ended, the wall bore a small metal box, a few inches off the floor. A power cable ran into it. The box was the size of a power point, but it had no sockets for a plug.

He went over to examine it and saw a small slit. A slit the size of a keyhole.

He held out his hand to Jo. She handed him the keys. He took the small chrome key, slid it in, turned it. Nothing happened. He pulled at the top of the box. The front cover flipped down on a hinge. Inside were two buttons: one red, one green.

He stuck out a finger, hesitated, pressed the green button.

From below him came the hum of an electric motor, the grinding of gearwheels. His left foot slowly started to rise, and he moved to one side.

A section of the floor rose, four foot wide and eight foot long, hinged at the back. Below it was a metal staircase, leading down into the dark. Jo came and stood beside him. They turned and looked with triumph into each other's eyes.

CHAPTER 47

They frogmarched Raul down the steps. The bravado had gone out of him, and he had become sulky and dejected.

'Lights,' she ordered; meekly he pointed to a switch on the cellar wall.

There was a second flickering of neon, much brighter than the worn-out lights in the warehouse above. The space down here was bigger than the barn, extending under the whole area of the concrete yard. At the far end stood four stainless steel tanks, twelve feet high, shining silver in the light. In front of those was a bottling line, a narrow metal conveyor belt with machinery for filling, corking, labelling.

At one side of the cavernous cellar was a small, square stack of brown cardboard packing cases, empty. At the other end were more cases, creating a huge cardboard wall the width of the cellar, reaching up to the ceiling. Along the wall next to the stairs was a neat line of cases, filled and sealed.

Hamish opened one of the cases and drew out a bottle. Green, orange and gold glittered in the neon lights. He held it in his hand, giving it a long look, let out a satisfied sigh and turned to Raul.

'No whisky, eh?' he said. Raul gave no answer.

Jo had been walking round the cellar. One of its walls had two wooden doors in it. They walked through the first of the doors and found themselves in a small room. In the middle of it stood a printing machine. On shelves round the walls were stacks upon stacks of labels, fresh and crisp from the printer, each stack about six inches thick, bound with a rubber band. Each in green and orange and gold.

Hamish picked up a stack and looked at it. From his pocket he took the label Seymour had given him in London, months ago. These labels were identical.

He went back out, and in through the second door. A bigger room, with more machinery. One for printing aluminium, the second for pressing the aluminium into the shapes of the caps.

There was a row of cardboard boxes along the floor. He opened one and pulled out a handful of caps, handed one to Jo. Hamish smiled ruefully in admiration.

'You've done a good job here, Raul,' he called out, wryly. 'Nice caps. Nearly as good as the real ones.'

Raul said nothing, his face empty.

Jo came out of the room with the labels, her face thoughtful. She had six labels in her hand. Wordlessly she held them out. All with the green and orange and gold of a Grand McCowrie label, but all very slightly different. One the same as the bottles they had seized in Holland. Another like it, but over-printed 'Duty Free'. Four more, printed specially for Brazil, Mexico, Japan, Spain, each carrying the name and address of the distributor in the country.

Hamish whistled.

'They're getting ambitious.'

'Yeah.'

He picked out the Japanese label. 'Wonder why they didn't use this?' he mused; then answered his own question. 'Well, they wouldn't if they sold it to Cheng as genuine. Greedy buggers.' He laughed. 'What a joke, if they'd told him it was fake and put the Japanese labels on, we'd never have picked that bottle up.'

'Japan wasn't what I was thinking of,' she said, and held up one of the other labels. Carefully he took it from her. After a moment his brow furrowed.

'Hey, wait a minute,' he exclaimed.

'Yeah. Just what I thought. Where's that little sod got to?'

*

He was standing nervously by the stairs.

They walked him over to the bottling line and sat him down.

'Raul,' she said, standing in front of him, her arms crossed, speaking softly so that he had to strain to hear. 'Raul, how long have you been selling to Spain?'

'We do not sell to Spain,' he protested, 'the only deal we make is for Singapore. The deal you know about, the consignment that is in Holland.'

'Ah. So what is this?'

She uncrossed her arms and held the label in front of his face.

'No.' He shrugged his shoulders, looking unhappy. 'It is only for the future, it is an idea only, we have just printed a few labels, we…'

'So where did you copy it from?'

'We copy from a genuine label, from a bottle which we buy.'

'Bullshit, Raul,' Hamish said from behind him. 'This label isn't on sale yet.'

'But it's true,' Raul said, his voice rising, 'that is all we do.'

'It's got the name of the new distributor on it. Look, McCowrie International. Who told you about the new distributor?' she asked.

254

'I do not know, it is João who found out these details, I—
' Jo's arm snapped out and smacked against the side of his
face.

'You've fucked us about long enough,' she hissed. *'Where
did you get it?'*

Raul struggled to get on his feet; Hamish put his hands
on his shoulders and pulled him back down.

'No!' he cried. 'It is true, João got the label, I had nothing
to do with it. I—'

Her hand swung out again, harder, landing on his ear,
knocking his head against the bottling machine.

'I wouldn't mess her about,' Hamish urged, 'she's a
stroppy little bitch when she gets going.'

Raul rubbed a hand on his cheek, looking apprehensively
up at Jo.

'I tell you,' Hamish persisted, cheerfully, 'it's really not
worth it.'

Jo picked up a bottle, held it by the neck, weighed it
thoughtfully as she looked at Raul. He flinched from the look
in her eye, tried to pull away, as she swung the bottle up and
down, feeling its weight. She gave the bottle a final swing,
watched it climb and spin and hang in the air and start back
down. Amber and crystal exploded into the silence as it hit
the floor.

The echo died away and there was silence.

Jo put out her hand for another bottle. Gripped it by the
neck and smashed it against the side of the bottling machine.
Held the jagged glass loosely by her side. Raul winced as
Hamish gripped his arms behind him.

'Better tell her, Raul,' Hamish said softly.

'It came through João,' Raul muttered faintly, 'through a
friend of João.'

'*Who?*

'I cannot tell you, I—'

There was a sharp smack as she slapped him again with her free hand, moved the broken bottle closer to his cheek.

Hamish stared at her over Raul's head, urging her on: *Go on, demolish the little bastard.*

'He's in Spain, isn't he?' she whispered. 'He's got to be.'

Raul's eyes were wide in fright.

She looked up at Hamish. 'If it isn't on the market yet – who knows about the new labels, the one with the new distributor on?'

'Well, the new company, of course.'

'Would that make sense?' she asked, puzzled.

'Not a lot.'

'Who else knows? The trade, generally?'

'Not yet.'

'*So who else is there?*

'Dunno. Oh, wait a minute,' he said as a thought came to him. 'Our old lot, they know, it's part of the litigation.'

'The lot you sacked, you mean? What's their name?'

'Morato.'

Raul's face flickered at the name, and his wide eyes glanced up at her. She stared at him for a moment, drinking in his apprehension.

'It is, isn't it? It's someone in Morato, isn't it? Who? *Who?* she demanded, pulsating with controlled anger.

As she looked at his face, saw the tightness of his lips as he tried to bury his thoughts inside him, her intuition started to whisper a message to her brain.

'Is Morato just the name of a company,' she asked quietly, 'or is it a person?'

She kept her eyes on Raul as she spoke, watched his

tongue part his drying lips to moisten them.

'Both,' Hamish said. 'Morato's the man who runs it.'

She smiled and crouched down, her face level with Raul's. 'It's him, isn't it?' she hissed.

Raul swallowed, started to stammer a denial.

'Say it, you little bastard.' She grabbed his collar and shook him. '*Say it!*

He looked up at her, shivered, hunched over, retched.

She pushed him away, her eyes narrowed. 'We'll get it out of you later,' she glared. 'One way or another, we'll get it out of you.'

CHAPTER 48

She went upstairs, signalled the back-up team in from the lane where they were standing guard, got Mario to lead Raul away and put him in the Peugeot.

'Well,' she said, as they looked round at the materials stacked against the walls, 'here it all is. It's all yours, lover. What next?'

Hamish smiled. 'Finally. After all that hassle. Finally, we've found it. And you know what? All that hassle with the law. It's been a pain in the arse. You know what I'd *really* like to do?'

'Tell me.'

'What I'd *really* like to do is just set fire to the whole bloody thing. Sit back and watch it burn.'

She gave him a wry smile. 'Oh wow. A lawyer speaks.'

'Yeah.' He looked deep into her eyes for a long moment. 'But I can't do that, now can I? So… this is what we do. Get your chaps in here. Film everything. Every bloody detail. Just to make sure the police have no excuse. Then when we've done that, we ring Senhor Vasconcelos, and we tell him to get off his arse, ring that colonel, and get them moving.'

*

It was after nine o'clock by the time they got back to the Sheraton, still fizzing with triumph at the way the day had gone. Hamish went straight to the bar for champagne, took it up to her room, and filled their glasses.

'Here's tae us,' he said, as they drank. He laughed. 'I suppose we owe a toast to Seymour, too,' Hamish said. 'Good old Seymour!'

'"Good old Seymour" – my arse!' she said. 'And by the way, I dunno know why you insisted on going through that pantomime in the warehouse. If it'd been up to me I'd have opened up the secret staircase the moment we got in.'

Hamish smiled. 'Well, we did make a deal with him. We promised we wouldn't let on that he'd ratted. And it'd be a shame to give those crooks the satisfaction of doing him over. And I enjoyed the, er, pantomime. Not often one's allowed to chuck plonk on the floor. And by the way,' he added with a sardonic look, 'I wonder if we should give him a small reward?'

'A reward? Are you joking?'

'Well, but for him, we'd never have got where we are now.'

'Oh come on, he's a crook through and through, he's been up to his neck in it all along. You're not going to reward him for that, are you?'

'Oh no. When I said "where we are now", I was being literal. Meaning here. In this room. With you.'

She gave him a long, cool gaze. 'Oh. Being literal,' she said, deadpan. She took his champagne glass out of his hand, walked across the room and put it on her dressing table. Came back, pushed him onto the bed. 'You know what?' she whispered into his face. 'This literal stuff. I must be getting to like that.'

CHAPTER 49

Back in London, Monday morning. The day was sunny and crisp, a day for avoiding London Underground, a day for driving with the roof down. As Hamish parked his car, fifty yards from the office, he was bemused to see a large crowd of people milling about on the pavement. He walked towards them and saw that it was the entire staff of the building.

'Hamish!'

Alec Johnston strode up to him in a temper. 'At bloody last!' he exclaimed. 'Where the hell have you been?'

'Portugal,' Hamish said with a straight face.

'I know you've been in bloody Portugal. But why can't you stay in touch? You haven't phoned me – you haven't even phoned Sarah. Sarah showed me *another* bloody bill that's just come in, this one's for *fifty-five thousand* pounds, what the hell do you think you're playing at? On top of which, Spicer came to see me yesterday, he wants your blood, he told you to deal with Japan as a number-one priority and you've done damn all about it. *What on earth* d'you think you're playing at?'

Hamish gave him a benign smile.

'*Relax*, Alec. Next time I see Spicer I'll tell him it's all sorted. The stuff in Japan was fake, it was coming from Portugal and we've just shut down their factory.'

Alec stared at him.

'Plus,' Hamish continued, 'Spicer can get stuffed, anyway.

He and his sidekick were trying to throw fifty million dollars of the company's money away. As you yourself acknowledged, when we had that little discussion. I've just saved the company's money.'

'What on earth are you talking about? Have you gone off your head?'

'Morato. That's what I'm talking about.'

Alec stood and stared at him, a frown gathering on his face. 'What's Morato got to do with Portugal?'

Hamish was suddenly conscious of a crowd of fascinated listeners. 'Come to my car and I'll tell you.'

He walked off to his car, opened the door and got in. Alec followed, got in, still frowning.

'Morato was backing the counterfeiters there,' Hamish said.

'*What?*'

'He was part of their operation. He gave them information, finance. He was even planning to put counterfeit on the market in Spain, copying the labels for the new joint venture company.'

'*Morato?* Bloody hell. I don't *believe* it.'

'You'd better.' Hamish fished in his pocket. 'Here are the labels. We found them in the counterfeit factory.' He dropped one in Alec's lap. 'We filmed the whole works. I can show you if you're interested. And we had a conversation with the man who was running the factory, bloke called Raul Cardoso. He wasn't too keen about telling us about Morato at first. But eventually we, ah, persuaded him.'

'Go on.'

'He had an associate called João da Oliveira. A smuggler. Who is, it turns out, an old friend of Morato's. We went to Cardoso's home – his address book had Morato's business and home phone numbers, so we photocopied it. And you will be happy to know, the police finally got off their backsides and impounded everything.'

Alec looked at Hamish in astonishment.

'After we left,' Hamish went on, 'Cardoso was stupid enough to telephone Morato and warn him. We were lucky enough to get a tape of his conversation.' Hamish dropped a cassette into Alec's lap.

'So,' Hamish concluded, 'by spending a modest hundred grand or so, we've saved the company fifty million dollars. Not too bad a result, I hope you'll agree.'

Alec stared at Hamish, speechless, eyebrows raised in amazement. Looked down at the cassette, gingerly fingering it as if it was going to bite him. Finally spoke, slowly, grasping for words. 'Hamish,' he said, 'are you quite... quite sure about this?'

'Yep,' Hamish said, trying to keep a straight face.

'Well!' Alec exclaimed. 'This is... astonishing. Better than I ever expected. Well done.' A smile started at the corner of his mouth, slowly turned into a grin. '*Very* well done!'

'Thank you.'

'I don't suppose...' Alec asked, 'I don't suppose you were able to, ah, get any of this into the shape of... formal evidence? A statement or anything... which we could present to a court in Spain?'

'Actually – no. I thought you'd enjoy doing all that. After all,' Hamish said with a gentle smile, 'you're dealing with the Morato case. I thought I ought to leave you something to claim the credit for.'

'Well.' Alec looked through the windscreen again, towards the crowd on the pavement. Then his eyes shifted back to Hamish and he smiled. 'Well, well, well,' he said again, with a deep sigh of contentment. 'That's the best piece of news I've had all week.'

Hamish followed Alec's glance down the street, looked at the crowd. 'What's everybody doing outside?' he asked idly. 'Has that office manager organised a fire drill or something?'

Alec's smile evaporated, and he passed his hand over his brow again.

'No,' he said wearily, 'it's the European Commission. They're doing a dawn raid on us.'

Hamish stared at him in astonishment. 'They're doing *what*? Why on earth?'

'Why d'you think? Spicer and his blasted discussions with his cronies in our competitors. Trying to carve up the market. The very thing you told him not to do, in case it satisfies you.'

Hamish's stare was blank for a few moments. Slowly it changed to a smile, then a grin; until he raised his head and let out a long bray of laughter.

'Silly bastard,' he said. 'You're right, I'd quite forgotten.' He looked at Alec with happiness all over his face. 'I did, too. I *told* him not to break the law.'

About the Author

David Cantrip was born in Greece, while his parents were on a diplomatic posting to Athens. He was then raised and schooled in England. He attended Cambridge University, where he read law. He went to the Bar (joining the same chambers as Sarah Caudwell, to whom this book is dedicated); and then became ensconced in the world of whisky, in both a professional and an appreciative capacity. He spent many years there, working in the UK and internationally. As well as whisky (and wine), he also enjoys fishing and painting.

Acknowledgements

My thanks to Heather Holden-Brown, an old friend, who was most helpful in providing advice and support from my book's inception.

Many thanks to James and Sara Gaskins for their invaluable help with the manuscript. Also, to all those who have worked on this book:

Martin Toseland, for his reading of the manuscript;

Justine Cunningham for her copy-editing;

Melanie Scott for her proofreading;

Nick Castle for his cover design;

Katie Sadler for her marketing advice;

and to Ian Hooper and his team at Book Reality for taking on this book and putting it together.